APOCALYPSE DRECKLY

APOCALYPSE DRECKLY

A Novel

N.R. Phillips

HALSGROVE

First published in Great Britain in 2005

Copyright © 2005 N.R. Phillips

To the man in the white linen coat.

British Library Cataloguing-in-Publication Data.
A CIP record for this title is available from the British Library.

ISBN 1 84114 478 9

Cover illustration by Charles Wood

HALSGROVE

Halsgrove House
Lower Moor Way
Tiverton, Devon EX16 6SS
Tel: 01884 243242
Fax: 01884 243325
E-mail: sales@halsgrove.com
Website: www.halsgrove.com

Printed and bound in Great Britain by
Cromwell Press, Trowbridge

CONTENTS

Acknowledgements   7

Introduction   8

Preliminary Observations   9

Tape One   11

Tape Two   31

Tape Three   51

Tape Four   70

Tape Five   87

Tape Six   101

Tape Seven   117

Tape Eight   132

Tape Nine   144

Tape Ten   158

Tape Eleven   172

Tape Twelve   186

ACKNOWLEDGEMENTS

Many thanks to Liz Tregenza for her patient and tactful proof-reading and comma clobbering. Thanks to the staff at Halsgrove and to Charles Wood for the cover illustration. My thanks also to those who are big and strong enough to have their legs pulled without squealing too loudly.

INTRODUCTION
– TO THE LADIES –

Whenever I reflect how disposed you are by nature to compassion, I cannot help being apprehensive, lest what I now offer to your acceptance should seem to have but a melancholy beginning. For it calls to mind the remembrance of that most fatal plague, so terrible yet in the memories of us all, an account of which is in the front of the book. But be not frightened too soon, as if you expected to meet with nothing else. This beginning, disagreeable as it is, is as a rugged and steep mountain placed before a delightful valley, which appears more beautiful and pleasant, as the way to it was more difficult; for as joy usually ends in sorrow, so again the end of sorrow is joy. To this short fatigue (I call it short, because contained in a few words) immediately succeeds the mirth and pleasure I had before promised you; and which, but for that promise, you would scarcely expect to find. And in truth could I have brought you any other way but this, I would gladly have done it; but as the occasion of the occurrences, of which I am going to treat, could not well be made out without such a relation, I am forced to use this Introduction.

In the year then of our Lord... there happened... a most terrible plague which, whether owing to the influence of the planets, or that it was sent from God as a just punishment for our sins, had broken out some years before... and after passing from place to place, and making incredible havoc all the way, had now reached the west.

(Introduction to *The Decameron; or Ten Days' Entertainment of Giovanni Boccaccio 1313–1375*)

PRELIMINARY OBSERVATIONS

That such a calamity should strike our little community was doubly disastrous for we are of so few souls, so closely knit that it was inevitable that the contagion should spread rapidly among the populace. We remember with shame the depravity of a few, the avarice of some, the delight of others, the veneration of the pious, the terror of the vulnerable on that awesome occasion. Best to forget, perhaps, the way in which the evil ones among us indulged their avarice and exploited the vulnerable. Unpleasant though it may be to recall these passions, bear with us as we remember the events as the terrible shadow fell over us in order that you may fully appreciate the contents of the narrative to follow. As the hour approached it was appalling to see honest people fleeing their homes; not anyone who was not infirm stayed within the security of their humble abodes or mansions for, like some terrible alchemy, the thing cast a spell over the whole population. All came out into the open air under the darkening skies and they merged with the hordes of strange tribes from other lands. There were those who gathered in the security of great crowds to dance to loud, all obliterating music. Some tried escaping to the countryside only to be met with the rituals of heathen cults. Fearsome figures could be seen clustered tightly together on the hilltops as they performed their sacred ceremonies in secret. The very heavens were confused! On some, it was said, there was a fall of rain like the black waters of hell, on others there were brief rays of sunshine, passing like a strange light of exposure over their sinful rites. Others were swathed in mists as in dreams of mystic worlds. The very forces of nature were held in abeyance. Fearsome events were foretold in the abnormal flights of birds and slinking cats scurrying in dark alleys.

(From the archives of Shimshai the Scribe, b.1930.)

Editor's note

Momentous and catastrophic events seldom occur simultaneously with the means of recording them in detail for posterity. It was therefore doubly fortuitous that at the time of the impending calamity there was also in operation the oral archive for which the unfortunate residents recorded their memories of the terrible tragedy and the events leading up to it. Future generations will be forever grateful to those members of the community who were willing to reveal such personal accounts of themselves at this terrible time.

However, in transcribing the following from the oral archive to book form, we were faced with almost insurmountable difficulties if it were to make any sense to the reader. Without wishing to appear condescending, we are obliged to point out that the dialect and idiom of some of the elders is almost unintelligible to the ear and impossible to read if written phonetically. These people also have little command of the Queen's English as spoken by you and us. Their insistence on saying 'just now' (pronounced 'jisnow') to mean some time ago and 'directly' (pronounced 'dreckly') to mean later, the exact opposite of the meanings in the *Oxford English Dictionary*, together with saying 'how' when they mean 'why', are but a few examples of their idiosyncratic use of the language. Therefore the following has, of necessity, been severely edited, although it must be said that some had a reasonable command of English when they chose to use it and they have been quoted (*ut supra*) more or less verbatim.

TAPE ONE

*Then came certain of the elders... from Tamar even to
the waters of strife... the river to the great sea.*

To all outward appearances, everything was perfectly normal. We
ordinary people went about our business as we had always done
but, in the alley-ways of administration, in dusty offices, emporiums
of business and from the highest authorities to the lowest, from central government down to parish meetings, momentous decisions
were being made by the elders of the community.

The elders are chosen by the people and elected in true democratic
manner after putting their wisdom before us that we might venerate
our leaders and mentors. They are twenty in number or thereabouts
and all, at their election to the chamber of the grand council, swear to
serve and represent our community in selfless devotion. Such noble
persons with high intentions are rare in any community and, with their
unassuming reserve, can blend into invisibility after the elections never
to be seen or heard of again until just before the next one, when they
again proclaim their dedication to public service and the man in
the street.

'We can't say that,' Old Steve said, 'or there'll be ructions.'

'Can't say what?' asked Collateral Fred.

'Man in the street,' Old Steve said. 'It's not allowed.'

'Oh?' Freddie said.

'What the hell are you talking about,' demanded Barnabas 'The
Bard' Baragwaneth.

'Person in the street,' Steve said.

'Person in the street,' Ceecil agreed.

'You're getting old and totalish*, Steve,' Barny said.

We all agreed on that, but Old Steve just shrugged. Nobody

*Don't ask! Eds.

believed anything he said these days, but what did it matter? To be old and totalish freed him from the absurdities of modern life. Barny ought to see that, but living out there, miles from anywhere, he was like a bleddy hermit, only coming into town for his necessities and completely out of touch. He's years younger than me, Old Steve thought, and takes life far too seriously for a man of his age. Time for 'n to get a good woman before it's too late. Old Steve leaned against the railings and looked down into the harbour. Half tide, just past the neap. Morning mist clearing and the sun breaking through on a windless day. Pleasure boats coming alongside the quay. Fishing boats going to sea. All normal. No indication of the calamity about to overwhelm them.

There was his son, Boy Steve, at the tiller of his open tosher as she headed out past the quay head, small enough to be handled by a one-men crew yet big enough to cope with our weather and ground swells. How times change. Old Steve's boat, the *Morwennol*, had needed three men to crew her, himself, the boy and Uncle Joe. But there we are, the boy prefers to work alone. Uncle Joe had drowned trying to save the boy, and the boy, it seemed, had never got over that, changing from a young, confident optimist to a reserved and dour man distant from all, especially his father. After the wreck, the loss of the lifeboat and the death of Joe, Boy Steve had sold their boat to clear debts, gain independence and buy this smaller craft, named *Morvoren*. She was a good sea boat, Old Steve knew, safe, and he never worried about his son out there alone. Alone? he asked himself. What 'ee talkin' about, alone? They're never alone these days. The radios and mobile phones are always on. They can be out there fishing, listening to the immediate weather forecast or *The Archers*, talking to a pal in Australia or watching telly. Not like my day. He turned his back on the harbour and looked to the land.

There were the bleddy tourists, beginning to crowd the harbour, hoards of them along the prom, the wharf, getting in the way on the quays. What it was going to be like when the darkness fell and they came in their millions, he dreaded to think.

There were the cars, loaded down with gear, the essentials for surviving a day in the hostile environment of a beach with dangerous seas and burning sun and no shops for two hundred yards.

Bumper to bumper, they progressed slowly among the hoards ambling along on foot, making for car parks already full. They were like fugitives from an overcrowded metropolis escaping to an even more overcrowded maritime paradise by the sea. No, he thought, it's me, dreading the things to come and fearing the worst.

There, in a light frock and little straw hat, old-fashioned as a poke bonnet, was Sarah Stevens walking down towards the plat. Never think she was the age she is, Old Steve thought, only three or four years younger than me. I don't know what she d' think about my son courtin' her maid, Katie. She don't exactly reveal much about what she d' think about anything. You would have thought that a woman like that would have married somebody, though she don't think much of me, that's pretty obvious. She must have admirers, besides me. She's never forgiven me, or I might've have become more of an admirer than I am.

And there's the mayor, pushing his way through the crush, accompanied by his clerk. Two worried men, or they ought to be, with so many impending problems on their shoulders, having to organise the logistics of the whole world descending upon this isolated community.

We are isolated. We have no communication with the outside world except by word of mouth. Sometimes the word is brought and sent by travellers from afar. Sometimes the word is written down and taken by carrier to the distant corners of the world. Sometimes we read the word in the form of printed papers that are purported to carry news from those corners. At times the word has been transmitted by flashes of light in coded impulses, or flags on sticks waved at peculiar angles to the body. Words are also sent and received by strange electronic pulses in the form of radio, television, telephone, fax, text, e-mail, and so many other forms of competing digital, analogue, monologue forms that the effect is to induce utter confusion and leave us, as we say, in isolation. Some read books, but they are few.

We are far flung. We are so far flung that, were we but a few leagues further flung, the ocean would engulf us and we would be under water. No! We jest! The ocean is kept at bay by a wall of granite, into which are indented curves of coves and harbours where the villages and towns snuggle in shelter from the winter gales. The settlement of which we relate these events is but a village if you come from some vast city, or a middling town if you inhabit a small hamlet. (Like a Danish flea.) There are twin quays, between which lies the fishing fleet and around which are clustered the enterprises of the sea. There is a ships' chandler selling Swiss army knives and plastic macs, a boat builder's shed converted to a cafe, a marine engineer's workshop selling buckets and spades, while behind all this are the quaint cottages of the fishermen, many of which are empty until filled by tourists in the summer. For centuries we have lived quietly, our peaceful way of life disturbed by nothing more than the lapping waves and the clippety clop of horses' hooves, together with the affable commands of the wagoners, like Dicky-drive-osses. ('Whoa now Duke, whoa now. Good boy, Prince. Tchk tchk. Git on Duke. Git on Prince. Git on. Git on! You bleddy sods. Git on!') There came the blasting of dynamite in the quarries and mines, the occasional howling gale with thunder and lightening, factory hooters, and air-raid sirens, while now we have the pervasive drone of self-drive motor boats, transistor radios and the dulcet tones of discos drifting across the moonlit bay. All this tranquillity to be disrupted by the coming of the dreaded umbra. Is there any wonder that people were apprehensive?

Are there twenty wise men and women to lead and reassure us? When we asked, nobody seemed quite sure of the number, for some are on the parish, some on the district and some on the county. Some serve on two councils and some on all three, which makes them very powerful men, or women, depending, among other things, upon their gender. The democratic system ensures that we are truly represented. The point is that, in true democratic manner, most of our councillors are elected to represent the people who are considered the most important and deserving in the community, themselves. Let us consider them, or some of them, who attended the first meeting after the acceptance that disaster was to strike due to their trying to overexploit the juxtaposition of heavenly bodies.

Following the initial euphoria, when, given widespread publicity, the event was seen as a God-sent opportunity to be exploited to the tune of millions, grave doubts began to be voiced. As the time drew nearer, and the full implication of the matter became apparent, the authorities became even more concerned. They looked into similar events in history and concluded that the massive increase in population since those days, together with universal mobility, could mean that we were liable to be completely overwhelmed. These doubts led to much confusion and eventually panic, following the warnings of chaos throughout the land, so a meeting of the elders was to be held when all had been given time to consult with the populace as to the measures that should be taken to ensure a satisfactory outcome for all.

The result of that tense gathering was the decision that, after four years of speculation since they had been warned of the implications, the time had come for action, not words. They therefore arranged for a further meeting of the whole council, after the planning committee had submitted a report, when the matter could be discussed in full. So it came to pass that an extraordinary general meeting of the wisest of wise men, i.e. the planning committee, was called for a.s.a.p.

There are some who say that the meeting was never held, that all the deliberations were made in secret, that we had no idea what was going on, who proposed what, and that the following account, like so much of what we relate in this document, is based on the defective recollection of biased individuals.

Some say, with a few dissenters, that in the council chamber where Tim Penberthy had overcome considerable opposition during his long service and risen to mayor for the third time, there was a good deal of heated argument, even before the meeting began, and he had some difficulty in keeping order. He decided that the business should be formal, as being the only way to keep control. As at the beginning of each council meeting, he looked at his fellow representatives to see if any had trouble in mind. He always knew by the look, determined or otherwise, on their faces, what to expect. He could run the whole show on his own given half a chance and, apart from D.D. Johns, he could twist most of them round his little finger, he genuinely thought. He gazed solemnly around the table that they might all appreciate just how seriously he took the matter before them and that they might respond with dignity. No chance, he thought, with this bunch of nits.

Of the members present, Tim represented the commercial element in the community, being a businessman and very small tycoon.

'Typhoon?' Zeke said. 'Don't seem much a typhoon to me. More of a puff of wind forecast as force eight, if you ask me.' Nobody was ever known to ask Ezekiel Endean anything. Which was quite surprising, come to think of it.

D.D. Johns was Tim's only serious opposition on the council, and therefore regarded with reluctant respect. DDJ had been there for such a long time that nobody could remember who or what he represented, although he had close business ties with the squire. He was getting on in years, was the father of the chamber and was as wily as a fox. He spoke with measured tones with several layers of dewlap wobbling under his chin. His speeches mentioned regret at the declining moral standards, and his sympathy with the plight of the underdogs and minority communities in our society, but he was on the right wing of the right wing and objected to any form of handouts to unemployed lazy buggers who had never done a day's work in their lives.

Freddie wha's-'is-name, known as Collateral Fred, thought he'd been elected to represent the fishing community after spending the pre-election campaign down on the quay listening to their complaints about quotas and scrounging mackerel. In fact he was elected by the tourist industry on the assumption that, as proprietor of a small guesthouse now converted to self-contained flats, he would have their interests at heart.

Boy Steve, son of Old Steve, had been persuaded to stand for election by his fellow councillor and long-standing girlfriend, Katie Stevens, to support her in matters of conservation, but was at absolute loggerheads with her over the matter of conserving fish stocks. His problem was that, while being a fisherman and originally elected to represent fellow fishermen, he was hardly ever able to be present at the meetings because of being at sea and was due to be ejected for low attendance.

Sheila and Arthur Brook were a husband and wife team who had come here as young, penniless, pot-smoking hippies, liked what they saw of the bohemian lifestyle of a few of the itinerants and decided to stay. Since then they had gradually acquired the morals and standards, together with a certain amount of the affluence, of conventional society, and were far-sighted enough to see that the town could not be preserved like an artefact in a dusty museum. Although nobody ever admitted voting for them, they had been representing incomers like themselves throughout their political life. There were so many incomers who regarded themselves underrepresented in the town that one or both Brooks had been on the council for some years and they always promised at election time and afterwards to make no rash promises except to do their utmost for the town and its residents. They were 'the Brooks' and were such a close team that they only counted for one rather feeble voice as far as most of us could see, although they had two votes with which to utter it, which some thought undemocratic. The fact is, however, that they nearly always disagreed over some small point, which became a bitter feud, and their votes cancelled each other out, so could be ignored.

Councillor Theodora Yeoman was a buxom widow we had originally elected to the dizzy heights of the local authority after her husband's early death. This was in gratitude to his and her family's long but eccentric tradition of service to the community. After her initial election, however, she became something of a vicarious iconoclast, representing those people who desperately wanted to kick some other candidate out, and who voted for her on the basis of strategy. As there were always those who desperately wanted somebody out, Theodora was always in and had been for years, believing that she represented the silent majority; though it's hard to tell how anyone could know who the silent majority are, them keeping so quiet and all. Theodora liked to think she was one of the more enlightened of our community, keeping up with the times, eschewing the old dialect and talking fitty. Her difficulty being that she wudn sure what was fitty, having been brought up to talk just like the rest of us, so her diction was a bit hesitant at times.

The third independent female member of the council was Ms Winifred Whistler, a spinster of forty years of age, representing women's issues in small parishes and the rights of the individual in an anonymous society, and was recognised universally by the wearing of a red hat, sometimes large, sometimes small, sometimes with a feather, at other times without, but always red. The wearing of a red hat had become so much a part of any ensemble for so many years since her secretly flamboyant youth, that she felt utterly ill at ease in anything else. This characteristic was so universally accepted as the distinguishing element of her personality that in anyone else it would have influenced the attachment of a nickname known throughout the community. It was, however, her apparent Christian righteousness, her duty to uphold the morals of the community and her unfailing attendance at her seat during every service at her chapel that meant she was known to all, in secret, as Winnie the Pew.

Winnie had kept her figure and fresh complexion by virtue of good living and plenty of exercise with the local ramblers who, despite her regular appearances at chapel, knew her to be 'a good sport' and game for anything. Our dear Lord, she maintained, never intended that we should not enjoy life to the full. Some on the council said that rambling was all she could ever do, in one form or another, but she had one secret admirer in the form of Ezekiel Endean. Zeke was a… well, he's one of we so we have to be careful, let's say a bit eccentric. Not being much of a lady's man, he kept his admiration to himself for years, but had been heard to solemnly proclaim on more than one occasion, with a wistful look in his eye, that 'red hat equals no knicks'. On the plat Ceecil nodded in agreement, 'Red 'at… no knicks!'

Denzil Trethewy was a retired farmer who lived out near Barnabas Baragwaneth and had let out his land. He was elected by his associates in the rural areas to look after their, and incidentally his own, interests. He couldn't see anything wrong with that. The fact that he had been set up by Squire Chygwin as a front man for progress, i.e. development, in the countryside completely escaped him.

Reggie Hammond, a semi-retired architect who only worked when he was sober, saw it as his duty and moral right to preserve the essential elements of architecture and culture which made the town the unique community that it was. He regarded architecture as an art form and headed his notepaper with the words 'Artist Architect' but, being overrun with artists and usually wanting detailed blueprints of nothing more than a proposed extension to the shithouse, we were not impressed. Being the most educated man, sorry, person, on the council he sincerely believed he was, *ipso facto*, the most intelligent, a mistake often made by people educated beyond their intellectual capacity, as you might say. Before meetings he invariably spent some time buying drinks for the frequenters of the local hostelries in order to be at the front end of public opinion so, while being very popular, was usually unable to offer much in the way of a coherent discussion.

Katie Stevens had been elected by the conservation lobby and, considering her background, got in to the surprise of everyone except those who knew her, that is most of the locals who didn't really give a damn about people's morals, provided they didn't preach to others. She was the illegitimate daughter of Sarah Stevens, and just as independent and determined in her quiet way as her mother, who nobody dared cross.

One regular attendant at almost every meeting, although not in fact an elected member of the chamber, was Winnie's secret admirer, Ezekial Endean, who sat in the public gallery, and was probably better informed about what went on in the council than most. He had once stood for election himself, with the campaign slogan 'Let's git a bit of bleddy common sense in there', and had been at the bottom of the poll. He had more common sense than most people could take from a forty-nine-year-old bit of a nutter.

'Well,' the chairman sighed. 'If we might get straight down to the business in hand, I would call on Mr Rainey, of the planning department to present his report. We might see just what preparation and progress has been made by our officials.'

Robin Rainey was used to dealing with the differing opinions and degree of ignorance in the various committees. He saw this coming crisis as an opportunity to impress the whole council with his efficiency and control under pressure. He rose to his feet in order to address the meeting, believing that this action would be taken as a show of respect, in which belief he was completely mistaken. Some councillors regarded him as a damn nuisance, with his brains replaced by a set of petty rules and regulations, while others thought he was too bleddy big for his boots and lost no opportunity for reducing him to where he belonged. 'Your officers,' he said, 'have undertaken an extensive and ongoing study of the developing situation and have made recommendations, which are contained in this report which I shall need to run by you.' He waved a bulky sheaf of papers. 'It is over seventy years since such a phenomenon was seen in this country,' he continued, 'and at that time three million people were said to have moved across the country to be there. With the increase in both numbers and mobility of the population, we should be prepared for double that number coming to witness the phenomenon. We normally expect to accommodate just half a million people at that time of year, when our facilities are stretched to the full. I have to say that our essential conclusions are that we are utterly unprepared for the event, and urgent measures have been proposed.'

'Well, what are they?' DDJ demanded.

'We have developed a doctrine for risk management of major incidents and, following recommendations from various civil bodies, we have proposed that all emergency services be on red alert, that extra police be drafted in and, in the event of total gridlock, all incoming vehicles be turned back or not allowed to cross the bridge. People are being urged to travel well in advance, to avoid snarling up the roads, and to be sure to carry enough food and water in their vehicles to see them through long delays. We are expecting people to go out in boats to avoid the crowds on shore, which in itself will put a strain on risk management and the emergency services. We are expecting ten times the usual number of 999 calls over the period leading up to and following the event.'

He was obliged to stop for breath, leaving a pause for unwanted awkward questions. Katie Stevens asked how such vast numbers of people could be prevented from swarming everywhere out of control, looking for the best viewing points, which were the historic sites on the hills.

Robin was ready for this one. 'We have made preparations for all ancient monuments to be cordoned off to prevent the admission of vehicles and...'

'What I want to know,' DDJ said impatiently, 'is what you have done to see that the event is fully exploited for the financial benefit of the community.' What a bleddy name, DDJ was thinking, Robin Rainey for God's sake! But very appropriate for a bird-brained drip like him. I should have known better and opposed his appointment in the first place.

Robin Rainey said, 'We have employed a national publicity consultant to see that we get the fullest coverage in every window of opportunity on all media. There are several websites and... '

'Never mind websites,' Denzil Trethewy said, 'are we going to allow farmers to set up camp-sites?'

'Provided the necessary facilities are available, we intend issuing temporary licenses to the responsible farming community for camping on suitable sites. Permission will be granted subject to certain assurances regarding health and safety. On one site for instance, where two thousand people are expected, there will be on-site marshals and twenty-four-hour security personnel.'

Katie Stevens was distinctly heard to mutter 'Two thousand? Good God!' while Denzil Trethewy, being in contact with the responsible farming community, wanted assurance that in order to accommodate so many people and bring much needed revenue into the rural areas they could do away with all this red tape and restrictions we usually impose on honest citizens trying to make a living, and asked 'Is every precaution also being taken to stop these here new-age travellers from trespassing on private land and setting up unsanitary camps, with the risk of the silly buggers falling down mineshafts while looking for somewhere to crap?'

Councillor Theodora Yeoman pouted in indignation. She turned to the chair. 'I implore you, Mr Chairman,' she said with her voice rising in shrill insistence, 'to maintain order in the meeting and curtail the use of profanities.' Theodora added that she herself was also very concerned about the risks to the local population if the invasion was not kept under control but even more so if the leading lights of the town could not control their language. 'I think,' she said, 'well, I mean to say, what I believe, what I'm trying to say is, that we're a God-fearing community.'

'A God-fearing community,' agreed Councillor Ms Whistler, Winnie the Pew, with enthusiasm. On the matter of the impending disaster and the invasion by aliens, she was anxious to be reassured that all matters of health and safety to the general public were to be regarded as being of prime consideration by the council and its officers.

She was assured by the planning officer, the tourist officer and the town clerk that every precaution was being taken. They were expecting the demands on public facilities, electricity, gas, petrol, water, sewage, etc., to say nothing of food supplies, to be unprecedented, so they proposed that all non-essential activities be curtailed for the duration of the event. The hospitals were all to be on red alert with ambulances, the police and the lifeboat standing by.

The clerk interjected to reminded them that 'While every effort had been made to accommodate representations made by the community, ultimately there will always be a number of factors that have to be taken into account before arriving at conclusions.'

Katie was tempted to congratulate the clerk on his brilliant deduction but, to avoid further procrastination on his part, said 'To illustrate the scale of the problem, I understand that a survey has indicated that half a million students will be arriving from all the UK universities, and there are one hundred and twenty-one applications for new camp-sites. Is it true that at just one site there is an application in for a music festival expected to accommodate thirty-seven thousand revellers?'

'Such surveys and proposals,' Robin Rainey said, 'have all been included in our action plan, but no decisions taken on the granting of licences.'

'One thing appears to have been overlooked in all this,' Councillor Theodora remarked, 'and it concerns me greatly.'

The town clerk, a wily and experienced council official of many years, looked at her over his glasses. One thing? he thought to himself, only one thing? My God, if only that were so! Scores, hundreds of things had been overlooked by these incompetent yokels. He couldn't think, right now, what any of these overlooked things might be but was quite sure they were waiting to plague him in days to come. Meanwhile, he kept his head below the parapet while obliging Robin Rainey to lay his own squarely on the block. If the chop came, it would never be the clerk's head that rolled. He looked to the chairman to ask Theodora what this particular one thing was that had been overlooked.

'Could you enlighten us, Councillor,' the chairman, Mayor Tim Penberthy said, 'over the matter of your concern?'

'What I d' want,' Theodora ventured, 'that is require, I mean I'm very concerned, I wish to inform the council, through the mayor, through the chair, of course,' she informed her fellow councillors, 'about the licensing hours.'

'Licensing hours?' the chairman said. 'What about them?'

'Well!' Theodora said, 'Just consider the situation, Mr Chairman. 'All these hordes of people. They'll all be at risk,' she said, 'of getting lost, well, I mean to say disorientated, and falling over the cliffs. To say nothing of the danger on the roads. I suggest, that is, I mean I believe, I propose, that all sales of alcohol be banned and all the public houses be locked up and kept under guard.'

'Locked up?'

'Under guard?'

'I am concerned, Mr Chairman, that these hordes of excited crowds will get completely out of control and go beresk.'

'Beresk?'

'I think,' the clerk whispered in the chairman's ear, 'she means berserk'.

'Berserk?' Mayor Penberthy said. 'I don't understand.'

'I am thinking,' she insisted 'of the consequences of consuming alcohol.'

'What consequences?' asked Reggie Hammond, whose red face was not entirely due to the effects of the strong ultra-violet light in these parts.

'I merely wish,' Theodora said, 'to draw the attention of my fellow councillors and their officers to the potential dangers of the consumption of excess alcohol during a period of darkness.'

Her fellow councillors, while trying to think of exactly what draconian measures she might be about to propose, allowed her to continue while they thought of some objection to whatever she might come up with. Several of them had already planned private gatherings to celebrate the event.

'I am thinking of people walking about the cliffs and beaches, getting lost on the moors, why doing all sorts of things, why, like driving cars, and trying to swim in the sea while... well, drunk!' Theodora said, 'In the dark!'

'Ah!' Reggie said, with some relief.

'I formerly propose,' Theodora insisted, 'that, in order to ensure the safety of the public, and to protect ourselves from public liability, we should rescind licenses and ban the sales of alcohol for the duration of the event.' She sat back in the assurance that her proposal would be seen as the most far-sighted yet put before this austere body.

'Ban alcohol?' Reggie murmured, not knowing how loud his murmurs were. 'Is the woman mad?'

'Does the Councillor realise?' Collateral Fred asked, 'Just how much revenue is brought into this area every year by the sales of alcohol?'

'We do indeed,' Winnie Whistler cried, with a nod of encouragement to Theodora. 'And it is a matter of some concern to a great many decent citizens.'

'We would lose thousand of pounds of revenue,' Freddie felt bound to inform them.

Councillor D.D. Johns reminded them, for he had seen the press, in the form of a bored junior reporter from the local rag, in the public gallery, that 'We should not permit greed to overshadow matters of public safety. I feel it is my duty, and indeed the duty of this council, to assure people that we care about their security at all times, regardless of the commercial pressures placed upon us. I personally am greatly assured by the fact that the government has allocated an extra half a million pounds to the local police and have confidence that this resource will be put to proper use in controlling the abuse of intoxicating substances and unruly behaviour and...'

'We have to let people enjoy themselves,' Freddie said.

'...on a point of order, however,' DDJ continued, scowling at Freddie for interrupting while the reporter was busy scribbling, 'the sale of alcohol will be dealt with under the licensing laws and is hardly a matter for this extraordinary meeting of the planning committee.'

'Some people, Mr Chairman,' Councillor Theodora retorted, 'have differing views on what constitutes enjoyment and the use of alcohol.' She also scowled at Collateral Fred. 'To say nothing of vested interest in its distribution and sale.'

'What we ought to be concerning ourselves with,' Councillor D.D. Johns insisted, 'are the preparations for controlling the unprecedented numbers of disruptive elements out in the countryside. I should like to know what our officers have recommended in the way of precautions.'

Councillor Denzil Trethewy agreed. 'You're stopping the buggers from going onto ancient monuments and all they places,' he said, 'the places what ought to be looked after by the National Trust and English Heritage and the like. What about stopping them from invading private property and camping in fields all along the road without asking nobody or paying a penny?'

'That's right,' Katie whispered to Denzil. 'Make them pay to go on proper sites. And since when has our heritage been English?'

'We have planned,' Robin Rainey informed Denzil, and here he paused for effect, that they might all appreciate the true ramifications of what was about to befall them, 'temporary villages of camps to accommodate ten thousand people each...'

'Ten thousand?' Katie said.

'....and we have requested that suitable barriers be erected wherever there is likely to be unauthorised entry on private land. After being advised by the police that chains and locks will be inadequate, we have arranged for all lay-bys and field gates to be blocked with massive boulders.'

'I would like to point out,' Councillor Freddie said, 'that if these people are exploited it will not do us any good in the long run. The hoteliers are not going to make anything out of it. This event,' he said with a degree of rue in his voice, 'is coming at the height of summer, a time when we're full already. We can't overcharge our regular customers and expect them to come back in future years. It's only the farmers with camp-sites who are likely to make anything out of it.'

'Nonsense!' Denzil objected, with a surreptitious glance at Boy Steve Trevorrow. 'What about they party who d' run boat trips and sell ice-cream and sun hats and the like? All they cafés and the hotels always do all right. It's a time for other people to be given the opportunity to make a bob or two.'

'On the matter of accidents,' Robin said, ignoring Denzil's remarks. 'We are aware of the possibility of these for all kinds of expedient reasons and, after consultation with the area health authority, we have been informed that all routine appointments for patients in the NHS have been postponed and leave for the whole NHS cancelled for the week. The same for the police, and other emergency services, and we are considering having the military on red alert.'

There was a brief silence after this. The military on red alert? As in a time of imminent warfare? All were suddenly aware of the enormity facing them. What, Katie signalled with raised eyebrows to Steve, have we let ourselves in for?

'Despite the assurances from our officers, our staff, I mean Mr Rainey, I am still worried,' Councillor Theodora insisted, 'that is, I mean, anxious, about the safety aspect of the event. I am really concerned about the possibility of people drinking and driving about on crowded roads being, well, benighted, I mean becoming overwhelmed by darkness. It could lead to innumerable fatal accidents.'

As chairman, Tim Penberthy felt he had allowed time enough for this discussion and wanted to press on to arrange a meeting to discuss matters of a more pressing nature, such as how to exploit the millions to be brought into this deprived area from the European Union by Objective One. There was also the need to discuss the advent of the millennium, the second great event of the year with its threat of disaster from the millennium bug disrupting computers and consequent communications from tourists trying to book accommodation for the next season. 'If the lady councillor agrees, we will ask the council's officers to look into the whole matter of safety and licensing for the event and consider their recommendations.'

All agreed, after Collateral Fred had made a proposal to that effect.

Theodora Yeoman, while objecting strongly to being referred to as 'the lady councillor', felt exonerated for broaching what had evidently been a contentious issue, and was grateful for the support of fellow councillor, Ms Whistler, although she was normally suspicious of that lady's self-righteousness. She suspected there might be some truth in Ezekial Endean's inferences regarding the wearing of a red hat and lack of underwear, although how he could be aware of that, she dreaded to think. Reggie and Freddie thought that by looking into the whole matter of licensing for the event there was the distinct possibility that opening hours and liquor licenses in general could be extended. So, everybody was happy with the outcome of what had evidently been a very fruitful meeting. They were about to bring the proceedings to a close, when Ms Whistler stated that she wished to raise a matter under 'Any Other Business', which she said was an omission on the agenda, and whose fault was that.

Chairman Tim Penberthy patiently reminded her that this extraordinary meeting had been called to discuss one subject but if she had a pressing matter he felt sure the council were prepared to listen. All assented and settled back to await a diatribe of complaints about one thing and another.

'And what,' Tim Penberthy asked her, 'is the matter that you wish to raise, Councillor?'

Winnie the Pew had an idea. It was an idea born of expediency, she assured herself, and one that was certain to meet with the approval of the full council if only she could get them to listen. Two birds, she mused, with one stone. The peace would be kept, unruly elements controlled, it would be a commercial success for local enterprises, and was a way of involving the highest powers without alarming the populace. More than a mere stone indeed, a veritable boulder of an idea to kill a whole flock of birds (with apologies to the RSPB, of course). The idea made her nervous, so brilliant and far-sighted was it. She was afraid, however, to breach such an idea in open council, to spring it upon them might be more than they could accommodate without warning. They would chuck it out as another hare-brained scheme of Winnie Whistler that hadn't a hope in hell of implementation. This time, she was determined to play them at their own game and get it all sewn up in committee before half of them knew what had hit them. Allies, though possibly treacherous, were needed. The potential advantages of the phenomenon were inevitably limited. Resources brought to the area would not be evenly spread if certain factions had their way. There was no point in recruiting (a good choice of words, she thought) no point in even attempting to recruit support from the farming community. That ruled out DDJ, and Denzil Trethewy. She could rely on Boy Steve Trevorrow, and Katie Stevens. The hoteliers would be indifferent as long as it helped with publicity. Collateral Fred would see his support as a good public relations exercise with the maritime element and could be relied on provided there was a chance of winning. Reggie Hammond would support her provided there was a chance of him being invited to the reception. Theodora Yeoman would definitely agree to the prospects of being surrounded by so many handsome young men, a prospect that Winnie herself had to admit was not unattractive. All in all, provided the appropriate authorities agreed, there was every chance of success so she had decided to put the matter before the council under any other business at this extraordinary meeting of the planning committee whether they liked it or not.

'What I wish to raise,' she said, 'is the Royal Navy.'

'Raise the Royal Navy?' DDJ spluttered, with astonishment.

'Raise the Navy!' Reggie murmured, loud enough to be heard by all. 'I didn't know they'd been sunk'.

Ms Whistler ignored them. 'Our community,' she said, 'has a long and close association with the sea.'

They had to agree with that, as all had seen the sea filling up the harbour on every tide.

'And our young men have a long tradition of serving in the senior service.' She paused for the nods of assent. After all, they were aware that the press, was still in the gallery. 'And, 'she continued, 'we have a long tradition of showing hospitality to Her Majesty's ships.'

Tim looked at her with growing interest. The woman, he thought, is about to talk sense. 'This, of course,' he said, 'is very true.'

'I hereby formally propose,' Ms Whistler announced, 'That we write to Her Majesty the Queen and invite her Royal Navy here on an official visit, to help us celebrate the forthcoming occasion.'

There was a stunned silence in the chamber. It was such an excellent proposal, with commercial possibilities right at the height of summer, that they were all kicking themselves for not having thought of it first, and for allowing themselves to be outwitted by a scatterbrain like Winnie the Pew. They were desperately trying to think of objections or amendments so that some, at least, of the praise could fall upon them.

DDJ's astonishment was because he had no inkling that Winnie the Pew ever had an original idea in her head. That this was due in part to the fact that he rarely listened to anybody else's words in council never occurred to him, although it came as a bit of a surprise to all of us that such a brilliant idea came from Winnie.

Reggie Hammond, who was aware that his contribution to the discussion had been minimal, and that a token support of the anti-alcohol brigade might enhance his fading reputation as a councillor, said, 'Good idea. They can keep their eyes on the trippers getting drunk out in the bay.'

Boy Steve Trevorrow was thinking that none of them knew what they were talking about, that there was really no chance of the Navy coming on an official visit in these straitened times and any discussion on the proposal would be just a waste of time. He was looking forward to having a drink with Katie in the pub after the meeting, so why not second the proposal and have done with it so that they could all get down The Ship before closing time. 'I second,' he said, lazily raising his right hand. The motion was carried unanimously.

Those genuinely in favour saw it as a return to tradition when the Navy put in a courtesy appearance every year and, should the situation get out of hand, with all those drunken hoards rampaging about the town, a way of using the armed forces to keep control with no expense to the ratepayers. Those against the absurd idea thought there was no way the Royal Navy would send a ship here in these times of financial restriction, so they could vote for it, get public approbation, and join in the general complaints about being neglected by Whitehall when the idea was turned down out of hand. Winnie was astonished that not a single objection was raised, that the idea received unanimous support, indeed, and went home a happy woman.

Tim Penberthy and DDJ could see all sorts of problems looming over the coming event, for which they might be held responsible and, remembering that councillors could be held personally liable for incompetence, had a little informal chat over a couple of brandy and sodas in the lounge of the pub after the meeting. They decided that, in view of the tremendous scale of the incident and its logistics, on top of normal council business, the extra pressures of controlling the event might well be beyond the abilities of morons like Robin Rainey, the clerk, whose evasive strategy had long been apparent, and the other officers. In order, therefore, that the council should be seen as far-sighted and efficient, the best thing would be to persuade them to head-hunt a high flyer who could take over all the organisational responsibilities and, while he was at it, all of the blame too if the whole thing, they agreed in a whisper, got screwed up.

When Zeke reported back on the meeting to anybody who would listen to him, we all knew that inviting the Navy here was another excuse for councillors attempting to get dined and wined at taxpayers expense. They had more than enough to cope with without a damn great warship out in the bay. Nothing would come of it.

'I ceant* see,' Ezekiel told us, when commenting on the coming event, 'why they're making such a fuss about it getting dark for once. I've been around for a few years and in all that time it's got dark every bleddy night.'

*Ceant = cehnt = cain't = can't = cannot; weant = won't = will not; sheant = shan't = shall not. The editors had considerable discussion on how to transcribe this key sound on the tapes. The vowel sounds are quite unlike anything in standard English and impossible to render by syllable, vowel or diphthong. It must be heard, so bear with us as we do our best to render it without resorting to phonetic symbols which you couldn't read either. Eds.

TAPE TWO

...the time is come, the day of trouble is near... Behold therefore I
will bring strangers upon thee, the terrible of the nations...

As we remember it, the headlines in the local weekly broadsheet on the following Thursday blared 'GUNBOAT TO CONTROL CROWDS'. This gave the junior reporter his first front-page feature but did not achieve a great deal in alleviating the growing panic among the populace.

To aggravate matters we had two local phenomena of our own to contend with at about the time when people first became anxious about the coming events. Shimshai was coming home and Quizzy Maggie died.

In recalling these momentous events we must emphasise that even within such a small community as ours there are many souls, each with their individual lives, their sorrows and joys, and we cannot here relate every tale that circulates among us and has been recorded for posterity. We have selected but a few, in the trust that these may represent the whole community in the events to be recorded.

We regret that there was one, indeed two, among us who by virtue of their standing as bards and historians of our community should have recorded the events as they unfolded, the one being Barnabas the Bard and the second the aforementioned Shimshai the Scribe. However, the interest of the first lies in the past, so the momentous present, as it happened at that fateful time, was lost to him as much as to the rest of us, as he became overwhelmed by the calamity and retreated into solitude. The second was of such a romantic nature that he failed to observe the mundane and allowed his imagination to soar to heights beyond the normal mortal ken. There was nothing the ordinary populace could do but gather together to await the passing of the event and then to relate our experiences to each other on these tapes as in a healing therapy that might enable us to resume some semblance of a normal life. So, bear with us as we endeavour to relate the events as we remember them and, trusting that at the end of sorrow there does indeed come joy, read on.

The first to know of the impending calamity, long before the rest of us, was he of academia, the novelist and scholar, Shimshai the Scribe, for he was exiled among the learned and obscure intellectuals who become aware of strange phenomenon through the interaction and communications of their peers. Upon consulting his charts and tables he decided that such a great event required his presence in the land of his birth and he wrote forthwith to the poet, Barnabas Baragwaneth, known to the rest of us as Barny the Bard, informing him of his intention.

Barny had a young friend, one Katie Stevens, who was trying to persuade him to become involved in a programme to record the voices of older people to be stored in an archive of oral reminiscences.

'All the old ways are going,' she said. 'The language is gone, and the dialect is going too. We have a duty to preserve it for generations to come.'

'I'm not so sure about that,' Barny said. 'The problem is that as soon as people's attention is drawn to their dialect they become self-conscious and stop using it. The best way to preserve language and dialect is to speak it. How many of us are prepared to do that and be regarded as backward illiterates by those in power, in schools and jobs? We have to abandon the old ways. Making recordings of old people is like… it's like having them stuffed and put on show in glass cases.'

He knew that this meant abandoning all their traditions, and was not really sincere in what he said. He was not very keen to be involved with old people and, on the day Shimshai's letter arrived, when she was with him at his home discussing the project, he was thankful for a reason to change the subject.

'Shimshai's coming home,' he told Katie.

'You keep referring to Shimshai,' Katie protested,' but I've never met him. Who is he?'

'One of my older contemporaries. One of those who went away to better himself. He's an academic, a writer. He's a bit of a character. A great guy, but he's got a bit pompous in his old age. It happens to academics.'

Barny is much older than Katie. Katie at this time would have been about twenty-nine and had known Barny for years. They were both interested in our history and culture and could speak to each other in the old language. Katie was an extremely attractive young woman, and Barny was well aware of it although she seemed not to realise it, and neither did she know that she was the one thing in his life that made him regret being old. This regret made him feel older than he was, which was, let's see, a bit older than Uncle Joe and a brea bit younger than Steve Trevorrow, who was sixty-nine at the time we're telling you about. You'll think that's very old if you're under twenty.

He had to be careful when talking to Katie about the past. The trouble with the past is that there's such an enormous amount of it and no two people remember it the same. His version, some of which included both Katie and her mother, he kept to himself, people thought, but there was much of it in his poetry for those who thought to look. Much of the past is best forgotten but when Barny remembered the days of their youth he wondered, as we all did, how two of the most attractive women this town has ever produced had never married. It was a crying shame, a tragedy, he thought, and often wished he'd been home when Sarah was young, or later, when all that stuff with Steve and Shimshai's woman happened, or that he could be twenty, well OK, twenty-five, years younger now, when Katie was herself so irresistible. Despite the difference in their ages, these two, as we all knew, spent a lot of time together and were very close. They had that rare open and accepting relationship that enabled them to be absolutely honest about each other. They shared personal emotions and sentiments that many a married partnership would have found too revealing. It was partly because of a shared incident that they never mentioned, had not mentioned for many years, but mainly because they shared an indifference to what other people, that's us mind you, thought of them. We were a bit jealous of that relationship, to tell the truth, which is not always advisable.

'He's always coming home,' Katie said. 'Why've I never met him? Will he record a tape, do you think?'

'Sure. He loves the sound of his own voice. He usually stays for just a day or so, but this time it's for good. He's retiring, although he won't like being called old. He wants to be home for the excitement.'

'Oh, that! I'm dreading it already. The council are having another special meeting to discuss the implications. It's going to be terrible.'

'Will Boy Steve be at the meeting?'

'Yes. The tides are wrong for fishing that day.'

'And how are you? You two?'

'Oh, you know. Not good.'

Shimshai was not merely coming home. He was also dying, he said! His demise was not altogether unanticipated. After such a long and uneventful life the end was inevitably near. And it seemed to us that he was determined to enjoy his death in the same way that he had enjoyed his life. Not a lot wrong with that, except that by doing so he could make life a little bit difficult for a lot of us. He tells tales, see? That's why the unexpected, and not altogether welcome factor in his demise was his choosing to come back here to die, the thoughtless tuss! As if there weren't enough of us dying already. We are dying too, always have been, but Shimshai has been dying the longest. It's his artistic temperament, don't 'ee see. He said he came back, came home, to retire and die, but the fact is Shimshai came home to experience the dark time and document the invasion and then die along with the rest of us, which might take quite a while.

Shimshai came home a while before the event, sometime after the end of the previous academic year, in fact, when he took early retirement to continue writing. Early in the sense that he quit before they threw him out due to the incompetence of old age. He's no chicken. Should have packed it in years ago, like everybody else. Anybody would think he's hard up. So he came home in the springtime, or was it early summer, say June, but the exact timing was neither here nor there. Some, like Ezekiel, reckon he was home in May, but Zeke hardly knows day from night when he's working on one of his crazy projects. Steve said he came before Maggie died and didn't go to the funeral.

It was the moon that drew Shimshai back. After so many years of prevarication he came home at last, as so many of us do who are obliged to spend our productive years away in the wilderness. How ironical that he came to see the moon obliterate the sun, which has been shining on us intermittently ever since he left.

Shimshai is home, they said, and he has brought his woman. Perhaps, the time of the darkness was not the most opportune moment to reintroduce her to so many memories. She was, after all, the truly innocent one among so many rogues, and he, Shimshai, the greatest rogue of all, for there is no greater crime than the theft of love.

That's what Barny the Bard said, 'No greater crime than the theft of love', when he was stuck in front of his new-fangled electronic brain trying to forget his past by writing it all down. He and Shimshai should have known that there is nothing more guaranteed to retain memories than the attempt to obliterate them.

Shimshai came home by train, for his woman – we'll never see her as his wife – came down later with their car, following the removal van and all their belongings, after he'd moved in and prepared his old home. It was raining when he arrived. Well, drizzling, but in some respects that's the best time to revisit the place and see it through a mist, so that details become obscured, as in his books where he ridiculed us all. The man was never hardly here. What does he know?

He carried a rucksack slung over one shoulder. That's Shimshai all over. An ordinary suitcase or a holdall or something would have been too conventional. He still thought of himself as a kind of non-conformist, although he's such a product of the establishment that he wears outlandish clothes to proclaim his identity. I'm a writer, they said, his clothes, slightly shabby, expensive when new, a white linen coat under that black, wide-rimmed hat worn in such a care-fully contrived indifference to fashion as to be right up there with the trendies. The mainline train was late but there had been no waiting about at the junction because it was so late that it arrived in time to meet the next connection on the branch line. There was a certain trepidation in his eye as he went past the taxis at the station, intending to walk down to his house. There was old Sam, the taxi man, waiting beside his car for trains, as he had done for years. They'll all be working still, he thought, resentful of my retirement, but he was wrong. Sam was just waiting to pick up one of his many grandchildren from the train.

From the top of the station steps, (ah yes, the steps) he looked down at the harbour, the view partly obscured by a new extension to a hotel on the road below, and went up to the bus station. The drizzle increased to slaggy rain and softened the outline of the quays, the headland and the white tower of the lighthouse across the bay blending into the distant mist. From this higher viewpoint he could see a few people, in bright plastic rainwear, looking into shop windows along the wharf, and some boys in black wetsuits diving from the prom. The place looked utterly devoid of local activities that he remembered. The boats in the harbour had no one aboard. There was nobody by the old slipway or on the quay or by lodge. He felt a sense of relief over that. In every community there is a centre to the lines of communication, like a spiders web radiating through the homes of the populace. For some it's the church, the chapel or the local pub but, in this society, in his youth, in the days he remembered most vividly, it had always been the lodges and the plat beside the harbour, where the men gathered after times at sea, or working abroad, to catch up on the news. Few of us there now would remember him but those who did would tell all about him, as items of news to be spread like vibrations along silken threads to everyone who still belonged to the old community. Poor old Shimshai had acquired urban values and saw our interest in his life and deeds as intrusion. He walked past the plat, head down against the rain, and saw no faces peering through the steamy window panes.

However, by the time he arrived at his front door, a good many of us knew of his arrival.

'Shimshai's home I see.'

'Is she with 'n?'

'No. She's coming pembye*. He wrote to Barny the Bard and told him his plans.'

At the time, Old Steve listened in silence; he thought he could

*i.e. by and by! See what we mean? Eds.

never face her. Even after all this time, but there had been many things in the intervening years that he thought he could never face. Losing his wife was one. She had been so tough and healthy he never considered she'd go first, but he had come to terms with it. The loneliness of old age was a different matter, one that he faced with some trepidation. 'I can't see what they want to come back here for,' he grumbled. 'There's nothing here for them now.' As Old Steve became more fed up with being old, the cynical side of his character became more prevalent with the passing years.

'What have we come to?' Old Steve queried. 'Leaning over these railings everyday, lookin' at the sae*. I've worked it out. I've seen the bleddy tide move in and out, twice a day, forty-three thousand, seven hundred and fifty-three times, allowing for holidays and days off sick.'

It's what you've been working for all your life, we said. You don't have to come down here. If you had money and all, you'd be going to your club every day. Looking at four walls. Expensive walls, and maybe a marble fireplace. Or you can stay home and watch the telly. Who d' want to see that every damn day for the rest of their lives?

'I went to Spain with Mary, one time,' Old Steve continued as Ceecil listened intently, 'and in a village I saw a pile of old men walking up and down in the village square. Up and down, in the shade of the trees surrounding the piazza, up and down, back and forth for hours on end. What a life!'

'They used to do that here,' Collateral Fred said with enthusiasm, 'I remember it well. Pace the bridge. That's what it was. Pace the bridge. The bridge on a ship,' he cried. 'Twelve paces from port to starboard and come about.'

'That's what I mean!' Old Steve insisted. 'We don't do nawthen these days, not even pace up and down, just lean over the bleddy railin's.'

'Times change.' Collateral Fred said. 'You have to keep up with the times.'

Barny the Bard burst out laughing, Old Steve followed, and there were grins all round.

'Wus funny?' Fred said.

'Wus funny?' asked Ceecil.

*Sea, for heaven's sake, sea!

Barnabas Baragwaneth, Barny the Bard, as a local historian is the one who d' reckon to be the one recording everything for posterity and, after some persuasion from maid Katie, had just begun working with her on the oral history project. The social historian, if you will. Did we say posterity? Ha! Posterity your posterior. Or, posterity my arse, as they say up London, all he's really doing is trying to find some order in his own chaotic mind.

'Where bound, Barny?' He don't come this way very often.

'I'm waiting to take Katie over to see my cousin.'

'Never knew you had a cousin.'

'Of course I have a cousin! Cousins,' Barny said, 'are like parents, or lustful desires, everybody has them.'

You speak for yourself, said she of the red hat.

Barny has no close relatives, so this distant cousin was so distant that he had to think back to work out how they were related. His grandmother and his cousin's father's mother were both grandmothers, something like that. He's closer to Katie than anybody else, due to events of the past, but his cousin and he had one thing in common, their love of that distant relative of the tea plant, the camellia. Barny grew a few out where he lived, but it's too exposed out there and they no sooner reached a good size than that north winds cuts them to ribbons. If there were no other reasons for staying out there on that exposed coast, his love of camellias would have induced a move to the more salubrious and sheltered side years ago.

His cousin was named Arthur Trezise, a gardener. He was the son of a gardener whose mother had been the daughter of one of the most famous plantsmen of his time. They'd all worked on the same estate. His employers knew hardly anything about him or his family, these days, for they were suffering hard times and were too worried about their own affairs to be concerned with the private lives of their employees, who were now more than taken care of by the welfare state anyway.

In the springtime, Barny would take Katie over to see the great garden where Arthur worked, with its wonderful show of rhododendrons and azaleas and, of course, to see what progress had been made in the development of his favourite flower.

He could see Katie over on the quay, waiting for Boy Steve. Boy

Steve was in a bad mood. We could see that, just by the way he was walking up'long with the crew. He had his waterproof coat slung over his shoulder and looked at nobody. He didn't even see three young female tourists as he passed them by. One in jeans, one in shorts, and one in a thin dress and a straw hat who looked at him with open admiration. He missed that and would have missed Katie if she had not obstructed his progress by standing in his way. His old man, all agreed, would never have missed any of them. Even now, the randy old goat.

'Hullo,' Boy Steve grumbled. 'What you doing down here?'

'Well, I came to see you, if you must know,' Katie protested. 'Before I meet up with Barny. What's the matter? You're looking black as the devil.'

'No wonder! I'm black as they devils in Brussels. The world's going mad and they're driving it even more insane every day.'

'What've they done now'? Katie asked as they walked up the quay.

'They've just killed two tons of prime fish and left them to rot and pollute the ocean for miles around.' He unslung his coat from the right shoulder and swung it angrily around his left. 'Jacky Tyke and they were over quota. And me and the boys in the toshers abm made enough to cover the cost of the trip. It's bleddy madness.'

'They dumped them?'

'Yeah. Dumped them, because they're over quota and would've been fined if they'd landed them. Again!'

Katie decided to say nothing more on the subject. They had more than enough discussions, arguments, and bloody rows at times, over the matter of the fishing industry, all of which had contributed to their growing apart. 'It's the same old story,' she said, not wanting any more of it. 'You ought to try to cash in on the big event.'

'There's nothing in it for us,' he said. 'We're usually busy at that time of year anyway. People aren't going to pay to go out in a boat to see what's better seen from dry land.'

'You wouldn't do it, but that doesn't mean that there aren't others who would. If only to get away from the crowds.'

'Maybe. What do you want to see me about?'

'I was going to ask if you'd like to ask me out.'

'Where to?'

'Can't you think of anywhere? There's the flower show, a horse show, the operatic society's show, the art galleries, the restaurants, even the pictures at a push, there's no end of places. We could even go for a walk.'

'Sure! And afterwards it would be night, night, sleep tight. No more your place or mine.'

'You don't have a place.'

'Tha's no fair! Sarah might have agreed to converting the top half of her house for you. But there's no way Da would do it. He says it ruins a fine old house. You know what he's like. If you'd agreed, we could have bought somewhere together a few years ago. Now there's no chance. You know what I'm getting at.'

'Yes. You're right. Sorry. But invite me out, Steve. We need to have a serious discussion.' And while he was fumbling for a reply, 'Ah, there's Barny. I'll see you later.'

'You're spending a lot of time with him lately.'

'We're working on the community archive together. An oral history project. Barny's recording old people's memories.'

He was, going about with a tape recorder interviewing old people, because, Katie said, he was so much closer to them. 'They'll be far more willing to talk to someone young, Barny reasoned, 'but I'll have a go.'

'Let's hope he doesn't record everything,' Boy Steve said. 'Not of his own past, anyway. Or ours!'

'He's not like Shimshai,' Katie said. 'We can trust him. I have to go.'

She gave him a perfunctory kiss on the cheek and skipped, like a young girl, over to Barny.'

Despite his sins, which were nearly all of omission and contrived amnesia, Shimshai was welcomed home nevertheless, for we knew more about him than he did himself and, no matter what had befallen him in the intervening years, he would always be one of us. Of his woman, we were not so sure, and neither was she sure of us. We had seen her so briefly, so long ago, that all our recollections

were sure to have been distorted by the passage of time. We knew
that their memories of us were of an age that has utterly disappeared
and, whereas we lived through the change and adapted gradually, to
return was often in the hope of stepping back through life, to days no
longer credible, so different were they from the present. They might
well be in for some surprises, disappointments even.

'Lots of us went away too. To hear Shimshai going on,' Steve said,
'you'd think he was the only one ever to cross the bar. I went away.
Barny went away. Lots of us went away. Only some were a bit
touched by the experience.'

'Like Henny Penny,' Katie said, with that infectious, childlike
laugh which she still retains. She was right, but mind you, we always
have to make allowances.

''lowances,' Zeke said. 'We make too many damn 'lowances.' We
weren't sure what he was talking about. 'I'll give 'ee 'lowances.'

'Give 'ee 'lowances,' Ceecil said.

Some became very grand of course, like Henny, living above his
station. Well, living above his shop to be exact. Henny was one of
those who went away. Who went away in more senses than one, if
you know what we mean. A bit touched!

And some can't tell truth from lies, like Shimshai. Shimshai's the
one. The one who really can't tell truth from lies. He has a leaning
to fiction but he's inclined to exaggerate, there's no doubt about that.
'How', we asked 'do you get away with telling so many lies about
people'. 'Easy,' he said. 'If they complain, I threaten to tell the truth.
That soon shuts them up'. What he actually said, when he wrote it
down, was, 'The inherent peril in accurate revelations will inevitably
quell the protestations of libel regarding minor economies of truth.'
Hee hee!

He came in here, that time when he retired and came back to live
here for good. Well, he thought it was for 'good', but some of us
had our own opinions about that. He still had this English way of
speaking at the time.

I've just been to see Henry,' Shimshai said.

'What Henry?' There's hundreds of Henrys.

'Henry Penny. I'm looking for a nice present for my lady to
celebrate the millennium'

He was like Henny Penny in some ways; they make a very good pair if you ask us, although we don't suppose you will. You can't blame him for the way he spoke, for if you deal with foreigners you have to speak their language, but to hear Henny going on was bleddy irritating to those of us who remembered him going to school with the rags of his ass (we don't say arse) beating his brains out. As if he'd never forgotten his roots and deliberately abandoned talking like we.

Now, you would think poor parents would know better then to lumber a cheeld with a name like that. No sooner could he go down the foreshore to play with his *Cok an Baban* than he was 'Henny Penny abm any'. Well, they never had much, that family but, perhaps because of those early taunts and poverty, Henny learned to ignore what other people said or thought about him and did all right. He was a bit out of it, mind, and forgot his roots, deliberately forgot his roots as an unnecessary encumbrance, and cultivated the manners of his masters, a bit like Shimshai really. It always pays off, and Henny did all right although we knew little about his time away, some of which was said to have been lived in the shadow of the Dartmoor sun. We had no proof of that. Put it this way, Henny did what Henny wanted to do and to hell with the rest of us, and there you are. Happiness.

Quizzy Maggie, on the other hand, had never changed one iota during her entire life. Well, she got older, no denying that. In fact she kept on getting older until she was into her late nineties. She had not the slightest wish to reach the ton, for she realised one day that all she had ever lived for was gone. She was a woman without malice, which was hard to believe for her interest in life had always been minding other people's business. We all knew that our own secret business was so utterly boring and mundane that we did our utmost to keep it private, while Maggie spent her life in devising ways of inveigling information out of people in order to enrich her own, even more boring, existence. A bit like a kind of unlettered literary genius, a writer without pen and ink, if you like. She found out everything about us, eventually. The incomers were no concern of hers, nor she of theirs. So, when she felt like it, she died. Nothing wrong with that, or with her, the doctors said. She died of old age. We thought she just didn't want to face the madness which was about to descend upon us. Poor soul.

In her youth she had one good friend, Tommy Blue, who might have been more than a friend, and who passed on years ago. We never knew if Maggie had ever been touched up, felt up, or fiddled around with, for she'd made damned certain that nobody ever knew any of her private business. She still had one fairly close friend even in her old age, for it takes one to know one, and Ezekiel Endean, just as nuts, and intelligent as Maggie in his way, had taken Tommy's place in her old age. Neither was anybody's fool.

Zeke said, 'The minnellium is months away, Shimshai. Beatin' on for two years. You're in plenty of time to buy a present.'

Maggie was ancient, although, as was to be expected with one so solitary and secretive, no one alive knew just how old she was until she died. She had outlived all her friends, few that they were, and when her acquaintances and neighbours began to go had nobody's business to pry into. That's hardly surprising seeing she was one of the last to live down there. She kept vaguely in touch with the distant world through her television and with more immediate events though Ezekiel Endean, who lived a couple of doors down the street and was her only permanent neighbour. Most of the houses anywhere near the harbour are nothing but holiday lets. But who d' want to live down there anyway, amongst all the cars, crowds, nosey people geekin' in your windows all day, and noisy buggers coming out of the pubs at night? Who d' want that, eh? Well, Ezekiel Endean for one. Almost the only one, but Zeke says 'This is mine, this is where I d' belong, and they can geek as much as they mind to, I'm staying.' One reason for his growing friendship with Quizzy Maggie, who he had previously regarded as a silly old busybody, was the fact that she was the only one in the street who could understand him.

'They ceant talk fitty down'long now,' he said, 'nown o' them. 'Not like we b'long to.'

'I's a brea crant when nobody ceant talk fitty, you,' Quizzy Maggie said.

Maggie received an occasional letter, for she had nephews and nieces out to California, where her younger sister went when she married a Yank from the 29th Infantry after the war. He went over on

D-Day and they never expected to see him again, so many of them were killed, but he came back here after the war and carted the maid off to the states. You didn't know that did 'ee. There you are, see, Maggie never let on much about herself or her family and Shimshai didn't know it all. In fact, Maggie was secretly following her young sister and her Yank out to Mester after chapel, to see they didn't get up to no hanky-panky, when some horrible little vandals up on the station steps threw a frenchie full of water on her head and ruined her brand-new hat. Now, who would do such a thing? Some say it gave her water on the brain, but others reckoned her brain was a bit washed out long before that regrettable incident of which the less said the better.

Her sister went out there to 'merica and never came back once but she had maintained her original identity and baked pasties for her children once a year until she died. When Maggie's eyesight failed, Zeke used to read the rare letters from her American nephews and nieces.

Shimshai's woman had a soft spot for Maggie, for once upon a time Maggie had shown her some compassion during a time of distress. Another thing that Maggie never spoke of, and neither did Shimshai's woman, so we didn't know of it either. Upon returning she went to see Maggie, who remembered her well and was glad to see anybody from her lengthy past. It was seeing Shimshai's woman with greying hair and a thickening waist that helped convince Maggie that she was old, had outlived everybody who was anybody, and that it was time to go. As one who had made funerals the height of her social life, her own, she said to Zeke in a rare moment of wry humour, was the only one she hadn't been to. She was the ideal one to do one of they tapes, we told Barny, but she wudn keen.

Shimshai's woman was still an artist. She and Shimshai were a very good pair, a better pair than ever she and Old Steve would have made. Both of them realised that but they had misgivings about meeting after all the years of memories of their passionate romance. When Shimshai mentioned that he would like to retire and come home, his woman had been reluctant but eventually succumbed to his persuasion.

'My roots are there,' he said. 'All my old friends.'

About the roots, tenuous though they might be, she had to agree, for his youth and most of his writings had been set here. As for the friends, she was not so sure. 'They might not welcome you,' she said, 'after all you've written about them.'*

'My books are all fiction,' Shimshai insisted. At which, like all of us, she merely smiled. He had come to believe it, and she allowed him to live in his own world of words, as she lived in her own of paint and colour. Her own early life had been so itinerant that she could claim no roots, so to retire here, where she could paint all that she had thought of over the years, would also be the fulfilment of at least half a dream.

When they had returned and settled in, in Shimshai's old house, we would see her go out with her easel, as in the old days, to sketch or paint the local scenes while he stayed at home writing. The spring sunshine warmed the pastel shades of the houses, the faces of the people and the granite stones of the twin quays, between which she often sat, back to the sun, immersed in her work. It was on such a day, when we were watching her, that she slowly became aware of a shadow falling beside her. At first she ignored it, for a glance or a nod could invoke unwanted questions or conversation. Alfresco artists must become inured to the curiosity or admiration of bystanders, and they soon went away if unacknowledged. This one stayed, and the artist became disconcerted at the immobility of the shadow, a little to her right, but kept mixing the colours in her palette. It was a moment she had anticipated with some trepidation, fearful of when he would appear, as so often in the past, looking over her shoulder at her work. She waited for that deeply accented voice to say hello, nothing more, as was his way. But there was no sound, not even of a sniff or a cough, or a sigh. Eventually the shadow moved, briefly casting shade over her canvas from the low, afternoon sun, but only to the artist's left, before becoming immobile again. After applying paint that was of a shade unintended, Shimshai's woman could resist no longer and turned to see, not him, but a woman, younger – in her twenties? – dark-haired, whose face was uncannily familiar, looking at the painting with equally dark, expressionless, eyes. She was wearing a ragged pullover under a fisherman's smock, dirty jeans and short rubber boots. No hat

*See postscript on p.202.

covered her untidy brown hair. A fleeting smile crossed the face, and, with an irrational sense of relief, the artist returned to her work and applied another stroke of the palette knife.

Now, we could see all this going on, and we thought, a brea crant here dreckly! When they d' each find out who the other was. We could hear no voices, not from that far away, but we could guess what they were saying, we thought.

'Do you use the knife,' Katie asked, 'always?'

'No. Not always.' It was a question often asked, meaningless, as a way of engaging in conversation that preceded the comment that the observer also did a bit of daubing.

'It's a technique that suits your subject,' Katie said. 'Sharp-edged shadows. The light and shadows on the water. Wet sand reflecting the sky. It's all there, but you have to look for it.'

Shimshai's woman turned to look at the observer and for once, found herself asking the question. For there was something in the other's eye indicating a genuine appreciation of what she was doing. 'Do you paint?'

'No. But I work part time at the gallery and I've watched a lot of artists. Living here, it's inevitable.'

'Yes, I suppose. There seem to be more artists here than ever. And have you any preferences?'

'No! Most of them are...' she paused, but, being Katie, not for long, '...shall I say... not to my taste.' She gave a little shrug of apology. 'I think there are some who are genuinely trying to be original, but without the skills. I haven't really liked any of them since Tony Connolly died.'

'You knew Tony?'

'Yes. I assume you did too?'

'You know me?'

'Of course! You're Shimshai's woman.'

Shimshai's woman laughed. 'Is that who I am? Then who are you?' she asked. 'What's your name?'

'Katie Stevens.'

Shimshai's woman shook her head. The name meant nothing to her. How could it? 'I must have been here before you were born,' she said, 'and then not for very long.'

'I know. My Ma told me about you. My Ma is Sarah Stevens. Do you remember her?'

Here it was, the past catching up. 'No. I don't think so. I probably saw her, not knowing who she was.'

'No? Well, she's older than you and moved in different circles, I expect. She had little to do with the artists' community.'

Now, it was about then that Old Steve came up and joined us leaning over the railings. When we say us, we don't mean all of us, that ought to be obvious. We are never all together all at one and the same time, but that's how we don't miss very much of what goes on. Some of us are always somewhere. You must see that, surely.

Stevens, Shimshai's woman was thinking, mother and daughter, same name. People usually referred to their fathers when identifying themselves in small communities. Perhaps there had been no father or, rather, no marriage? This Katie seemed a pleasant person, someone she might wish to befriend. It seemed advisable to avoid the subject of events of thirty-odd years ago. 'I suppose strangers are always recognised,' she said.

Katie liked the demeanour of the other woman, she had a frank look in her eye equivalent to her own. She could be trusted, Katie thought, with secrets. 'Not any more,' she said, 'there are too many of them,' and realising her blunder, broke into laughter. 'Sorry,' she said. 'I didn't mean you.'

The other also laughed. The times she had heard that, 'sorry, I didn't mean you'. He had always said it. Lying to her and himself. She was, and always would be, a stranger. Not only here but wherever she lived. 'Do you work in the harbour too?'

'Not really. I help Boy Steve sometimes.'

'Boy Steve?'

'Old Steve Trevorrow's son.'

We could see, by the body language what they d' call, that here was a shift in attitudes. Old Steve turned his back to them, with a grim curl to his lips like a ground swell runnin' over Gowna, and didn't see the odd wink or two that passed from one to another.

Maid Katie watched Shimshai's woman pack up her painting gear and they walked together over the foreshore to the quay steps. On the way they stopped at Boy Steve's fishing boat, the *Morvoren*, and

Katie clambered aboard to lift out a canvas bag. On the quay they passed a cluster of suited men with clipboards and tape measures who spoke to Katie with deference. Robin Rainbird said, 'Good afternoon, Miss Stevens', and she stopped briefly to discuss the proposed work. 'Council officials,' Katie explained, 'measuring up for temporary safety-railing that may have to be erected for the day. Utter waste of money,' she said to Shimshai's woman. 'All for two minutes and five seconds of darkness.'

'It seems,' Shimshai's woman said, 'that we're to be overwhelmed. We're thinking of going away for a few days to avoid it all.'

'If you do, you can charge a fortune for letting your house,' Katie said, 'but you'd better go early and return late for, from what our experts are saying, all the roads will be blocked with traffic, and trains and planes are expected to be fully booked weeks in advance.'

'Your experts?'

'I'm on the local council. We've employed extra staff to co-ordinate it all. They've been three years planning to avoid total chaos, but still have no idea what to expect. I even heard that Concorde has been chartered to fly through it and the QE2 and other liners are expected to add to the flotillas of ships around the coast. We'll see.'

On the council? Shimshai's woman was thinking. Not your usual idea of a local dignitary.

'And how is Shimshai?' Katie said.

'Do you know him, too?'

'No. Not really. He won't know me. He also left before I was born.'

'Come up and meet him. Come and have tea with us,' Shimshai's woman said.

Maid Katie made a gesture towards her grimy clothes, a gesture the other dismissed with a sweep of the wrist. 'We just might get him to reminisce about the good old days,' she said, 'as if he ever stops. And he's always happy to talk to an attractive woman.'

'Aren't they all?' Katie said.

That things were 'not too good' between her daughter and Boy Steve was a matter of some concern to Sarah Stevens. After nearly ten years together they were no nearer to marriage or even a stated commitment than they had ever been. Unlike many women of potential grandmother status, Sarah's concern was not that they might part, but that they might decide to stay together in an unsatisfactory union that would bring joy to neither. She had seen it happen before and could she have her time over again would, in at least one case, have done her utmost to prevent it. No partner is better than the wrong partner, of that she was sure. She never mentioned any of this to us, or to Katie for, apart from being a very private person, she had brought her daughter up to make her own decisions and was reluctant to offer advice that might have been regarded as persuasion. The eighteen-year difference in the ages of Katie and Boy Steve was less apparent as the years passed, and she was sure that was no longer an obstacle in the way of their relationship.

She watched through the big bay window, wet with drizzle, as Katie came along the terrace to the house where both had lived all their lives. She smiled at the recollection of her parents and what they would think of their daughter and granddaughter if they could but know. So pious they had been, good, God-fearing people who had brought Sarah up to be the same. Yet, here she was with an illegitimate daughter who was committing fornication with total indifference to God or the Devil. How the world had changed, Sarah thought with a slight disbelieving shake of the head, and in such a short time. Who would have believed it? She was no longer God-fearing herself. She had a far more intimate and understanding relationship with him than fear. It was one of, she said, mutual respect. Only old Margaret Pender ever admonished her. The only one who had dared, for Sarah was renowned for her quiet assertiveness in all walks of her life.

'You'll have to answer for your sins,' Maggie had said 'when you're called to meet your maker.'

'I 'spect so Maggie,' Sarah had said in that quiet, resigned voice, 'and my answers are all ready. But I have a few questions for our maker too, if he'll be kind enough to answer me.'

'I told her,' Sarah remembered joking with Katie, 'my question to our maker will be about quality control.'

This had been beyond Maggie's understanding and she went off muttering about the sins of the mothers being 'zackly the same as they of the fathers in the eyes of the Lord'.

Katie came in, removed her wet clothes and flopped into a chair. 'Whacked,' she said.

'You haven't walked all the way from Barny's.'

'No, halfway. Took the bus the first half. Looking forward to the summer.'

'Summer!' Sarah said. 'From what I hear it's going to be terrible. All they people.'

'It's just another example of the world going mad. I doubt if it'll affect us much.'

'Well, I don't know,' Sarah mused. 'They were saying down town that everything will be in chaos. Millions of people panicking and no food and no water. The roads and railways all at a standstill. It sounds awful.'

'I don't believe it. It's just media talk. Blowing everything up beyond all reason.'

'I hope you're right,' Sarah said, ' The place could be devastated.' And, in an attempt to discover a little more about her daughter's growing involvement with Barny the Bard asked, 'And how is Barny? I d' hardly ever see 'n.'

'OK. He's still reluctant to become fully involved with the oral archive. But he did suggest I ask Quizzy Maggie for an interview. Wus she called again?'

'Margaret Pender. She weant do no interview with you,' Sarah laughed. 'She d' hate my sight, and yours too I 'spect.'

TAPE THREE

Therefore, thou son of man, prepare thee stuff for removing...

Shimshai the Scribe, trying to reconcile past and present, also wrote:

We were equally culpable. Right from the very start. We were all in it together! There is no doubt about it; and, while some never mention it, as if they were not involved or wish to forget it, others never stop re-examining it, as if they were the only ones who had ever experienced anything, and grumble the same old grumbles over and over. Our small community is as varied as any other, although we were subject to influences which brought out certain common qualities. With the two industries of mining and fishing in our past, we have been well aware of tragedies that bring a community closer as well as the divisions that these two competitive industries engender. You would think, after all this time, that we would have resolved the old conflicts, sorted the old problems and learned to live together while we strove for a common goal. No chance. Only the mad among us are universally regarded with compassion and endearment, for they epitomize all our follies. Not even in the face of an invasion from another world were we united in the common cause. Another world? From several other worlds! The oracles forecast an onslaught unprecedented in times of peace. The authorities took precautions. The warning propaganda went out over all the available media. But, as we knew full well, there was no way of knowing when or where the invasion would occur. The defences were puny, and all directed against the invaders taking over open country. There was no way of keeping them out of the towns and cities.

Well, that's Shimshai all over. In fact, in all of this, as in impending and actual disasters throughout the world, life went on as usual for most of the populace. Shut away in his attic he was not very much in touch with any of us and still lived, as he had done for most of his life, in his imagination. Like many who left small peripheral places for life in the central conurbations, where societies were comprised of disjointed fragments from far and wide obliged to communicate in the language of the common denominator, he had lost his accent. We never forgave him for that, although, unlike Henny Penny, his loss was uncontrived and inevitable. He assumed his reassimilation was universally accepted, and it was. What he couldn't see was that it was not without reservation on the part of some of us. He was never brought face to face with Sarah Stevens, for instance, for which he should have been very thankful had he but known of her ferocious loathing of him and his woman. With Steve Trevorrow, from whom by connivance and perseverance he had stolen her, he appeared to be as friendly as ever. On his frequent brief visits in the past they had maintained a fragile friendship, for each conceded that the outcome of their past involvements had been for the best all round, in the end. They met, up on the plat, or in the pub, and joked and laughed or discussed the various plans of developers to gobble up the last juicy sites about the town, just as any two friends might do anywhere. There was one subject they never discussed; whether in public or in private they managed to avoid the one thing that might fracture this friendship forever. Now that Shimshai's woman was living here, it seemed inevitable that her name would arise in conversation between themselves or with others of us. It didn't happen. We never mentioned her in their presence and neither of those two was likely to, so their friendship, on the face of it, continued unimpeded. However, whereas Shimshai had become insensitive to the realities of life, shut up in that attic, and assumed that his woman and Old Steve would have no problems when they met, Old Steve was terrified of their inevitable next encounter. Maybe, he thought, it would have been easier were Mary still alive, for then the old restraint would still be there, instead of which he was free to quarrel or kiss, to hate or, the most dreaded emotion of all, to love her.

Barny Baragwaneth, who was younger and wiser than Old Steve, was also having trouble with his emotional life at the time we're recounting here. His wisdom, possibly misplaced, enabled him to appear to us untroubled by anything except his past. How could we have seen it otherwise, for his past was all we knew about? His interest in the heritage of our people and places meant that, despite his initial reluctance, he soon became as enthusiastic about the oral archive as Katie herself. We soon got fed up with him asking us to remember the past, old people, old times and practices. Our computers were giving us enough problems without going into all that stuff.

Barny came to realise that Maggie Pender, with her undiluted accent and dialect, was the perfect subject for the oral history project although he, like everybody else, had avoided her for years. After several visits and discussions, mostly conducted on her doorstep, and with some persuasion from Katie, Maggie had eventually agreed to be recorded for posterity when she could find the time. 'I'm a very busy wumun,' she said.

Only the ancients among us know of Maggie's past, and then only from events related to them in their youth. We heard vague stories of her cherished father being lost overboard from a sailing lugger caught in a sudden squall in the days before engines and shipping forecasts. We heard of her mother, always neurotic and insecure, soon dying of grief while Maggie in her late teens was left to bring up an infant sister all alone, unable ever to form a close relationship with anybody and becoming increasingly weird. The young sister resented what she saw as Maggie's over-protection and rebelled against her, marrying her American serviceman after the war, leaving her sister even more isolated. Old Tommy Blue had been very close to Maggie in their youth, we all knew that, but her growing eccentricity put him off, people said, and he married somebody else. Not many of us knew her whole story, and the rest saw Maggie only as an old busybody or, in the case of Shimshai, a figure of fun. Well, she was a figure of fun, but no need to put her in his book as a figure of ridicule. That's not on!

Barny the Bard, himself no babe in arms, had been brought up in a house near Maggie's and, while not knowing all about her background, remembered her from his childhood as being, even as a young woman, when the thing hit her on the head, very eccentric. It was this very eccentricity, her isolation, and her individuality that interested Barny now, especially after hearing these details of her past, and he looked forward to his interview with increasing anticipation of capturing on tape something of the genuine accent and heritage of our community. With Katie's help he drew up a list of discreet but leading questions to ask when Maggie agreed be interviewed.

Katie is a walker. She thinks nothing of ten miles over the moors or along the cliffs, and her favourite walk is along the coastal path and then inland to Barny's hamlet to spend time listening to his music or planning the recording of the oral archive before walking back through the fields to home. With all the preoccupation of the coming event looming over them like a black cloud, Barny found hardly anyone wanting to talk about the past. Until the lunacy was over, he told Katie, he would retreat into his own solitary existence out in the countryside, drawing up lists of likely interviewees and transcribing the tapes they already had. His cottage lay snuggled in a cluster of farm buildings to the west of town, where the contours sloped gently from the high moors, through the cultivated fields, down to the granite cliffs and the sea. This was where he now felt most at home, though his own past was all back here, in town, shared by us all except for his time working 'out foreign' and a short episode with a beautiful girl much his junior of which we knew very little, only the bare facts. He had written a book about the incident, not yet published and unlikely ever to be, for he had written it for himself as a catharsis and considered that in it he had revealed more than is expedient about himself, and her, and kept it locked away. That Shimshai should have published his book, in which he had exposed himself and his friends, was something Barny could not condone. Perhaps it was because Shimshai was away at the time and had intended never to return, never to become part of the community again. Katie, when she found Barny in a more communicative mood, would occasionally remind him that it was he, as much as any, who ought to record his personal reminiscences of his background and life.

'There's nothing to tell,' he would say, 'nothing to tell.' Which Katie, and Boy Steve, having been involved with him at the time, knew to be so tragically true.

'Nothing to tell' Barny said, not, 'Nothing happened'. Too much had happened and it was all too traumatic to recount to anybody and, as a consequence, he had become even more reticent about the past than Old Steve, who was as tight as a clam. 'Nothing,' he should have said, 'that I can tell.'

Barny spent many hours in his garden. His vegetables were in neat rows, weed free and the soil hoed to a fine tilth. From the cultivated section a grassed path led through a thick escallonia hedge, on the other side of which was an area of apparent neglect. There was a small area of grass, hardly a lawn, full of weeds but mowed short and even. In summer the white clover and blue self-heal of this little patch hummed with bumble bees, while buttercups and daisies and short-stemmed dandelions dotted the grass with yellow and pink. This area was completely enclosed by the escallonia, with a few taller shrubs and lank perennials hanging over the grass. It was sheltered and in full sun and, on the northern side, Barny had constructed an arrangement of granite and a horizontal slate slab, into which were drilled a series of holes of various sizes. In the centre of the slate slab was an old fashioned bell jar, of the kind formerly used as protection for tender crops or cases for stuffed birds, and in front of this a shallow earthenware dish.

'My shrine,' he had explained to Katie.

She knew that few of his friends were invited to visit this part of his garden for, despite his superficial gregariousness while in town, there were aspects of his life that he revealed to very few. Beth, from over the road, had free access, and Old Steve Trevorrow, who could be trusted, had once been taken here to share an intimacy.

'A shrine,' Katie had said when first shown this construction 'is usually for worship. I thought you were an atheist.'

'I am,' he had told her, 'in the sense that I don't believe in an almighty creative God. I worship life and beauty, and the wonderful marvels of our planet and the universe, whatever their origins.'

Sometimes there would be some item on the shrine. It might be a flower from his garden or a seashell from the shore. It might be a piece of stone he had found or a bird's egg or a golden feather moulted by a finch. Sometimes, in acknowledgement of the achievements of his fellow humanity, there might be some artifice he considered to be of great beauty or intricacy and sometimes, under the glass, a page of poetry of a sheet of music. He would stand or kneel before the item and attempt to understand the significance of things. In which he had never succeeded. If he wished for moments of reverence and thanksgiving for the miracle of life, and there was nothing on the shrine, he might take a blade of grass or a daisy from the lawn and wonder in awe at their form and function. Occasionally he would be inspired to write his poetry, but the purpose of the shrine was to stay in touch with the reality of the world and what he secretly called his higher self, that part of him that was above the petty trials of everyday living.

It was in the summer time, when his chores were done, that he brought paper and pen to this secluded sanctuary with the express purpose of seeking inspiration and wrote whatever came into his mind. As the afternoons became warm he discarded a sequence of clothing until he lay on the grass with nothing between him and the sunshine or a cooling breeze, or any of the forces of nature, but his own tanned skin.

Barny's old cousin, Arthur Trezise, the one that Barny took Maid Katie to see, worked as a gardener for Squire Chygwyn. Barny had eventually persuaded his cousin to record a few reminiscences for the oral archive. He went over there and coaxed him to relate the experiences of a lifetime's dedication to a single garden, apart from the time when he was called up in the Second World War. Of that episode he would say nothing, except that it was best forgotten, although Barny had once seen a box of medals in one of his sideboard drawers. Around the estate there were magnificent trees that he had planted as diminutive cuttings or seedlings taken from other estates. He knew the history of every shrub and tree in the garden and could describe their attributes and requirements as if they were his children. Regarding his employers he was more reticent, saying nothing about his relationship with them over the years. He did relate, but not on tape, a story of an older cousin who worked on an estate a few miles away. His parents died and left him a small miner's cottage. As he was living in a tied house with a job for life, he decided to sell the cottage and bought a little old Morris minor, or was it a model T Ford? No matter. When he drove up to work in it he was sacked, for having ambitions above his station. 'Can 'ee believe it?' Arthur said. Times have changed.

Further comments on his own boss he would not make, except to say that he was a very dedicated gardener, but a very disappointed man. 'All this,' he indicated a large nursery of camellia seedlings, 'is the old man's attempt to breed a blue camellia. He's not succeeded and will probably die a disappointed man. It comes of having ambitions above your station. He idn God. You abm put that on tape have 'ee?'

The estate workers had finished the new entrance to the field and were laying out rows of markers to define the camping and caravan sites. A corner had been levelled off in preparation for portable toilets and a mobile shop.

'He's hoping to make a few bob out of it,' Arthur said. 'I'll be glad when it's all over and we can get back to normal.'

Now, it mustn't be thought that we are all tarred with the same brush. Not all of us are of the expected stereotype, to be seen leaning over railings, pushing handcarts, unloading fish, mining for tin, painting masterpieces, working in hotel kitchens or queuing up at the grand portals of the social security offices. Neither are we all old and poor. Some, believe it or not, are young, work in offices, on building sites and in factories, just like you party. One of us was a plumber, but you're unlikely to see him in a painting or a book. Some of us you'll never see, and if you did you'd never know it. We are talking, now, about those of us who provided for the poor, provided employment, provided homes, provided everything. Those of us who belong to the hard-working upper classes. The wealthy ones.

The squire is one of us who is quite well off. His family owns thousands of acres, twenty farms, property in town, shares in banks, and has a whole lot of interests in other ventures that the rest of us know nothing about until we come up against them. The squire would own a hell of a lot more if it were not for three other wealthy families among us with whom the squire's lot have been at war for five generations.

Arthur Trezise's ancestors had worked in the grounds of the squire's big house for most of those generations, although relations with Arthur's employer had recently deteriorated. The squire was of the new breed of powerful men, those who wielded the big sticks and carrots through the hands of others. There was a time when his family made fortunes from mining and they still retained all the rights to the minerals beneath the towns, villages, and isolated cottages, in case of a resurgence of the industry. There was another fortune down there, adding to its value with the passage of time with no death duties, inheritance taxes, or any other claim on it from revenue officers of any administration or generation. And good luck to them, the rest of us say, admitting that we would do exactly the same under identical circumstances, but without the pretence of benevolence. They also had interests in the seines and fish-curing houses, but these had been disposed of just before the industries went into decline after all the mullet, pilchards and herring capable of being caught by the means at the fishermen's disposal had been caught, once and for all. The squire was of the breed that used to appear as the rich and powerful in historical novels, the kind that Barny and Shimshai can't abide, but they sure as hell do not wish to appear in modern ones, the kind that Shimshai d' write now.

The squire served on all the important committees and councils of the area. Not in person, for this was out of keeping with the new strategy of remaining inconspicuous, out of sight, like a predator lying in wait for prey. Out of sight, and appearing out of touch some of us might be, but some of us are never out of control of other people's destiny. Once upon a time these few were in total control over the rest of us and were famous throughout the land. There we are. Times change. Only common people allow themselves to become famous these days, pop stars and the like, tasteless and brash, while the actual power is self-effacing in a world where personal lives of the temporarily rich and famous are the stuff of scandal.

The squire served and controlled by proxy, through the likes of Denzil Trethewy and D.D. Johns. His tenant farmers and business associates were elected to the local council by those with agricultural interests in the belief that they would be better represented by one of themselves. It was Squire Chygwyn, however, who determined the outcome of decisions made in secret, particularly on matters of planning, for his forbears had the foresight to acquire the cheap agricultural land surrounding the little towns and villages, all of which was now in demand for the expanding housing estates. They had retained interest in some of the most important sites in the towns, had interests in the more profitable retail outlets and the grander hotels of the area. As a man with the interests of the community at heart, he was anxious that the impending event be handled with discretion and skill to the benefit of us all. With camp-sites capable of holding ten thousand people being spoken of, he made it known that he was in a position to offer help to the authorities in several areas. At a price, of course, but the hoards would pay. He spoke to his tenants, who were probably in a better position to assess the possibilities than anybody, and urged them to exploit the influx to the full.

Barny and Katie found his cousin working in the walled garden behind the big house.

'Hullo Arthur.'

Barny was never fully at ease in the company of his cousin. Although they had much in common, with their mutual love of horticulture, Arthur was the true son of the soil. He knew not only about crops but about cattle and horses, sowing and ploughing. Barny, on the other hand, was more attuned to the sea, having been brought up within the area of its spray, and some of his forebears had worked in the mines. He had never earned his living from either, but the affinity was there. There are lots of us like that these days.

'Loh Barny,' Arthur said. 'Loh Katie.'

Arthur was round-faced, with full cheeks and a kindly eye. His countenance in its normal expression bore a slight smile, as if happy with some secret wisdom. On the day that Barny and Katie went to see him however, so Barny told us, he was less than pleased with life.

'Things aren't what they were,' Arthur said. 'It's all rush and pressure now. The old man idn like his father. He's getting more impatient and anxious everyday. If it wasn't for agricultural subsidies on the farms, which'll most likely be done away with soon, the tenants could hardly pay their rent. I think he's worrying that if the growing villages don't put value on the estate for building land, he'll be going bust. Don't tell 'n I said so, mind.'

Barny was amused to hear Arthur refer to Squire Chygwyn as the 'old man', for his employer was a good fifteen years his junior. When addressing him directly, Arthur called him 'Mr Simon,' or 'Squire', the only one still to do so, and could say it as if speaking to an equal, a rare attribute in servants. He had better relations with the squire's son, who was off travelling the world before settling down to carry on the estates.

'I don't see much sign of anybody going bust around here,' Katie said, looking at the three large off-road vehicles in the yard. 'I expect he'll do very well out of the eclipse.'

'That!' Arthur said, 'He's talking about turning the lower mowhay into another temporary camp-site.'

'Well,' Katie said, 'why not?'

'Well, depends what you mean by temporary. Some of the tenants are hoping the temporary sites will be granted planning permission as permanent camping grounds.'

'We'll see about that,' Katie said.

'How are the camellias?' Barny asked, for this was where their truly mutual interests lay. They were both, together with the squire, camellia men. Barny was just an amateur with a few in his exposed garden but both the squire and Arthur had devoted a large part of their lives to them.

'Come and have a look,' Arthur said, and led off through the garden gate. 'He d' want me to forget the camellias this year, and plan layouts for the campers, helping the men with building temporary access and one thing and another.'

'He must be expecting an invasion,' Katie said.

'He is. Spending a fortune on preparations already. I'm dreadin' it,' Arthur muttered as he led them to a sheltered area between the hedges of escallonia and eleagnus, where there was row after row, after row, of small camellia seedlings. He turned to Katie. 'We've been working on these plants for thirty-five years. Trying to breed a blue camellia. And we're nearly there. A blue camellia, blue as a gentian, can you imagine it?' Arthur gave Katie a wry look and a rueful smile. 'We're nearly there,' he said. 'Nearly there. It's the only reason I stay on. I should have retired years ago if it wasn't for these little chaps.'

They walked on among the rows in silence. Each little plant was carefully labelled with a coded number. Together with the work of the squire's ancestors, nearly two hundred years of selective breeding lay in these plants. Scores of beautiful varieties had been propagated and grown in gardens throughout the world: pinks, whites, yellows, yet never a blue. 'But we're nearly there,' Arthur murmured, leading them on. 'Nearly there.'

'Would you,' Barny asked with some apprehension in his voice, for he knew Arthur well enough to expect refusal, 'be prepared to put all your memories of camellia growing on tape, as part of the oral history project?'

Katie was becoming aware that, as one whose life's interest had been in the historical heritage and language of his people, Barny the Bard was becoming more enthusiastic about the oral history project than Katie herself, and she was amused by his being repeatedly frustrated by the old folk's refusal to co-operate. 'Who d' want t' hear all about that old stuff,' they'd say. 'Pile of old slop.' Or, sometimes, they'd agree to do it 'dreckly' and died before he recorded them.

They became aware of the roar of diesel engines from beyond the shelterbelt.

'You won't hear much over that,' Arthur said.

'I don't mean now. I mean a proper recording, over a couple of days.'

'I'll think about it,' Arthur said, and led them the trees to where there was a view down the valley towards the sea. At least, Barny thought, it wasn't a downright no!

By a gate in the lane leading to the pasture there was a huge bull-dozer grubbing out the stone 'hedge'.

'What are they doing?' Katie asked.

'Putting in wider entrance,' Arthur said. 'And a new hardcore road up to the camp-site. They're expecting ten thousand people to be here.'

'My God,' Barny said, with dread in his voice. 'Ten thousand!'

'The old man's down there,' Arthur said. 'The one in the scruffy tweed jacket.'

The squire was standing on the high ground above the bulldozer. He was thin, gaunt, slightly stooped at the shoulders, wearing an old tweed jacket and baggy grey trousers tucked into muddy rubber boots. A woollen scarf hung lopsided from around his neck and his hat was an ancient cloth cap, frayed at the peak. He looked shabby and worn, and would not have looked out of place among the poorer of his tenants or the queues at the social security office in town.

'The poor old sod,' Katie said with a laugh. 'But he'll afford a new hat after ten thousand people have paid for a couple of nights' kip among the cow shit.'

After tea with Arthur and his wife, they left and returned to town the way they had come over, on the bus, just for the ride and to see the view from the open top. They were surprised to see that their friend, and Maggie's friend, indeed everybody's friend, Ezekiel Endean, was also on the bus, sitting on the back seat. On his lap was a small parcel wrapped in thick brown paper that he was guarding carefully from passengers staggering up and down the aisle. He had also chosen to go the roundabout way along the lanes through the countryside, over the moors, along the coast, and then the long descent into town. The bus wound its way along the coast road, past Barny's house, but Barny stayed aboard. 'I want to borrow a few books from the library,' he said. 'I'll get the next bus back.'

They saw tractors moving huge granite boulders into gateways and lay-bys in preparation for the defence of the countryside when the time came. The farmers are panicking, Barny thought, and there's weeks to go yet. 'It's like world war three out where I live,' he told Old Steve. 'The lay-bys are all blocked off, boulders in farm gates, the ancient monuments barricaded. I haven't seen so many precautions against invaders since they dismantled the tank traps and barbed-wire entanglements in 1945.'

They were halfway home, with the opportunity nearly lost before he broached the subject he wanted to discus with Katie and which was the true reason he had brought her with him on the pretext of seeing Arthur's garden and asking him to make the recording.

We all loved Katie. Just as we all loved her mother, Sarah. Some, well one anyway, loved Sarah a lot more than the rest of us. For, despite the fact that we all pretended that no one knew who her father was, Katie was not dumped by a migratory stork way off course, and neither was she found under a goosegog bush.

Goosegogs don't do well here, anyway. The damp makes them mildewed just as they're sweet enough for picking.

Sarah was getting old now but, while always feeling a little apart, had been more of the community than she ever knew. Some are like that. They are so utterly at ease with themselves that they never find it necessary to question themselves on anything. She was one of those women whose presence altered the behaviour of men for the better. She was demure in appearance, without make up, plainly dressed. We're talking now about when she was young, mind you, beautiful without glamour, but with a figure to turn men's eyes, together with an air of childlike innocence, belied by candid and mischievous eyes if you were ever brave enough to look directly into them. She could come up on the plat, a thing which was prohibited for women in the old days, and talk with the men as equals, and they forgave her trespasses more readily than the women did and, secretly, every one of them wished that it was they who had trespassed with her in those distant days and fathered the child themselves. There had always been an unseen mischievous streak in Sarah. In old age people tend to let their wickedness have sway and to hell with the consequences. She did it by retaining the most innocuous manner, while developing a candid element in her conversation that forced people to think twice before speaking in her presence. She did not suffer fools or naves gladly except in her own delight in putting them down.

Her daughter was a bit of a misfit, with all of her mother's mischievous qualities. She was too independent a thinker ever to fit into a preordained slot in any community. Katie was self-sufficient and self-reliant. Yet she was also loved by all of us, and also more particularly by one. Despite being begot and raised entirely within the community, she belonged nowhere and was at ease everywhere. She was a child of her times, and would suffer for it if circumstances led her along the wrong track, or on a wrong tack as you might say, into the storms of life which excite the waves of emotions and are best avoided by staying safely moored in harbour. But Katie was too adventurous to avoid getting into deep water through fear. Sarah, however, was aware of a change occurring in her daughter, as if she were harbouring a secret.

So, no one knew who Katie's father was. Her mother had never apparently had a permanent lover. There was all kinds of speculation at the time. Some said she had been assaulted. Some that she hadn't known what brought cheldern. Some made up all kinds of yarns to explain why the most prim and modest girl in the town had produced the most beautiful child all by herself. Well to tell the honest truth, the fact is that we are now perfectly well aware who Katie's father was, but some subjects are best avoided in public, both for the sake of the living and respect for the dead. It came out in the course of a flaming row, but we don't talk about it. It's a matter of some interest that the things we never talk about are always the first to become widely and intimately known to everybody.

As the bus began the descent into town Barny asked her, 'What about you and Boy Steve?' No point in beating about the bush once he had found the courage to do it. Boy Steve was as much of the community as she was, more respected than loved, mind you. Known for a bit of a temper. More like his father in some respects, as Katie was like her mother.

'Nothing,' Katie said. 'There's nothing about me and Steve. It's all finished.'

'I thought it might be, but does he know it?'

'Not yet. We've been together too long without commitment. I think we were not suited from the beginning.'

'Well, he is a lot older than you.'

'It's not that. We're both getting older. We just don't get on. We weren't really committed, right from the start. It was the opposition from our parents, as much as anything, that threw us together. Out of rebelliousness I suppose. Steve is still in love with me. I think. He's never said so, but we weren't really suited, you know.' She said this with a direct look into his eyes. 'I know you wanted it,' she said. 'And so did Joe.'

'I wanted it because I thought you did. Both of you.'

'I was too young to be sure.' She shook her head and looked at the gorse beginning to fade on the hedges, the dark ploughed furrows in the fields. 'If it hadn't been for all that other stuff... things would have been very different. I still find it difficult to accept.'

'Does anyone else know the truth about all that?' Barny asked. 'We swore not to tell, you remember.'

'No. Just the three of us. Not even Mam.'

'How is Sarah?'

'She's like you, Barny, like Old Steve, getting over the past! She must never know, Barny.'

'Never from me,' Barny said. 'She'll be disappointed about you and Boy Steve.' And it was here that he took the chance. He was too old, had learned from too many mistakes, not to risk making more. Life is dull without risk and adventure. 'You know,' he said, 'how I feel about you.'

She placed the palm of her hand on the back of his as it rested on his knee. 'I know, Barny,' she said, 'zackly how you feel.' And they exchanged a couple of rueful smiles as the bus stopped at the library down town where Zeke also alighted and said a brief 'Yow! A' right?' without stopping.

'I wonder,' Katie said, 'how much he knows. He's a dark horse.'

Back at the estate, Squire Simon Chygwyn was musing to himself as he inspected the work proceeding in the lane. The more one does for some people, he reflected, the more they want. We provided all their needs and gave them employment, housing, recreation, a certain amount of education, ideals, higher and higher standards of living, morals, everything. So, he reasoned, when the opportunity arises to recoup some of that expenditure it should be firmly grasped. The prospect of ten thousand people inhabiting this site, even for a couple of days, was the result of most exciting venture he had initiated for years. If he only charged then a quid there would be a significant return on the capital, he told himself while restraining his avarice and glee. It was not the done thing to exploit others' misfortunes. *Schadenfreude*, he believed, was not for the English gentry.

Quizzy Maggie lived in her parents' house, the interior of which was rarely seen by anyone else, and had kept all their old furniture and ornaments. The oven of her old black slab, with polished brass and smoky grate did eventually burn out and, being obsolete and irreparable, had to be replaced by a gas cooker but almost everything else in the house had been there for over a hundred years.

'You ceant move in theer,' Zeke said, 'for fear of scattin' somethin' over. Theer's ornaments everywhere.'

Zeke probably knew every item in the house from his bit of dealing in small objects of interest, though what they used to talk about when he went to see her must be a matter of some considerable conjecture. Towards the end she gave him a key, and in fact it was he who found her dead.

'Sittin' in the cheer by the fire,' he said. 'I didn' knaw she was gone. Thought she was a bit quiet, mind. Thought she was slaypin so I crept out the scullery and made a cup of tay. I took 'n in to her and gave her bit of a shake to wake her up and she capsized on the bleddy floor. Dead as a bleddy dodo.'

'Damn!' Barny said, when he read the notice of her death and funeral tacked on the wall of the lodge. 'Another one gone and never recorded a word,' he told Katie. He phoned Old Steve and asked if he would do a recording before it was too late. Steve told him to go to hell. 'Record yourself, you old tuss,' he said. Barny didn't think that was a good idea. Not with the memories he had.

Quizzy Maggie was put under after a very good send off, considering that hardly anybody down'long knew her, for all we locals turned out in our best clothes to pay respects, a thing we never did when she was living.

The house and contents were left to her relatives in California, who sent condolences and sympathetic words by e-mail to Maggie's solicitors: 'Sell the goddamn lot and transfer the dough' or words to that effect. No! We tell a lie! Not everything went to California. What did they want with a pile of old mahogany furniture and Staffordshire dogs when out to America, her sister had assured her, everything is brand spanking new and everybody seems to be a millionaire. (Truth to tell, her sister's husband's family were in the business of making hats and, before Zeke began reading Maggie's letters for her, she had written, in an blurred hand, saying that 'everybody seems to be a milliner'. There was a little codicil in Maggie's will which said that, apart from the aforementioned assets, everything, after one thousand pounds to the chapel, all the residue, all the ornaments, junk and aspidistras, should go to 'My good friend and confidant* Mr Ezekiel Endean, and whatsoever he may choose from my personal effects as a token of my affection.' Make what you like of that, we thought.

After the chapel (and the solicitors) had their share, for which they were very grateful, there wasn't much cash and Zeke had no use for most of the stuff which was eventually taken to Henny Penny's antique, or junk, shop, depending on your point of view and Henny said that out of sympathy for Zeke, who was a bit too simple to make much of himself, he paid a pretty good price for a load of rubbish. He was expecting a great deal of business to be done during the madness of the eclipse, he said, and needed to stock up with whatever he could get. There were few items of personal interest to Zeke. She had a few rings and things which had been in the family for a generation or two, which he kept as genuine reminders of her, and an item he brought down to the railings to show us.

'What do 'ee think of that?' he demanded. 'What do 'ee think that es?'

'That?' we said, 'why it's a bit of glass, that's what that es.'

'That,' Zeke said, 'is worth a bob or two.'

It looked like a cheap flower vase to we. About ten inches (twenty-five centimetres, Maid Katie said) high. A tall thin thing that would fall over so soon as ever you put flowers in 'en. Now, Zeke prided himself in being a bit of a dealer. He knew that everything has value if the right buyer can be found. The trouble was he could rarely find the right buyer and depended on Henry Penny to act as middleman.

'Henny Penny will know what it's worth,' Zeke said, 'but I reckon that will fetch a hundred quid, more maybe.' He held the vase in the palm of his hand at arm's length, turning it slightly from side to side. 'That,' he said, 'is called a sweet pea vase. Nearly a hundred years old and a valuable antique that is. Must have been Maggie's mawthers. Oogly bleddy thing, idn a?'

Henny, although eager to examine Zeke's acquisitions, always felt a certain trepidation when he saw Zeke looking through his antique-shop window, and did not welcome his presence in the shop. For one

*We liked that!

thing, Zeke's outlandish mode of dress, in clothes which were bought from charity shops or jumble sales, would, Henny thought, deter potential customers from crossing the threshold. He looked so disreputable, with his second-hand clothes, his scruffy beard and darting eye, like someone guilty, Henny thought, of petty crime. Henny detested petty criminals and their crimes which robbed honest citizens of their possessions and time. The crimes in Henny's life had never been petty, and he was one of the perpetrators of the fourteen billion pounds worth of white-collar crime per annum, and regarded it as legitimate activity. If the system was so infernally complicated, Henny reasoned, that even the government officials couldn't understand it, then who was poor uneducated Henry Penny not to make the occasional mistake in accounting. He had realised, in his early childhood poverty, that honesty was the worst possible policy and determined to live by the best policies whenever opportunity arose. He had, as we said, done all right, but we didn't quite know how. He was just as daft as Zeke in his way but was, so he believed, infinitely more sophisticated. The idea of Ezekiel Endean coming into his shop and behaving as an equal was totally abhorrent, especially if there were customers in, but must be endured if the occasional treasure that Zeke produced was to be procured. Henny, in his tweeds and cavalry twill could no more believe that he was out of fashion and that Zeke was among the avant-garde of contemporary attire than he could believe that Zeke had a quick wit and an analytical brain. He always endeavoured to arranged Zeke's visits to the shop when it was shut, saying, 'It gives us some privacy to evaluate a fair price. I wouldn't want to make a rash offer which was too low. I mean, occasionally you do bring in something that might be of some interest to a collector at the lower end of the market.'

'Oh,' Zeke said, being as laconic as Henny was loquacious. 'I see.'

Henny was older than Zeke, and thought his background and upbringing was unknown to his supplier of odds and ends, but we told Zeke all we remembered about Henny, including him going to school with a piece of bread and jam in his hand. Our reason being that we all knew and tolerated poverty but not the snobbery that made previous paupers fabricate their past.

'I've got somefin' this time,' Zeke said.

'Oh yes,' Henry drawled in his carefully cultivated upper-class English accent.

Zeke unwrapped his little parcel. He placed his item on the counter and stood back, with his darting eyes vacillating between the eyes of Henny and the tall blue vase which he had been left by his good friend, Maggie.

'I reck'n,' Zeke said, 'that tha's worth a hundred pound.'

'A hun…' Henny said, unable to restrain a derisive laugh. 'You mean a hundred pence, don't you?'

Zeke knew all about Henny's tactics. He said nothing while Henry picked up the vase and examined it closely. 'Ah!' Henny said, 'I see what you mean.' He held it against the light. 'Fenton's celestial blue, eh? The trouble is,' he said, 'that these things have gone out of fashion. Two years ago, well, maybe you could have got a hundred for it. Now...' He shook his head. 'Fifty'.

'Hundred!' Zeke said. If it was worth a hundred then, it was worth a hundred now, he reckoned. He didn't begrudge Henny making a profit if the right buyer eventually came along, but things don't loose that much value in so short a while, not in these prosperous times.

'Seventy-five,' Henny said. 'Where did you get it? I don't handle stolen stuff.' He did, but not from petty thieves, of whom Zeke was not one, except for a bit of wrecking, but that doesn't count.

'Quizzy Maggie left 'n to me. I'll take 'n up'long,' Zeke said.

'Very well. You do that! Take it where you like, but I can assure you that you won't get more than fifty anywhere else.' Henny placed the vase amongst Zeke's wrapping material, dismissing the deal as a non-starter.

Zeke thought about it. Was it worth going all the way up there on the bus or train, paying the fare, buying dinner, losing a day, being paid by cheque, and possibly not getting any more. After all, he reasoned, seventy-five quid in the hand is seventy-five quid in the hand. Tax-free, nothing said.

'Cash?'

'Cash,' Henny conceded with a sigh, 'if you insist.' In fact he already had a buyer in mind.

TAPE FOUR

The time is come, the day draweth near, let not the buyer rejoice, nor the seller mourn; for wrath is upon all the multitude thereof.

Despite her earlier misgivings, Shimshai's woman was very happy to be back here. Perhaps, she thought, if Old Steve's wife, Mary, was still alive I wouldn't have come. Shimshai, she knew, like many expatriates, harboured a life-long dream to end his days in the surroundings of his youth and she, having no roots or attachment to any place, eventually agreed to come back to the art colony where she had first found her inspiration and style. She often wondered what they all thought of her but not being close enough she could never know. I can't change, she thought, I'm still the same woman who fell in love with that handsome fisherman with the cynical sense of humour and forced him to decide between me and his wife. In truth, I loved him more for refusing to abandon her, and Shimshai loved me more than ever I deserved. So he said! He has the abiding ability to make me laugh too, and for that and his undemanding companionship, I will love him also till the end.

We see her, now and then during our brief summers, out with her easel and paints, sitting by the sea, or at the end of a street, busy painting and oblivious to us all.

I see them, she thinks, from the corner of my eye, which is as blue as ever, or full in the face as they approach me. They will see my greying hair and the young will ask who I am. Shimshai's woman they'll say, and leave it at that. They might stop and look with their critical eyes seeing the daubs of paint, as they have seen so many daubs of paint applied to canvas and board in these narrow streets and wild, spray-soaked headlands, and pass me by, another artist come to steal images of themselves and their environs. Perhaps they see only the paint, only the brush or the palette knife smearing the colours and shades over the canvas, like clouds and beams of sunshine crossing the heather of the hills. Perhaps someone will see the bedrock beneath, the substrate under the superficial, changing, seasonal, modified topography. Perhaps they will see themselves and me and change and permanence trapped by pigment. He will never stop and look, stop and talk. Not while the others are there to see.

Katie had seen her around, found out about her and thought she would like to get to know this woman. So she did. Katie was, we think, about twenty-nine years old. She had her mother's quiet determination, or pigheadedness, depending whether she was for or against our own opinions. She became friends with Shimshai's wife after she stopped to look at the painting that time, nearly finished, of a wave, just a wave, passing with hardly a bit of spray or foam as it surged around the quay head at low tide. Katie had seen many a painting of waves. Here, Katie thought, was someone who looked at things, who could see below the surface and fathom the depths.

We only found out later what she'd been painting and what they had really said to each other. It wasn't boats after all. Our surmises are understandable, however, for most artists sitting in the harbour are painting boats. You can see that for yourselves.

'What's that a picture of?' Katie asked.

'I,' said Shimshai's woman, 'am not too sure,' as she leaned back and dropped her eyelids in contemplation.

Now, if she'd said 'a wave', or 'the sea', or 'Can't you see?' Katie would have passed on, left her to it and remained a stranger. The paintings of waves that Katie had seen before, wave after wave that had swept over countless canvasses were, could have been, she thought, of far greater technical perfection than this one, but here was more, here was emotion in the motion of water like the secret depths of sentiment that forced one to look and ask the questions. She gazed at the picture for some time while the artist added a slight modification here, a deeper shade there, a highlight.

'It's about memories,' Katie said at last, 'the lingering waves washing back on the reminiscences in the froth of their wake.' And Shimshai's wife turned from her painting as a woman awakened unto herself. She came out of her reverie to look at the young woman standing beside her.

'Yes. Memories.'

They smiled at each other, Katie remembered, and there was an instant rapport between them that some of us couldn't understand, considering their different backgrounds.

'You're quite right,' Shimshai's woman mused. 'I thought I had overcome that... nostalgia, memories! Believing that they were only for the young.'

'Do you always use the knife?' Katie asked.

So it was apparent that Shimshai's missus was settling in very well. She came down to the harbour and spoke when she was spoken to, was very civil, got on with a bit of painting, joined the arts club, went on cultural outings and kept out of Steve's way. Most everybody had forgotten what went on between them anyway. It was remembered as only a bit of summer madness at a time when everybody was nearly as crazy as they are now.

'I've bought her a millennium present,' Shimshai said on one of the rare occasions when he deigned to grace us with his presence on the plat.

'Time enough for that,' Zeke said. 'You've got nearly eighteen months.' It was a lot less than that for most of us, but Zeke said, 'I don't care what they d' say. The minnellium is at the end of the year 2000, not the beginning.'

We all looked at 'n. How could everybody else in the whole damn world be wrong and Zeke the only one that's right.

'Do you...?' Zeke said.

Ah! Now, look out here! If Zeke d' say 'do you' in that tone of voice instead of 'do 'ee' like he d' belong to, then we're in trouble. Time to lock up and go home 'cause he'll gibm bell tink till we're fed up to the back teeth.

'Do you,' he demanded, 'celebrate a cheeld's first birthday the day she's born? Do you celebrate the beginning of her second decade when she's only nine? Now do 'ee? Course you dammee don't! The end of a century d' come after a hundred years, not ninety-nine. It's exactly the same with minnelliums.'

'She's always been a bit of a collector,' Shimshai said. 'Just little things. Button hooks and bits of glass.'

'It's very simple,' Zeke insisted. 'They counted wrong from the very beginning. I mean, the very end, looking back. They've done away with a whole year, ceant 'ee see? They counted wrong and can't wait till the proper end like sensible people would 'a done. What kind of glass?'

'You would think,' Steve said, 'that they'd be only too pleased to move the millennium on a year when all this other stuff of the eclipse is threat'nin us.'

Freddie looked at Old Steve with a puzzled frown, thinking that half his contemporaries were losing their marbles. How did Steve think you could alter the calendar? And for God's sake, Zeke, Minnellium! At my age, and when I look at my contemporaries, he thought while smiling smugly to himself, I reckon I'm very lucky to have kept all my facilities.*

'I have it here,' Shimshai said. 'Will one of you look after it. She's sure to find it if I hide it in the house.'

We watched Shimshai unwrap a small object made of blue glass that was familiar to the rest of us and hand it over to Old Steve who held out his hand just a nana-second before Zeke. Steve examined it carefully, turning it over that we all might see the light glinting through the tints.

'Bought it from Henry,' Shimshai said. 'Very lucky to get it. I'm sure he doesn't know its true value.'

'How much was a?' Zeke said.

'It cost me three hundred and fifty.' Shimshai was less circumspect in revealing his private affairs than Zeke could ever be. We assume it's because he doesn't want to appear aloof after coming back from his rarefied academic world. 'It would fetch a lot more on the London market,' he said.

'Three 'undred an fifty pound,' Zeke said quietly. 'Tha's a lot o' money.'

'Well, it's worth a lot more.' Shimshai said, 'I beat him down fifty.'

'Fifty,' Zeke said in a voice barely audible. 'You beat 'n down fifty!

*He makes the editors *sic*.

He was asking four bleddy hundred! For that?'

'Just something else to collect the dust,' Steve said. 'I'll put 'n away in a cupboard for 'ee.'

'I thought of getting her a cat,' Shimshai said.

'You can have Maggie's,' Zeke said. 'She had three. I'm fed up looking after them. Can I have a look at that thing a minute? Sweet pea vase, idna?'

People thought Zeke was a bit touched. Well, Zeke was a bit touched, but he was no fool. He knew about electronics and metals, both scrap and precious. He knew about jewellery and the value of old postcards. He could mend things. He could get video recorders to work and could set the controls on the digital watches of all hands on the plat.

Zeke made a living. More than enough, for his needs were few. He did a bit of this, and a bit of that. He couldn't drive a car but he had an old handcart, which he could push into little back lanes between houses where a car or a van could not enter. Sometimes he delivered stuff, sometimes he took stuff away. He was a dealer, like Henny Penny, and he kept in touch with the world via the Internet but his business premises were the streets, and the pavement outside the bank.

Zeke would come into the lodge now and then and, 'Here!' he'd say. 'What 'ee think of that?' Showing us a bit of jewellery or perhaps an old watch wrapped in a piece of rag. 'Have a geek at this, Ste,' he said, one time, showing Boy Steve a rusty old iron corkscrew.

'Beautiful!' Boy Steve said, with a wry smile.

'Ivory handle, look. I can git twenty quid for that,' he assured an incredulous Steve.

For Zeke to show anything to anybody and state a price was a rare occurrence. His business deals were discreet and secretive, and his unlikely appearance made him the perfect anonymous go-between.

Another time it was, 'Have a geek at this one'. We craned our necks to see what he had this time, wrapped in a piece of torn linen. A glass paperweight. Zeke passed it round, for us all to have a look. It was very pure clear glass, with a design of floral circles, in delicate pinks and blues.

'It's a paperweight,' said Collateral Fred. He's very observant at times. 'What's it worth?'

Only Collateral Fred, with his obsession with the world of high finance could have asked that but he should have known better. Trade secrets were trade secrets to Zeke. If you wanted to know what it was worth, then make an offer. He wrapped it up and shoved it deep into the pocket of his voluminous overcoat. 'A brea bit,' he said. 'How about this?' And he brought forth yet another piece from the murky depths.

'Ha!' Barny said, 'A Dinky Toy Bedford van. I had scores of them when I was a kid.'

'You should've kept them,' Zeke said

Now, we knew that, in an honest way, Zeke was just as big a bleddy rogue as Tim Penberthy, the mayor, who had always sailed very close to the wind in the course of his business deals. It was Tim's folly that he believed he was a bigger bleddy rogue than anybody else. But whereas Tim would deliberately break the rules, or the law, as the necessity arose, Zeke had no idea what the rules or the law might be, and had no wish to know, either, for the knowledge would have been a restriction of freedom. He had a few things worked out all right.

Henny later paid Zeke fifty quid for that paperweight, after assuring Zeke that it was probably worth about seventy-five, retail, if a collector could be found. He, in turn, passed it on to a dealer up-country for three hundred. A reasonable profit, considering the gamble he had taken, he assured us. Henny heard later that the dealer up-country sold it for six hundred and fifty and thought he had been diddled something rotten. Daylight robbery, he told us, and avoided mentioning it to Zeke.

As we've explained, and as you can see, from time to time Henny took things off Zeke and made the grave mistake of not always paying a fair price, thinking that Zeke was unlikely to return to the shop before the item was sold. Usually Zeke didn't mind, for only small amounts were involved. But... three 'undred and fifty quid for a fifty quid sweet pea vase was three 'undred and fifty quid no matter which way you looked at it. Friend or no friend.

After Old Steve put Shimshai's woman's sweet pea vase carefully in his pocket Ezekiel shuffled off the plat with his hands deep in the pockets of his overcoat and a dejected expression on his weathered face. We watched him go, with his head bowed, and saw the bottom of his overcoat flap into the air as he moved a discarded lager can out of his way with a vicious kick.

Then Boy Steve walked past, and we could tell by his manner he that was also having a bad time. Down on the wharf he fell in with Katie, who came out from Salubrious Place with pile of books under her arm. Apart from the financial problems, which all fishermen claimed to be having ever since they two brothers gave up the job to become fishers of men*, it was pretty obvious he was at loggerheads with Katie too.

'They have bleddy great factory ships out there vacuuming up everything in the sea and the boys with the hand lines, who could go on fishing forever and not deplete the stocks of mackerel, have been restricted too. It's bureaucratic madness. I'm just about ready to sell the boat and give it all up.'

'That's exactly what they want you to do,' Katie said.

'I know. I know. They Brussels bastards. The more of us who give up, the less compensation they'll have to pay those who they force out. There's fewer boats fishing every year.'

'You're too efficient,' Katie said, risking another argument. 'What matters is the amount of fish landed, not the number of boats. With the industry's sophisticated gear you could catch all the fish in the sea with a quarter of the boats. The fleet's redundant.'

'I know that too. But why should it be our fleet that suffers? The continental fleets are growing all the time.'

'Are they?'

'Yeah! They're growing as fast as ours are shrinking.'

'Well, you have to admit that some of that's due to our men selling their quota to the continentals.'

'All right! All right! I know that. Sometimes I think they did the best thing. Got out while the going was good.'

Katie was fed up with him. She knew they would never marry long before we did. What she didn't know was why he had never asked her. It puzzled her, whenever she thought of it. Maybe he knew she would refuse him. They had been together in a state of

According to St Mathew.

stagnation for too long.

'I think you should give it up. Until there's some sort of conservation policy the industry's finished for small inshore fishermen like you. Use the boat for something else. Or change her for a purpose-built passenger boat.'

'Father wouldn't like that.'

There it was. He was moored to the past, with ties like anchor chains that kept him from ever sailing on. Looking at the wake instead of the far horizon, just like Old Steve, his father. Believing that progress was detrimental to their identity instead of taking their identity forward to a new self-assurance in the world.

'What would *you* like?'

Boy Steve shrugged. 'I came in to this, gave up the prospects of secure jobs, to enjoy following a traditional way of life. Looks as if that's no longer possible. What do I do? I don't know.'

'I don't know either.'

But she did know. She knew what she would do, she would exploit other creatures of the sea apart from edible fish. There were dolphins out there, there were basking sharks, there were whales, there were seals, there were hundreds of thousands of sea birds that twitchers from all over the world were prepared to pay good money to see. It was the way things were going in our increasingly urban society. People were willing to pay just to have a glimpse of things that he took for granted. But the realization would have to come from his own reasoning. He was not amenable to suggestion, seeing only the hazard of change. She left him and went home to Sarah, passing Ezekiel Endean on the way.

'Hullo,' she said.

Zeke seemed also to be an unhappy man, an unusual state for Zeke who was known for his bad temper but it was a bad temper he thoroughly enjoyed and he grumbled with a twinkle in his eye. He shuffled past with downcast eyes.

'Loh,' Zeke said.

He trundled on down to Maggie's.

Now, as we have seen, Maggie was one of that sort that can never throw anything away. Zeke had taken a load of stuff from her house, but there was still a lot to get rid of that even he didn't want. So when the American relatives got in touch with their estate agent, Tim Penberthy, to dispose of the remaining contents, he had a quick look around the house and brought in a firm of house clearers, and they in turn filled a lorry with stuff which nobody wanted. Some items went to Henny Penny's antique shop, via Zeke, some by the side of a country lane. Tim knew all about licenses and regulations regarding dumping of rubbish but he knew nothing about what happened to Maggie Pender's stuff. That was not Tim's problem. The house was emptied and that was that. Which was all very well, but when the roof was inspected by a surveyor for a prospective purchaser he found a pile of junk in the attic, which the house clearers never found and didn't look for. It was a priced job after all and the junk was threatening, the surveyor said, to bring the ceiling down. Tim knew the Americans were likely to make a fuss about paying for a second house clearance that should have been done in one trip, so he called on Zeke.

'I say, Zeke!' he said when he saw him.

'Say what?' Zeke said. 'What do 'ee say?'

'A little job for you,' Tim said. He still thought he was doing you a favour by asking for work to be done.

'What do 'ee want done with 'n?' Zeke said.

'Well,' Tim said, 'I thought you might find something useful amongst it. 'You can dump the rest. Put it in the council skip,' he said.'

'Nothing there,' Zeke told us when he'd been up in the dusty old attic and had a look, 'but a pile of old pictures. Tins of dried up paint. Might have known it.'

'You can sell the frames,' we told him. 'They're very old.'

'Es,' he said. 'I b'lieve they are. I think I'll hang on to them for a bit. They might be worth a bit more, pembye.'

If some have their way, the days of the lodge are numbered. The times of walking up and down on the plat outside are gone. Gone forever. The bleddy tourists have taken the plat over. Either they fill up the seats, which should never have been put there in the first place, or else they feed the damn gulls which fly off with beaks full of bread and shit all over 'ee. The old men can no longer pace up and down and are forced to go for a stroll across the wharf and along the path above the beach. That's the only way to get any exercise these days, and then only in the winter. Sometimes we go along the top of the beach in summer, for there is much to see, but you ceant move on the prom in summer. Summertime we get up there early and stake out our territories on the railings. And the railings are not what they used to be. As we lean over them with our backs to the harbour, keeping an eye on the road, or with backs to the road as we keep an eye on the harbour, we don't miss much. Everybody will pass by sooner or later, and we have learned over the years to interpret the signs they leave in their tracks. It is a talent as highly skilled as that of Bushmen trackers, for the signs can be as obvious or as obscure as those of elephants after rain or leopards over deserts of stone.

Sometimes they leave no more than disturbed air after a brief dismissive wave, implying a busy life, as from Collateral Fred off to check his investments, or Tim on the way to negotiate a sale, unless there is an election pending, when they'll come and yarn for hours. Occasionally there's no more than a smile, as from Katie, or a waft of perfume lingering on the air from behind the ears under the red hat of Winnie the Pew. At times we have to interpret the innuendoes of conversation after people stop for a yarn. A pause here, a hurried denial, a slight hesitation after a question, an over-assertive affirmative. We too, as individuals, also have to be careful to leave no tracks if we wish not to be pursued but, under the scrutiny of skilled eyes, ears and noses, little is overlooked. From the vantage point of the plat, right there where everybody passes by sooner or later, we watch each other, taking turns, the observers and the observed, looking for signs. There is no escape from the scrutiny. This one might be getting too arrogant, this one too pompous, or that one (for it must not be thought, as many of you do, that our scrutiny is malicious) needing succour and sympathy from the community.

Now and then Boy Steve's father passes by instead of coming to have a yarn. We could see that Old Steve was fed up with getting old. The cynical side of his character became more prevalent with the passing years, and that was due to a long, barely tolerated marriage and intolerance of fools. He only became aware of his own potential when it was too late to utilise it, and saw himself surrounded by known incompetents who had somehow managed to achieve their aims by bungling through. He also knew that he'd never had much in the way of aims or ambition, and couldn't decide whether this characteristic had been a good or bad influence in his life.

His daughter went away to college and hardly ever comes home, and we never saw much of his wife in latter years. We used to see her passing by now and then, when she was getting on and full of remorse, and we didn't like seeing her, to tell the truth, for her passing was a reminder to us all of the regrets in our lives. Like many of us, she also discovered herself too late, which in itself is nothing unusual, but she knew that her life had been spoiled by the suppression of that which was wanton and wild. We couldn't tell what was going on in her mind, of course, but Steve knew. To remember what she, and many another, were in their prime; to recall the youth and vitality and the potential for hedonism all wasted and gone from the ageing bodies and minds, is to induce regrets that the old among us restrained ourselves too much in our youth. When Mary died, however, we knew just how much he missed her, by the dimming of the twinkle in his eyes, as if they too were hidden behind a shadow.

Old Steve's saving grace was that he had not lost that acerbic sense of irony that most of us had suffered from over the years. Like the time when we, all hands, watched a, let's say, well-covered man trying to put up a wind-break and deck-chair on the beach below the plat. Such endeavours had provided many an amusing interlude over the years. The wind-break, being just a bit of coloured canvas between a few poles, was fairly easily erected. It was, however, erected to the leeward of where he was establishing the family territory, and wouldn't even shelter them from a quietly broken, gentle, force three fart, but that's quite common. The deck-chair presented more of a problem. Having gone back to his car to get it, he first tried to erect it one-handed while the other held on to his beach bag, towel, shoes, lunch-box and cans of cold beer to keep them off the sand. No chance! The frame of the chair was a bit tight, so he kept one set of toes on the outer section while trying to lift the inner. 'Look at that tuss with the deck-cheer!' Steve said. He couldn't see how these people managed to get to middle age without meeting disaster in their youth. That the toes were about to become painfully jammed in the chair was painfully obvious. After it happened, all the encumbrances were abruptly discarded as the man hopped on one leg with the other dragging the chair over the sand before he fell over and freed his toes while in the recumbent position. After limping round the chair he picked it up turned it over and had another try. It seems to us that putting up a deck-chair is a very simple process. Lay it on the sand, up side up, pull on the top bar of the canvas frame and it simply falls into position. Could anything be easier? This man, probably like many others whose lives are embroiled in the complicated aspects of modern living, couldn't see the basic simplicity of it. He turned it and unfolded it, folded it up again, put the legs back to front and front to back, jammed a thumb or two until, more by chance than anything else, after all, a chimpanzee would get it right given enough time, the thing fell into position. With all hands on the plat watching, he arranged his belongings in a neat semi-circle, beach bag there, towel here, and beer within reach. Then, with both hands steadying the frame, he flopped into the chair. Now, one, as the English say, should never do that. One should never flop into one's deck-chair, and one should never put one's hands on one's frames, even if one intends to lower oneself gently into one's seat. As we say, it is all very simple and basic. The chair bust! The canvas ripped and the frame collapsed. Two sets of fingers jammed in the frame, and the man ended up completely entangled in the chair, halfway though the canvas with a tangle of wood all around his neck and thighs unable to free and untangle himself, for both hands were trapped in the wreckage, until liberated by a passer-by.

'He should have known better,' Old Steve observed, 'than to attempt such complicated tasks without the user's manuals.'

'User's manuals,' Ceecil nodded in agreement.

Freddie said, 'I didn' know you could get user's manuals for deck-cheers.'

Of all the creatures passing by, the most dangerous marauders are officials bearing tidings of good will. They came up on the plat in the spring of the year, wearing regulation blue anoraks with the council's logo emblazoned in gold, and bright day-glow yellow jackets lest they be run over on their way here by teenage kids on skateboards. They looked around at the historical memorabilia on the walls, old photographs and amateur paintings of ships and the sea, the ancient tortoise stove belching smoke, a framed collection of hitches, bends, splices and whippings in hemp and skillivan. They surreptitiously assessed the potential of the site, the position, and the view. This lodge, they said, is a truly superb institution and perpetuates one of the last remaining traditions of the town's heritage. They were greeted affably by the few who were present, Zeke, Old Steve, Ceecil and Barny, who listened to propositions about possible grants to maintain the building and perpetuate the traditions of the town and that they would be receiving a letter to that effect in order that the propositions might be 'formalised and finalised'.

'OK' the officials were told. As if we were unaware that in fact they see the lodge as an anachronism in this changing climate of progress and initiative. Here we are, right on the harbour front, old and decrepit (some of us), becoming extinct, occupying the most valuable real estate, in terms of potential per square metre, in the whole of the town. The time had come for considering if the property might now be put to more efficient use.

'It can't go on like this,' the Brooks agreed. 'We have to look to the future.'

Nobody minds looking to the future. What we object to is bringing the future forward by twenty or fifty years, to make it right up-to-date.

The Brooks were trying to persuade Freddie, after agreeing with Reggie Hammond, who in turn was mentioning an idea leaked to him in confidence by the tourist officer, that the historic old building should be protected and preserved under a conservation order.

Freddie, for once, kept his mouth shut and opinions to himself, for he, like the rest of us, knew that what the tourist officer really wanted was to kick us over to the old people's day centre and convert the building to make the ideal tourist information bureau, where all the town's publicity departments could be brought under one roof with computerised hands-on internet communications with the targeted market in time for the eclipse, i.e. right now. The difficulty was that, through some historic blunder, the building seemed to actually belong to its users, all those dopey old men standing around minding everybody's business.

We, even those of us who never go near the place, therefore asked

Barny, as our local historian, bard and expert on matters traditional, to write a formal letter to the council expressing the importance of maintaining the status quo for the foreseeable future.

'Dear Sirs,' he wrote, 'Bugger off!' Or more erudite words to that effect.

Some time later, Katie went with Shimshai's woman to the family house that Shimshai had retained after the death of his parents many years ago. Over the years he had made a few visits, sometimes staying for months, but always alone. His woman stayed away. His was a name that Katie had been familiar with for all her adult life. He was a writer, people said, but his books were all out of print and forgotten. He had exposed things best left undisclosed. Told tales. A dangerous thing to do in a small community if you value your life. Your life in that community, we mean. There is more than one kind of death.

Katie's ma, Sarah, was reluctant to talk about him. Even she, who had few secrets withheld from her daughter, would dismiss the subject. 'I didn't know him very well,' she would say. 'He lived away.' Which merely encouraged Katie's curiosity, as Sarah should have seen.

Shimshai lived on the high ground (he would, wouldn't he?) overlooking the harbour and bay, just a few doors away from where Barny the Bard was brought up. The front door was still the original, with heavy brass fittings, and the small hall floored in black and white tiles, while the inner door was glazed in leaded lights that threw patterns on the carpet inside. All the original features of the whole house were still here, Katie thought as she was led through into the front sitting room. It was so like Sarah's, with an old black grate surrounded by lotus-flowered tiles and an oak mantle piece, that she wondered what else they could have in common. The furniture was old, worn on the arms, the carpet a bit bare. This Shimshai was either a traditionalist or else nothing had changed because he never lived here long enough to change things. Perhaps he and his woman didn't notice such things. What would the kitchen be like? She's trying to make a good impression, perhaps, or we would have gone out there. No, she thought, that's my interpretation of what I would do.

'Sit down and enjoy the view. I'll call him and make some coffee.'

Another gesture by Katie to her dirty clothes.

'Oh, never mind. A house is for living in. Take a seat.'

Katie noticed, when she was left alone, that there was no sign in the room of the influence of either writer or artist. There were none of her paintings on the walls, neither were there shelves full of books. There was a novel on the floor by one of the chairs, and a crumpled newspaper in another chair was opened at the crossword, nearly completed. I suppose, she thought, he'll ask a string of questions to be polite, but it's his woman I want to get to know.

Shimshai had spent too long sitting on his backside at this time. He was healthy enough, mind you, but that hill he had to climb every day took it out of him. Do him good, we say. He had a slightly sad countenance, clean-shaven, thin of hair, grey. His smile was enigmatic, there, all over his face, yet revealing nothing, like, Katie thought, that of a man who had already disclosed too much. He greeted her warmly, however.

'And how is Sarah?' he asked.

'Fine, thanks. She's a tough old bird. I suppose you knew her before you went away?'

'Not very well. I think she's about five years younger than me. Five years is a big gap when we're young.' He was being evasive, not welcoming her question.

He must be about seventy, Katie reckoned. She wasn't far out. Shimshai was sixty-nine at this time, Barny was younger.

'You'd be the same age as Old Steve,' Katie said. And she watched his face for a sign of reaction. You never know with older people just what their relationships were. She saw the sharp glance between him and his woman.

'We're very old friends,' he said. 'We went to school together and have kept in touch, intermittently, ever since.'

There again was that smile that hid so much. Katie decided not to pursue the matter. She looked out of the window, where the late sun was casting long shadows of boats' masts across the harbour sand

'You'll have a good view on the day,' Katie said.

'It might rain.'

Now there, Katie thought, was the affinity with Old Steve. That cynical view of life. She laughed and said she didn't want to keep him from his work. He went back to somewhere up above where, it transpired, they had a workroom each.

'He works in the attic and I have a back bedroom converted to a studio,' his woman said. 'All his books are up there where there are no distractions. It would be impossible if we didn't keep our work out of our marriage.'

Until then, Katie had not been sure if they were married. They discussed a few more trivialities of daily living, with Katie's mind elsewhere, far back in her mother's youth, until, in a pause when she thought Shimshai had been gone long enough to be out of earshot and concentrating on whatever his work might be, Katie, having made the decision to be frank, asked abruptly, 'What happened?'

'Happened when?'

'Then,' Katie said. 'Whenever it was. Whatever it was.' As a woman with secrets, she could see them in others. 'All the things my mother avoided telling me.'

Shimshai's woman was just a little disconcerted by this. 'Would you like a drink?' she said.

'Gin and tonic!'

There were not many smiles coming from Shimshai's woman now, Katie noticed. She liked that, and raised her glass slightly as she sat opposite her. 'Cheers!'

'You and Boy Steve,' Shimshai's woman said. 'Are you lovers?'

Here was one as frank as Katie herself, requiring frank answers if this conversation was to continue. 'No. Not now.'

That seemed answer enough. 'His father,' Shimshai's woman said, 'and my husband were, still are, great friends. It was thirty years ago that they both fell in love with the same woman. Steve was already married, so Shimshai got her.' She smiled a wry smile as she looked at the lengthening shadows. 'Still has her,' she added.

'So, we were in love with father and son.'

'Yes.'

'But I,' Katie said, 'am no longer in love with the son. How about you and the father?'

'No. I got over it.'

Katie thought that reply too abrupt, too certain, and watched in silence as Shimshai's woman rose and quietly pushed the door with her foot until it slowly closed. She leaned back in her chair and a blank, dreamy expression came into her blue eyes. 'I did get over it but I have never known such passion since,' she mused aloud. 'Such physical passion and emotional passion that threatened to destroy me... us... with its intensity. The combination of love and lust that those who have never experienced it can't imagine. The madness it induces. We could never have sustained it and everything else would have been anticlimax. We were better apart, although it was agony at the time. I thought my life was over. Without Shimshai I might well have committed suicide. Is there any more madness than that? He has loved me with more fidelity than I deserve. He is a sweetie. A term of endearment he loathes, so I never tell him.'

There was a long pause in the conversation, as if both had revealed too much, until Katie said, 'You call him Shimshai, too?'

'Yes. He even calls himself by that now, although it began as a nickname I believe! He loves it. Shimshai the Scribe! Apparently the locals gave him the nickname when he first claimed to be a writer. Just never call him Shim.'

'Is he religious?' Katie asked.

'No. Why do you ask? Are you?'

'Not in the conventional way,' Katie said. 'My mother is. Very! Primitive Methodist, like all my ancestors. She told me who Shimshai was when I asked about the name. He's in the Book of Ezra, Chapter 4, Verses 8, 17 and 23: '...and Shimshai the scribe wrote a letter..."

'Well, I didn't know that. I don't know the Bible, and I'm afraid I couldn't quote Chapter and Verse.'

'Did you know that my mother was also madly in love with Steve when they were young?'

'No.' Shimshai's woman said. 'Indeed, I did not know that.' Wondering if she would ever understand the complexities of the relationships in this community.

'She still is,' Katie said. 'I think'.

'So there we were,' Shimshai's woman mused with an ironic grin, 'His wife, Mary, your mother, Sarah, and me, and all loving Old Steve Trevorrow. He was a very popular man.'

'He didn't know about Ma.'

TAPE FIVE

Mischief shall come upon mischief, and rumour shall be upon rumour...

We've heard them say that Her Majesty's Ship, *Median City*, was steaming up across the Bay of Biscay, one time, in a steady force seven nor-wester. Captain Mathews and First Officer Tomlinson were on the bridge drinking black coffee. They had been sheltering north of Cap Penas off the Costa Verde during the weather system's southerly spell, knowing that they'd have to plough through it when the wind veered. If they'd had their way they'd have been well on the way to Portsmouth by now, in the lee of Lyme Bay, but their orders had been to stay on station. Some landlubber had decided to keep them there watching for fish poachers, drug smugglers and incompetent yachtsmen in weather when all those actions were well nigh impossible. The fishermen had long since run before the wind for home, the drug smugglers were all making fortunes in Bulgaria, and the yachtsmen, not being as incompetent as some admirals would have you believe, were drinking gin and tonics in the marina at Santander. It was raining but, as the ship plunged into the weather sending green water over the decks, there was no way of determining how hard. They just kept her slow ahead to make life as easy for the crew as possible, anticipating a spell ashore with their families after two months at sea.

According to reports, their radar was indicating not another vessel anywhere within range when Captain Mathews was handed a signal by their telecommunications officer. Captain Mathews had a morbid fear of signals handed over by his sparks. These messages were always from someone who did not want to speak to him directly. They invariably contained bad news in these days when he could have been phoned up on the bridge and spoken to personally by anybody in the whole wide world. He read it through in silence and shook his head with a prolonged sigh as he handed it over to Mr Tomlinson with the ominous words, 'We are going into action, Number One.'

Tomlinson's features brightened up at the prospect of some excitement but, as he read though the message, his expression changed to one of deep foreboding. 'Not another one,' he groaned. 'Are we the only ship on active service in the whole of the western approaches.'

Captain Mathews pressed forefinger and thumb down over his eyebrows, drawing them together in a series of furrows to match the waves pounding against the port bow. 'Seems like it! We'll just have to put on a brave face and make the most of it,' he said. 'Duty is duty, whatever the danger.'

What we are talking about here all happened in our yesterdays. Now, yesterday is a long time ago in anybody's memory, sometimes yesterday is further back than yesteryear. The events we are relating here occurred a long time ago but we aborigines remember them as if they were but in last night's dream time. All accounts of the approaching preparations for the dreaded day differ to such an extent that we wonder sometimes if it ever happened at all, so perhaps we can be forgiven for discrepancies in detail.

Shimshai said the sun was shining on the day and he's the one who's supposed to be so observant, with his novelist's eye, and remember everything about the place, though he wasn't here. He never was here, hardly. Never was here, yet wrote about us as if he was one of the family. Everybody's family. Boy Steve said the sun was shining weakly through an overcast sky and the sea as flat as a pancake, like a sheet of glass, until the ground swell rose up in the afternoon. Ceecil reckons it was raining cats and dogs, but we can't be expected to remember every little detail, and Ceecil is... well, we all know what Ceecil is. Perhaps the day was showery, but where, the question is, was Nelly when the light went out.

Shimshai, on the other hand saw it in an entirely different light, for darkness to him is anathema (whatever that might be). He sat down one evening and, as a writer and observer of the human predicament, he told his woman, began recording his preliminary observations of the whole sequence of events as they occurred, in preparation for book on the subject. Intending that the opportunity for the creation of a contemporary work of literature should not be lost, he wrote:

Tonight, the moon is full. As darkness fell it rose from the thin cloud over the Eastern Shore like a Chinese lantern rising from the mist of opium smoke, red, and unreal, as seen from the harbour wall, so huge and utterly silent. The noises of the night were muted in the maze of narrow streets behind us, with the first bright stars appearing in the blackening sky. For a short while the initial meniscus of orange light, beneath the lowest band of cirrus, seemed to bend the horizon, as if it might drag the whole of earth heavenwards along its nightly arc. We watched it rise. From our windows overlooking the sea, or from the harbour wall as we paused in our work and play, we saw the reflection spread in a tapering glitter across the bay and through the masts of boats at anchor in the shallows...

Which, Barny thought, was a fair enough start for a literary man, but then Shimshai's head got stuck on a block, writer's block, but it was another night, another day he was talking about. Life is hard for the solitary writer starving in his attic who can't tell jisnow from dreckly.

Shimshai apart, our little community has produced a lot of talented people; some from among ourselves and others from outside. It's as if the whole ambience of the place encourages the creative side of its residents. We remember musicians who could make music on peeweeps fashioned from the fresh springtime twigs of sycamore trees, painters who could cut in the abstract boundary of a boat's waterline with a hand as steady as a rock, and stone carvers so clever they could split granite with a feather.

Most of them were never heard of in the outside world, and neither are most of those outsiders who come in, but occasionally some come here from far away and are inspired to such creative energy that their fame spreads far and wide. Comparisons are odious, somebody said, although we can't think why. However, there was one who found his inspiration among us and became world famous all over the parish. No names, no pack drill, so we shall simply call him Alfie. We could call him Wally, but at the time of these recollections no famous person could be a Wally. We had a Babs, and a Bernie, and a Borlie too, not to mention a Ben and Bry and a Barny. Barny is not famous yet, and neither is Shimshai. But then, unlike Alfie, they're both still alive and kicking. Barny writes poetry and Shimshai is still writing the book he started after he began to take life so seriously. If he dies before it's finished, Old Steve said, it will be published post-humorously.

Alfie died a while ago. Quizzy Maggie knew him well, and Old Steve vaguely remembers him from his boyhood as a little man in a battered cloth cap going about his business with a faraway look in his eye as if he saw things denied to the rest of us. He was a compulsive painter with not enough money to buy paints or canvass. He used old bits of wood or card for his canvasses and paint salvaged from dustbins for his colours. He painted what he saw, in a way that no other ever did, unless the other was less than six years old. He was a primitive, with such a distinctive style that his work is instantly recognisable and became extremely valuable after he died, so to have one of his little bits of old, expensively framed cardboard on one's wall is to proclaim to ones friends that one is an art lover of the first order, and very rich. One of Alfie's paintings will fetch ten times more money than Alfie earned in his whole life.

We have a great institution where the works of our geniuses are exhibited from time to time, and a few of us go along there now and then to enrich our life's experience by contemplating these works at leisure. At leisure, but not at ease, for there is hardly anywhere to sit. Never mind. It's where Katie works as a part-time attendant so, being the way we are, the place became known to the locals as Kate's Gallery or as merely The Kate. Katie was intrigued, but not surprised, to see Ezekiel Endean enter the gallery on the opening day of the Alfie retrospective. Zeke was so unpredictable that nothing he ever did surprised anyone any more. To fill the space, the show was shared with two other local primitives, for few collectors were prepared to let their Alfies be taken out of the air-conditioned bank vaults where they lay accumulating value each time another one of Alfie's works was exhibited.

'Hullo Zeke,' she said. 'We don't see you here very often. I didn't know you were interested in art.'

'Hulloh my cheeld,' Zeke said. 'I aren't! I jes come in to see if they'd like to buy some nice frames, and thought I might's well have a quick geek while I'm here.'

'Well, what do you think of them?'

'Not much,' Zeke said. 'They're like kid's stuff.'

'That's why they're so interesting, Zeke. Alfie saw things with an innocent eye. He wasn't influenced by any other painter. He was unique. I wish I could have known him.'

'He was before your time. Why, he was before mine too. Maggie knew 'n well though. And Steve, Old Steve, can remember 'n from when he was a boy. Bit simple, wudn 'uh?'

Some people, she was tempted to say, think you're a bit simple but, in the implied sense, it wouldn't be true of anyone who knew him. His apparent simplicity was, in fact, just that. He was simple in the sense of being uncomplicated. Katie knew, better than any other, just how intelligent Zeke was and regarded him as one of her closest friends. She had to tell him, however, that it was highly unlikely that the gallery would be interested in old frames. To which intelligence he nodded sagely. 'Nobody don't value nawthen, these days,' he said. 'I'll have to take them to Henny Penny.'

He seemed reluctant to go, spending a long time over the Alfie's, as if seeing them with a new eye after Katie's words. From time to time he leaned very close, looking at the brush strokes and textures on the old wood panels and cardboard. 'Crude,' he mumbled, 'bleddy crude. Paint put on with a bleddy tar brush.'

Katie had to leave him there, for an emergency meeting of the gallery's management committee was being held that afternoon. A member of the management committee, up London, had raised the possibility of crowds pouring into the gallery to view the eclipse through the wide windows if it came on to rain. It was essential to discuss and plan for crowd control, security, surveillance and the closing of the doors at a moment's notice if things became too hectic and the priceless works of art were put at risk.

After all that, the last thing Katie wanted was a meeting of the council that evening at which the question of temporary camp-sites was to be raised. She went along, however, if only to ensure that D.D. Johns and Denzil Trethewy would feed the information back to the squire that there was no point in spending thousands of pounds on facilities when there was absolutely no possibility of 'temporary' permissions for emergency camp-sites becoming permanent. The whole day was hectic and she was thankful that Steve was at sea, with no possibility of further argument, and she could go to bed and get up early, for she had the morrow off, when she intended to walk out to Barny's place.

Barny wudn like the rest of us, but then, come to think of it, none of us are. He lived out of town, for one thing, and he wrote poetry for another. While not being totally isolated, his house was pretty remote, we thought, out there in the narrow belt of farmland between the moors and the sea. He had a couple of neighbours, living in a house across the lane, who were close to him, especially her, but Barny was becoming more of a recluse with the passing years. Not a hermit, and certainly not to the exclusion of his friends, who could always be sure of a hearty welcome if they ever knocked his door. Not that many of us did very often. Who wants to go all the way out there for a cup of tay when we've got plenty of tay at home. What did he look like? Well, he was quite ordinary really. Quite good-looking in his youth he was, and about five foot nine or ten, whatever that might be in euros... you'll have to ask Katie about that. He had a short beard that still had more brown than white streaks, hair getting thin, teeth all complete and white. He was very fit. Not an ounce of fat on him. 'If he was a uncut stallion,' Ezekiel said, 'you'd look at his feet and teeth and buy him.' It was all the gardening and regularly walking the five miles into town. A lot of us envied his good health but were not prepared to do all that exercise and eat so much healthy food to attain it. He wouldn't stand out in a crowd in town; his clothes were such that they were never noticed, ordinary. Like most people, he was obliged to buy whatever was the passing mode and replace them when worn out and another fashion was past its trendy peak, maybe ten years later. At home, he wore shorts, or a lot less, and sandals in summer, and wellie boots in winter. Not, as you might say, a dedicated follower of fashion. He was very reluctant to talk about his past, his personal emotions, religion, or poetry. However, reluctance, or reticence, as we know, is not the same as silence, so by one confidence divulged here, another shared there, we knew pretty well all about him between us.

Despite his apparent settled way of life, Barny had a past. He had been in love. Twice. Well, OK, three times counting the one we never mention. His first love was a local girl he has now forgotten all about after believing, at the time, that he could never live without her. We can't remember who she was either, but a lot has happened since then and memories, even invented ones, dim with time.

The one we never mention and everybody talks about, and he writes about in his poems and stuff, came into his life at about the same time that Katie was getting close to Boy Steve. No need for details here, but he was devastated by her departure and swore never to become so closely involved with anyone, female or male, and give so much of himself away ever again. We've all heard that before and not a few of us thought he should have had the sense not to become involved with a party young enough to be his daughter in the first place. The rest of us, most of the men, we mean, thought what a lucky bugger he was to have had her at all, the randy old sod! While some of the women among us thought he was gone mad and blind not to see the opportunities under his very nose.

He probably had a few adventures when he was working abroad as a highly qualified electrical engineer in his young days but they really are never mentioned. Altogether an undisclosed part of his life. Interesting! We know he was in Nigeria and Arabia for a while, earning high enough wages to allow him to semi-retire early, doing odd jobs as an electrician before being forced to quit, he said, by rules and regulations and the premium on his public liability insurance in our increasingly litigious society. The truth is that at his age he was quite happy to do not much, but found the days too short for even that. His poetry output had been prodigious, and once he won a prize for it, but that disastrous love affair had left him dumbfounded in the poetical sense. The fact also is that he still wanted to live life to the full, but as to live it as a young man. Getting older, with too much retrospection, was a pain in the ass, he said in his eloquent way. Life should be about the future. Well, we don't know about that, but it was one reason that, originally, he was not so anxious to be involved in the oral history project that Katie was so keen on. Old people are only interested talking to the young, he said, they say I know too much about them already, and would inhibit their memories. More likely to restrict their imaginations, he told Katie, they can't reinvent themselves with a contemporary. Besides which, they keep dying off and reminding me of my own mortality.

He had known Old Steve and Uncle Joe and Shimshai and the rest of us as older schoolboys, together with the girls, such as Mary and Sarah, back just after the wartime. They'd had an adventurous youth, he realised, and he really should make the effort to get some of them to talk to tape. He became acquainted with Katie just after he came back home, for she had always been an admirer of his poetry and they shared a common interest in the language and old culture of their people. He was a bit surprised when she paired off with Steve's son, for he didn't think they were really suited. But there we are, there's no accounting for taste and, after that dreadful business in the mine, he was very happy that she had someone to see it through with. In recent years he had seen a good deal more of her, found himself confiding in her, and thinking of her a lot more, and in ways that, to tell the truth, he thought, she probably would not approve of, being her mother's daughter and all.

The morning after Ezekiel went to Kate's gallery, Barny looked out of his curtainless bedroom window and saw the sun rising over the hill into a clear blue sky. He rose early, as always, ate a leisurely breakfast and did his housekeeping, reluctantly tis true, but he did it. Then he worked up a sweat turning over a bit of his vegetable garden for an hour, had a shower and prepared his crouse of a bit of cheese and a pear and a glass of *rioja* and then went for a read and an afternoon snooze beside his shrine in the part of the garden he had made secluded by planting an escallonia hedge twenty years before.

So, while Katie was walking along the cliff path, Barny was lying on a rug in his garden. Between snoozing and scribbling his own stuff, he was reading a book. The spring sunshine was deliciously warm, there in the shelter from the wind. And as the sun passed

around his camelias he removed more of his clothes to enjoy the freedom of movement and the air and sun on his skin, feeling the
warmth of the sun on his back, and he put the book down and rested his head on his arms under a battered old straw hat. Those images
of Katie, his wishful thoughts of how they might be if he were twenty years younger, that he resisted with increasing reluctance, came
into his mind. Katie, he hoped, had no idea how he lusted after her.
It began when she used to come and see him for help with her stud-
ies of the language. He couldn't help, he thought, his own desires,
whether right or wrong. Nothing would come of them so what's the
harm. Katie was so like her mother in looks and figure, smallish and
firm, radiating health, but he wondered if she was quite the same in
temperament. He hoped not, for Sarah had gone through her life
alone, totally without carnal desires, it was believed, except for just
the one occasion when Katie was conceived. Although it was impossible to judge, Boy Steve had never struck Barny as being much of a
lover, and he wished many a time in his improbable fantasies that
Katie might come to him as an older, more experienced man and ask
him to make love to her. Thinking along those lines now, imagining
her body beside him, he lay there daydreaming for some time, letting
one erotic fantasy after another flow through his mind until he
became aware of the distant doorbell ringing as if in a dream.

He hurriedly rose and put on his shorts, cursing whoever had
disturbed him until discovering it was Katie herself, dressed in a short
skirt and a teeshirt, carrying a small rucksack, and wet with sweat.

He greeted her in the old language which they often used when
alone. 'Katie!' he cried, *'Wolcum! Da tha welles omma.'* (Welcome.
Good to see you here.)

'Deth da,' she said. *'Fatla genes?'* (Good day. How are you?)

'A wrusta kerdhes? Pur poth osta!' (Did you walk? You are very hot.)

*'My a wra kerdhes yn uskys hag yma an howl ow spalanna yn cref. Allaf
vy entra?'* She asked. (I walked quickly and the sunshine is strong.
Can I come in?)

The request was a formality. 'Of course you can come in. *Yth esen-
vy owth obery yn an lowarth.'* (I was working in the garden.) He was
in a flurry of embarrassment. 'Would you like some tea? Shall I put
the kettle on?' he spluttered.

'No!' she said. 'Never mind the kettle. As I said, I've just walked from town. I needed some time to think over a few things, and I needed to get away from the panic that seems to be gripping every-body on the council and in the gallery. But five miles in this heat! I'm boiling hot,' she said. 'Pour me a gin, with lots of tonic and ice.'

'Go into the garden. I'll bring it out. And one for me too.'

When he returned to the secluded garden he found her stretched out on his rug before his shrine. She glanced at his clothes scattered about the lawn

'*Pur poth yu hedhyu,*' he said. '*Yth essen vy owth obery yn noth.*'

'*Yn noth?*' She laughed. 'Sorry. didn't mean to disturb you.'

Barny laughed with her and took a sip of his drink, feeling the sun on his back and penetrating his shorts. 'I often work naked,' he said. 'Enjoying the sun, as you know.'

'And why not?' she said. 'It sounds very sensuous.'

He found himself unable to meet her direct gaze, and put the drinks down on the grass. Such impertinent candour, he thought, however, could only be countered by an equal frankness. 'Yes.' He said. 'I won't deny it. What with the sunshine and the warm breeze, the smell of the flowers and the hum of bees, the sound of that lark up there, can you hear it? The whole day is sensual. So, yes! Very sensual. I only wish I could write poetry depicting such sensuality, but I can't, I'm too inhibited.'

'Oh, come on! You're one of the most uninhibited and sensual people I know.'

There was something in her eye that was challenging him, he thought. 'At my age I need all the sensuality I can get lest it deteri-orates and dies of neglect.'

Katie grinned at him. She was used to his references to his age. 'You're lucky to be in such good shape,' she said. 'Most men of my age are nothing like as fit as you.'

He accepted the compliment with a nod. 'True,' he said. And they laughed together.

'One of the things I like about you...' she said, and shook her head, unwilling to say more.

'Go on.'

'I was going to say, your lack of inhibitions, but I'm astonished to hear you say that you are inhibited... in your writing anyway. Stuff that no one sees. That surprises me.'

'Yeah! Me too. But I am. I'm not alone in being afraid to put some things in writing.'

As Barny and Katie avoided each other's eyes and looked around the garden the leaves of the escallonia, dark green in their own shadows, glinted like silver where the sun struck them in the hedge. They sipped more of their drinks, enjoying the cool bite of the gin under the hot sun.

'I hate inhibition,' she suddenly said. 'Why can't we just be what we are. What we want to be. I should love to be as wanton and capricious as my mind is. You know, just to have the opportunity. We, I, feel sometimes as if I'm going through life in a straight-jacket woven from the threads of other people's morality.'

If that's what you feel, he thought, why don't you take off that wet teeshirt and let it dry out? How can I keep my hands off her? Christ, how I hate being old. 'You don't have to be inhibited here,' he challenged, glancing at her tanned muscular legs.

He was thinking how luscious the sun would be on them both in the nude. How he would like to slip off his shorts and her wet teeshirt and run his hands so gently over those soft and rounded contours of young and beautiful skin, and excite her with words of love and endearment. He was obliged to change position to cover his rising lust.

Katie sipped her drink There was a long silence between them when he thought he had overstepped the boundary and offended her by his revelation. He could think of nothing to say and could take his eyes off her only by determined self-control. He stretched out on his stomach.

'Barny,' Katie said at last.'

'Yes? I'm sorry. I was miles away,' he lied, 'It's the sun, making me sleepy.'

'After what you've just told me, I want to confess something too. To confide in you. I know I can trust your confidence.' A short laugh. 'After all, we've shared one secret for a long time. But, promise you won't be shocked.'

'I can't do that in ignorance of what you want to tell me. But I'll try not to be.'

'Well,' she said in considered tones. 'It's me and Steve. I don't know what to do. It's not very good. I mean, we're not very good. You know, I have to say it, in bed. No. No, don't say anything. I came all the way out here to tell you what's bothering me and I don't want to be put off. The thing is, I've always been, I've always thought, I was unrestrained. That life, and all aspects of life, were to be enjoyed to the full. Yes, like my mother.'

Barny nodded encouragement. He had not expected this. Why didn't she talk to her mother. Sarah the superior and resourceful who was supposed to have life sussed.

'I mean,' Katie said, 'with my upbringing I should be able to talk to my boyfriend. Shouldn't I? I can't though. I feel repressed. We don't... he doesn't ... It's just not exciting.'

She had said it. Without specifically stating it, she had told him she was emotionally and sexually frustrated.

All the lust Barny had for her died away. He was irritated by her confession. It put him in an unwanted position of avuncular responsibility. He wished she had told him she was a raving nymphomaniac and enjoyed every sensuous moment of copulation with total abandon and didn't give a damn about Boy Steve or Sarah or anybody else. Then he could have seduced her, or even have been seduced by her, with a clear conscience in mutual joyous delight in their naked bodies and sensuous minds. Oh, hell! he said to himself. Getting old is a bind! How I hate it!

But how could Boy Steve, how could a man, how could men, be so useless, so heartless. He sipped more of the iced gin and let her go on.

She also became aware of what she'd told him, and what she had revealed to him. She stopped talking and finished her drink before leaning back on her elbows on the rug beside him, stretching the dry-ing teeshirt, with her legs out in front of her. 'Perhaps I shouldn't have told you,' she ventured eventually. 'But I don't have anybody else to confide in. Not with stuff like this. I don't know what to do. Is it my fault Barny? Am I inhibited without realising it?'

'Looking at you now, I should think you're anything but.'

'And there's the problem. I couldn't even do this in front of Steve without embarrassing him. And he's my lover.' There was desperation in her voice and a hint of a tear in her eye. 'I can't be doing with it. Not all my life, Barny. Not all my life. I have to tell Steve we must end our relationship. It'll break his heart.'

'I'll top up our glasses, shall I?' He put his arm around her shoulders and kissed her hair. 'Hearts mend,' Barny said.

Now, we know that Barny was telling a great lie there. *An gowick braws.* His own broken heart had never mended. It was patched up, yeah, but the crack still showed. We could see unrepaired hearts all over, if we minded to look.

He mixed the drinks, with his mind on other things, delaying the onset of further conversation about matters he'd rather avoid, wondering how he could get her to relax, enjoy the day and accept that relationships don't always go on forever. Eventually he brought them out with ice clinking in the glasses and placed them on the grass beside her, looking into her eyes. *'Yn noth?'* he said.

She looked up at him and smiled. *'Yn noth!'*

Still holding her gaze, Barny sat beside her on the rug and chucked her damp discarded teeshirt over a young camellia and lay back beside her with the warm sun gently soothing all their pains.

'Oh yes,' she sighed. 'That's better. Ah yes!'

The bit of fine weather that began the day Katie went out to see Barny – and they, well, who knows what they did, but not what you're thinking, that comes dreckly – lasted for a while, so we made the most of it. Down'long, the warm sunshine had brought out the cats, what's left of them. Everybody seems to be going in for dogs, these days. The regulars on the plat had turned out to take a turn about and see who was who. There was no room to take a turn about, so we leaned over the railings, thinking that at least we could see what was what. Boy Steve put the *Morvoren* alongside the quay on the rising tide to land his catch. A young woman in a summer frock and straw hat stayed behind when her two companions moved on up the quay. She watched Steve's strong arms hauling the baskets of fish up over the railings. His old man noted with relief that, judging by the number of baskets hauled up, it seemed that he hadn't done badly this time. Whether the trip was worthwhile depended on what was in the baskets and the price on the market of course, but that was always an unknown quantity until the money was in the bank.

There, as we watched, was Shimshai's woman carrying her little easel, her canvas and box of paints. There was Zeke, still wearing his long overcoat despite the sunshine, trundling his old handcart with a pile of junk from Maggie's attic. There, along the wharf, bleddy tourists were settling themselves down in deck-chairs for the day, skirts and trousers pulled up to reveal daring lengths of ankles and legs in varying shades of grey, white or blue. Some even removed their shoes and managed to stay respectable. The prom was already getting crowded, with the seats full up with people reading newspapers and doing crosswords. Passenger boats were being brought alongside the steps to pick up the first trippers of the day. On the foreshore sand the clothes were progressively removed as flesh warmed up and inhibitions cooled. There was Theodora Yeoman, pulling her rickety shopping trolley over the cobbles. The whole harbour was full of colour and movement. Shimshai's woman would have an inspiring morning.

Freddie said, 'I thought Boy Steve was fishing round land.'

He's completely out of touch, Freddie is. Out of touch with everything but his collateral. 'He was round land for the winter,' we told him. 'In the trawlers. And he d' work his own boat for the summer.'

'Is a wonder he can get a berth.'

'He can always get a berth. The damn boats are going to sea short handed. They can't get crews'

'They're going to sae, not short-handed, but undermanned, I tell 'ee. Undermanned!'

'Well, you don't like to think it, but that'll cause trouble. It's all right while it's all right. But things go wrong out there. And when they do, they need all hands.'

'They need all hands,' Ceecil said, and laughed at some personal, secret joke.

TAPE SIX

They have blown the trumpet to make all ready...

Another emergency meeting of the council had been called under the chairmanship of his worship the mayor, and Zeke made a point of being there in the public gallery to keep an eye on things. The whole business was getting completely out of hand as far as he could see.

The town clerk had explained, before sending the letter to Her Majesty, that they ought, as a matter of protocol and political expediency, to offer hospitality to her ships rather than request the reverse but, to be realistic, there was really very little likelihood of their offer being accepted. So, when the reply came and, at the mayor's request, the clerk read out the reply to the town's offer to entertain the Royal Navy, they listened with some trepidation. While expecting to be refused, some were thinking that the clerk's letter was somewhat ambiguous, and what if she decided to send the whole bloody fleet to be entertained? It would bankrupt the town! It seemed, however, that Her Gracious Majesty evidently respected the wishes of her humble subjects, stuck out here miles from anywhere in a forgotten corner of her diminishing empire, and saw fit to command just one of her warships to pay an official visit.

The news was greeted with unbridled enthusiasm by most present at the meeting before the full text of the communiqué had been read, while a few, like DDJ and Collateral Fred, with feet firmly planted astride port and starboard, advised caution that the exercise might incur an unacceptable cost to the ratepayers if it was allowed to escalate into an uncontrollable shindig. The mayor was obliged to call the meeting to order when Winifred Whistler and Theodora Yeoman were on their feet laying into Reggie Hammond who'd been overheard saying, in an aside to the Brooks, that it would be the best opportunity they'd had in years for a good piss-up at the ratepayers' expense.

When order had been restored, Reggie assured the mayor that the expression was a figure of speech, a colloquialism, and he meant no offence. He merely meant that the whole town could join in the celebrations to which they had made generous contribution.

Tim grumbled an acceptance of the apology and asked the clerk to read the remaining paragraphs of the letter. These were received with somewhat less enthusiasm, for the official visit could not be on the day requested, as the ship was scheduled for duty elsewhere on that day.

On that day! And here we have more confused memories. Or is it just the distortion of words travelling from mouth to mouth down the ages? Did the infamous message 'Send reinforcements, we are going to advance' really become passed on as 'Send three and fourpence, we are going to a dance'? Who knows? What we do know is that the Navy came, sometime, no doubt about it for we have the photographs. There is one photo in particular, of that which is normally kept securely hidden and a top secret, that only very, very few privileged persons were ever allowed to see, but it proves beyond any reasonable doubt that these incidents that we herein reveal and relate did occur.

We maintain that the communiqué informed the council that Her Majesty's ship could visit on 10 August. It also informed them that the usual protocol was to hold a full civic reception by the city (that's what it said, according to Zeke, 'city') followed by the dignitaries being entertained aboard ship in traditional manner. Captain Mathews would be in attendance in the wardroom, etc. etc.

After the altercation with Reggie Hammond, Winnie decided it was expedient to keep quiet for the rest of the meeting. That she would receive due recognition for her enterprise in the fullness of time she had no doubt. It would be her day, the triumph of her political career, and she was not having it spoiled by anybody. The reception and ceremonies ashore in the town hall would be attended by the whole council and witnessed by all the townspeople, together with the thousands, nay millions, who had come for the main event. The whole council would not be entertained on the ship, however, and Winnie was maintaining a quiet determination that that man Hammond would go aboard Her Gracious Majesty's ship only over Winnie's dead body.

As the details were completed in the following weeks, it became apparent from the diplomatic communications from the Admiralty that only two officers would attend the ceremonies ashore and that it was 'advisable' to restrict the number going aboard for the reciprocal entertainment to just ten, who, it was strongly hinted, should represent the whole community and not necessarily only the council.

Drawing up the shortlist, which meant throwing most of the council off, was a job Tim, the mayor, tried to fob off on the town clerk, but that gentleman would have none of it. 'As I shall be going myself', he said, 'it would be interpreted as questionable by those omitted from the invitations.' Tim conceded defeat but was gratified to have it inadvertently pointed out that he would have committed political suicide by forgetting to include any paid council officials in the ceremonies. He would have to go, reluctantly, but as mayor it was an inescapable duty. Limiting the final list, after a great deal of behind the scenes lobbying, was not as difficult as he had anticipated for many business people would be unable to give up the time. They were anticipating a very busy week in which their casual staff might not be relied upon to turn up for work due to disruption of transport. They had read that, in other countries, the police had closed all the roads during such an event. Others had decided that the odds of losing their dignity during a bout of seasickness were too likely to risk. Denzil Trethewy, for instance, declared that he had never been on a boat in his life and wild horses could not drag him out there. Some councillors, in anticipation of the impending chaos, had long since booked short holiday breaks on the continent to retreat from it all, only to learn that the thing would follow them there and the only escape from the penumbra was at the north pole or south of the equator. Katie Stevens expected to be working, for a good percentage of the crowds were likely to visit the gallery. Boy Steve was unavailable. As a member of the lifeboat crew, he had agreed to be on duty and was expecting a busy time running short trips around the warship to raise money for the RNLI, while being on standby in case of emergencies. Zeke reported to us that Boy Steve also pointed out that high water here would be around midday but none of the others saw the significance of it.

'Who could believe it 'en you?'

'What have we come to, here? Don't know when high water es!'

'Things aren't like they was.'

'Not like they was,' Ceecil said.

At a later meeting, Tim found himself getting desperate to fill the list. There would be himself, the town clerk, Winnie (of course), Freddie, Theodora, and DDJ as father of the council. The Brooks were always free. It seemed that Reggie Hammond would have to be included despite his promise to Winnie that he be blacklisted. As a concession, for Winnie threatened to make Reggie's disparaging remarks generally known (they already were but she wasn't aware of it), Tim thought it might be a good idea if Winnie and Theodora be permitted to choose escorts from among the prominent members of the community, thus making a gesture to the women of the town and letting himself off the hook. This is not the way these things were recorded in the minutes, but nobody reads them anyway so what do they matter. The point is that no objections were raised, who would dare, so the proposition was adopted and recorded as unanimous. The council went on to discuss other items on the agenda, anticipating problems during the celebrations of the eclipse and major chaos to be caused by the dreaded millennium bug. Upon Tim and DDJ's suggestion, the council had appointed a high-ranking retired civil servant to manage the logistics and had more or less left it to him, the point being that nobody knew what the hell to expect or prepare for, so were reluctant to make comments in public that would make them appear completely out of touch and control of the situation. It was reported that all emergency services were to be on red alert. Traffic in and out of the area would be controlled by the military. Barricades were to be placed at vulnerable sites and all access to the countryside was to be strictly controlled lest the situation get completely out of hand. We were afraid that our limited resources, in such a small community, would be stretched beyond breaking point, and that we would be powerless to stop the total disintegration of law and order, but the councillors were assured that arrangements were proceeding with military precision, and every contingency allowed for, so the remainder of the meeting was a routine procedure with little further in the way of discussion. For which the mayor was very grateful.

After the meeting Winnie found herself walking down'long with Ezekiel Endean at her side. We saw them go past the plat, Zeke with his flowing beard and overcoat and Winnie in her red hat. They were followed a while later by Boy Steve and Katie, on the way to the pub. It was evening, so Shimshai had come out, like a crepuscular troglodyte, for his constitutional. Steve was there as he had no wish to spend the evening at home alone in front of the telly. And there was Freddie, and a few others who had managed to squeeze in along the railing between the few early bleddy tourists. We watched Zeke and Winnie, and made no comment. Even Freddie had nothing to say about them. Some natural phenomena are beyond our understanding. Shimshai didn't know who they were, having been incommunicado as he put it, while researching yet another book. He was, however, so he said, anxious to re-establish himself as a member of the community and frequently asked questions on the plat about passers-by. There were some that he damn well should have known, Old Steve told him. 'How can 'ee forget so and so, he was like a brother to 'ee?' He lost patience with Shimshai sometimes, telling him he was a silly tuss and stuff like that but he never, as far as we know, ever raised the subject of all that other business or asked about his woman. Shimshai knew who maid Katie was, having met her at his own house, remember, and when she went by the plat with Boy Steve, that time, he turned to Old Steve and asked the question he should have avoided.

'Who's that young man?' he asked. Although Boy Steve was not that young by this time.

Old Steve looked at 'n like one mazed as a gurgy. 'You don't know who he is?' he asked incredulously.

'No. I don't know him.'

'Well!' Old Steve said, ' I thot everybody knod who he is.' And he turned with a quick glance around to ensure that there was no one within earshot who shouldn't overhear what he was about to impart. 'He!' he said, nodding back over his shoulder towards the passing couple, 'is the one...' pausing, reluctant to utter such a thing now. 'He's the one,' leaning forward to whisper in Shimshai's ear, 'that my wife Mary had by a married man after our wedding. And you mean to tell me you never knew it?'

Shimshai was shocked. He knew he had been a little out of touch over the years, but to be informed of this was indeed a revelation. His whole relationship with Steve, who he had always regarded as one of his oldest and closest friends was thrown into question.

Freddie attempted to make an embarrassed contribution to the revelation but was silenced by a fierce look from Steve.

'Less said about it the better,' Old Steve continued, with a sigh of resignation at the anomalies in life. 'Less said the better.'

'Less said the better,' Ceecil agreed.

And the subject was dropped, leaving poor Shimshai in a state of silent perplexity as he and Old Steve strolled slowly down to the pub.

There weren't too many in there, which was a change. These days the pubs are usually so crowded, Steve told Shimshai as they were waiting for their pints, that nobody goes to them anymore. There was a time, he said, when old Young William went in to the barber's, only to find it was empty and he could have his haircut and shave right away. 'I'll come back dreckly,' he said, 'when there's a few more in. Who d'want go to the barber's and not catch up with the news?' he explained, 'I can shave m'self and me misses can cut me hair.'

'Those days are gone,' Old Steve lamented as he led the way to join the others in the bar. Sitting at the far end of the bench, near the window was Katie, Boy Steve, Zeke and, biggest surprise of all, Winnie the Pew with a glass of wine in front of her.

Shimshai found himself sitting between Old Steve and Boy Steve, who was next to Katie. Opposite sat Winnie and Zeke. Winnie was evidently a little nervous at being there, in the pub, but Zeke was looking at her like a cat who'd got the cream and could hardly take his eyes off her to greet the newcomers.

'It's years since I've been in a public house,' Winnie assured them, 'but they're not like they used to be, are they?'

'Not a bit,' Old Steve said.

'Needed a drink after all that talking in the meetin,' Zeke explained, apparently forgetting her silence throughout most of the proceedings. 'Do her larynxes a world of good.'

Shimshai wasn't sure about Winnie's larynxes, or of Zeke, either.

Zeke had been but a boy when Shimshai left here. The man was evidently very eccentric, to judge by his old-fashioned clothes, but his tastes were totally idiosyncratic, although apparently he had no idea that he was in any way different. He was certainly not stupid, and his darting eyes missed very little. As a writer, the bearded Shimshai, who was wearing faded green corduroys, his linen coat, and a yellow silk scarf under an open necked shirt, all topped by that black, broad-brimmed hat, found the little man of great interest, as he did his companion, Winnie. True characters were rarely encountered these days, Shimshai thought, and it was good to be back among so many. He was very much aware, however, that it was advisable to determine just who was who in any company here and to be sure not to put one's foot in it by making inadvertent remarks. He remembered being put in his place many years ago by one of their contemporaries, 'Uncle' Joe, for considering himself superior and being as Joe put it 'a bleddy shitbag'. The revelation about the relationship between the two Steves had reminded him of this and he had little to say. Winnie asked if he was looking forward to the eclipse and he mumbled that he might be away, for he needed to go to London, intrigued by the relationship between her and Zeke yet reluctant to determine what it was.

What Shimshai didn't know was that indeed all hands were intrigued by the relationship between Winnie and Zeke. As far as we knew neither had ever been seen alone with a member of the opposite sex before, and we were watching them as intently as he was. The only person who seemed totally relaxed in the bar was Katie, who chatted to Zeke and Winnie about the forthcoming visit of the Navy.

'All Winnie's idea,' Zeke pronounced. 'Only one on the council with any brains.'

Winnie grimaced coyly in embarrassment and smiled at the man in the black hat, having no idea who he was, for no one had bothered to introduce him, all assuming that everybody knew everybody, as they should have done anyway.

Boy Steve and Katie glanced at each other with a smile. 'Thanks, Zeke,' Boy Steve said.

'Aw! Didn' mean you two. How's your mother, Katie?'

'She's fine,' Katie said. And here, for some reason, Shimshai saw Kate glance at Old Steve before continuing. 'She keeps very fit, but I think she gets a bit lonely now that I'm not with her so much.'

'She always comes to chapel,' Winnie said. 'Most Sundays.'

Boy Steve had to catch the early morning tide and Katie was working next day so they went off after one drink, with Boy Steve just giving Old Steve a brief nod as they left. Not, Shimshai noticed, a very good relationship there. Which was hardly surprising.

There was a time when, if Boy Steve and Katie went past together, they'd be arm in arm, but not now. They knew, Old Steve knew, and Sarah knew, that before long they would have a flaming row and be enemies for the rest of their lives if one or the other didn't initiate and manipulate a conversation about their imminent break-up. Each thought the other was still committed to a continuance of that which should have been finished years ago and was reluctant to inflict pain on one so close, even if the old love had faded away. We could see that, and we were pretty sure Sarah would have seen that, for she would be as happy to ease them out of an unsatisfactory relationship as she had been keen to foster it at the beginning.

'You're still seeing quite a lot of Barny Baragwaneth,' Boy Steve said to Katie. 'A lot more of him than you do me.'

'I told you! Ask me out. Let's go somewhere.'

'We're going nowhere,' Boy Steve said.

Katie stopped in her tracks. Now, she decided, was the time. Right now. 'Let's go down along the quay,' she said.

Now in this seafaring community the quay is not just for landing fish. The truth is that landing fish has never been their original function. We might's well make it clear that most of our little harbours – despite the propaganda put out by publicity officers who don't, some say, know what the hell they are talking about and use every mortal thing to make us appear picturesque and surrounded by heritage and do their damnedest to bring in more and more people and weant be satisfied until the bleddy tourists are standing shoulder to shoulder over the whole of the bleddy landscape and want to see the quays crammed full of cars and... and... Eh? Oh 'es. Sorry about that. Where was we? – were never built for fishermen. All of our quaint old harbours were built for the embarking and disembarking of stuff other than fish. Most of the stuff was minerals and equipment needed for the extraction of those minerals. The minerals shipped out were copper, tin and stone; the stuffs shipped in included coal, timber, iron and tiles from Holland used as ballast. There was also a considerable amount of human traffic, for these centres of activity were our gateway to the outside world long before the coming of roads, railways and airports. The harbour, then, was the centre of communal life. We didn't go in much for your village greens or squares or circles or plazas. There was hardly ever enough level ground for such things, anyway. So the harbour was our business centre, community centre, amenity centre, shopping centre, medical centre, playgroup centre, courtship centre, and old people's home (gerrycentre!). So we'd like you to understand that going the short distance, down along the quay, could be a journey of some significance.

Boy Steve turned about. They walked slowly along the wharf. Their whole relationship had been doomed from the start, he thought. The age difference between them was too much. He turned to look at her, remembering that she had been only eighteen or so when they had first become acquainted, while she was still at college. She didn't look much different now. He was eighteen years older, and felt it. Yes, he thought, doomed from the start.

The night was clear, they noticed, with a sky full of stars. Aquila the eagle hung over the dunes across the bay, carrying the thunderbolts of Zeus across the Milky Way. The tide was coming in and a few couples, arm in arm, were ambling back up the quay as they passed the old squat lighthouse and piles of monofilament nets, white and glistening in the lamplight. Neither knew that it was here, on such a night, under the same constellations, so many years ago, that Old Steve, this Steve's father, and Sarah, Katie's mother had exchanged their one and only kiss that should have bound them together for ever. And perhaps, in ages past, their grandparents, great-grandparents, ancestors of generations gone had exchanged first kisses here on the quay, or among the rocks from which the quay had emerged, as their predecessors wrenched a living from this untamed land and sea. Times change and we have to change with them, each moment demanding a slight concession until a complete metamorphosis transpires and we are no longer the people we were. This happens in generations or in a single life. Neither of these two were as they were at the time when they were bound by circumstances too distressing to recall.

She was so self-reliant, he thought, that she could well have coped with their predicament alone. He was so self-centred and withdrawn, she believed, that she was rarely in his thoughts. If they married, they would live the remainder of their lives growing apart, becoming remote as strangers. Even that which had thrown them together at a time when they were little more than kissing cousins was never, had not been, mentioned for years.

They reached the end of the quay and leaned on the railings. Reflected light from many windows sparkled across the water and the sound of a slight swell washing over the quay steps could be heard clearly above the muted sounds from the disco behind the roofs. The night was made for love, for tender declarations of eternal devotion, and these two, both so dear to us, were about to part after many years together. It was a night to speak of the beginning and the years between. It was Boy Steve who took the first tentative step.

'You never mention him,' he said, 'but do you ever think of Joe?'

Katie took some time to gather her thoughts. This was not what she expected. 'I would be lying,' she said, 'if I told you he was always in my thoughts.' Her voice as soft as the breeze that was wafting over the town from the west. 'Most of the time I don't give him a thought. Just get on with life, same as you. But when I do think of him, of that... time, I wish I knew before, before all that, that he was my father. To have known him as a casual acquaintance for all my early life only to discover, then, who he really was... it was such a responsibility, somehow, as if he was some kind of anonymous benefactor. I... we... owe him so much, don't we? She waited for a response from him. It was not forthcoming. 'Do you think of your mother?' she challenged.

'Not much. She's been gone six years. Da d' miss her, though he never says so. They weren't all that happy together. She and Da were always at loggerheads. These days people would end the marriage and think nothing more of it, seems to me. Your mother detested mine, as you know, and to tell 'ee the truth, Katie, I d' wonder if we would've been together if it wasn't for the sake of defying the opposition of our parents.'

Katie turned to look at him. They seemed to produce handsome men in his family she thought, thinking how like his father he was; good, honest, reliable men that are becoming hard to find. She could do worse than stay with him, get married, have a family. No! She dismissed the possibility. They weren't right for each other. They would either grow further apart or end up in perpetual conflict, quarrelling over trivia. Better to live alone, as Sarah had done, quite happily. 'Do you regret the years we've been together, then?' Her question was too abrupt, and she immediately regretted it, hoping he would not interpret it as a further challenge.

He too turned, from looking at his boat riding easily on her moorings, and leaned back against the railings. He had, Katie thought as she looked at him, been very near to spending most of his life in prison for her sake, but he never mentioned it, never used it as justification for demanding her loyalty.

'Fishing is a weird sort of life,' he said. 'I don't know why we do it. We work the most unsociable hours you could possibly imagine, day and night, seven days a week, all controlled by tides and weather. You can't join societies or clubs or plan ahead for any two consecutive weeks. The only friends you have are among your fellow fishermen, the only dependable social life where you can meet casual acquaintances is in the pub. It's unreliable, and you never know where the next penny is coming from. It is a way of life that demands dedication, and that mostly from the wives.'

Katie had never head him speak like that before. He'd given up the prospects of a career as a biologist to live this life, and rarely used language that indicated his education. It was as if he considered the two as incongruous, and he wasn't the only one to think so. There's a brea few among us like that. Katie was glad that he'd not gone fishing for her sake. Just like so many here, like his father, his grandfather, her father, her grandfather, he loved the life and could not imagine doing anything else. In addition to all this he had been a member of the lifeboat crew for years. She respected and admired him above all others, but could she spend the remainder of her days with him? She was silent as he gathered his breath and wits.

'I've loved every minute I've spent with you,' he continued, 'unpredictable though it's been. But I thought it was too much, to ask you to marry me. Every time I came ashore I expected to hear you'd found somebody else. I just can't imagine you being a, well, a fish-wife, with your social life restricted by mine. Not many women can put up with it these days. Especially women like you.'

She dug her elbow into his belly. 'There aren't any other women like me.'

'Ow!' he said, grimacing in pain. 'Well thank God for that,' he gasped. 'I'm sure that men will be glad to hear it.'

'Do you think all that is news to me? Do you think I don't know what it would be like, married to a fisherman? Don't you think you could have asked me and let me decide.'

He thought carefully before answering. 'Don't you ever consider what a refusal would have done to me if I went down on my knees and proposed? You bloody feminists can't have it all your own way.'

'I'm not a feminist!'

He looked at her and shook his head in disbelief.

'Not in that way,' she said.

He couldn't resist a good laugh at that, but could see that she was perplexed by her own values, wanting some of the new, some of the old. 'Do you regret the time you've given me?' he asked. 'It's been a big chunk out of your life.'

'No. I don't do things I'm going to regret. Not consciously. Not very often. Ha! Sorry about the dig in the guts. No. I don't regret our time together, what we've done. It's things we've not done that I wonder about. Have we missed out on life in some way, just being here, going on in the same old manner, day after day?'

'Are you looking for somebody else?'

'I don't know. Are you?'

'I don't know either.'

They had told all. Or rather all that could be told at that moment. 'Come on,' Steve said. 'We'll finish this some other time. I have to be up at four o-clock.'

Winnie sipped her wine very slowly. She wasn't exactly a tee-totaller, but alcohol went to head almost immediately, making her become giggly and foolish, she told Ezekiel.

'Don't think I'm narrow-minded or anything like that, Ezekiel. I just, you know, a lady has to consider her self-respect and I wouldn't want to do anything silly, Ezekiel, 'cause we all live together here and I'm like you Ezekiel, a respected member of the community, and as members of the council we have added responsibilities over and above, you know, the ordinary mortal...'

'Will 'ee have another drink?' Zeke said.

'Oh no I think this is quite enough for me thank you, Ezekiel, I don't use much alcohol you know and I have to walk home dreckly and I wouldn't want to be found in the gutter in the mornin' now would I, though I like to have a good time now don't get me wrong, Ezekiel, a good time I mean in the proper way of behaving. I mean I'm no good time girl what they d' call...'

'I'll just get another half,' Zeke said. 'Hang on here.' He was delighted to see, out off the corner of his eye, Old Steve, Shimshai and some more of us regulars looking at him and Winnie sat so close and cosy in the corner. If only, Zeke was saying to himself, if only I'd a knawd how easy i' was t' ask her to go for a drink I'd a done it years ago. She wudn a bad looker for a forty-year-old, he thought, with a figure that would have done justice to a party half her age. It was all that walking the cliff paths. He was also delighted to think, as he waited for his half to be pulled, that he, just by his very proximity, could make a woman, especially Winnie, so bleddy nervous that she might at any minute become overwhelmed by uncontrollable excitement and wet her knicks. If she had any on, my God! Zeke himself was trembling a bit when he returned to his companion with his half pint of bitter spilling over his fingers.

'I'll walk home with 'ee,' he said. 'Make sure you don't end up in the gutter.'

Shimshai and Old Steve said good night to the incongruous couple as they left the bar, although Zeke was evidently so besotted with his companion that he hardly spoke to anybody else, even to bid them good night. Shimshai and Old Steve left in the bar together were also a bit of an incongruous couple, we thought, and wondered how they could have stayed such close friends after the trouble over Shimshai's woman. Steve still wore his old navy-blue garnsey with the ribbed pattern over the chest that had been his family tradition for generations. He was one of the last to be seen in such a garment, for everybody else was going in for fleeces that had never, he said, been anywhere near a bleddy sheep so how can they call them fleeces when they're nawthen more'n a bit of old fluffed-up plastic.

Shimshai was aware that Steve was very quiet tonight, and put it down to the revelation about Mary's child. It was something that evidently upset him, even after all these years. He felt somehow guilty in the shared knowledge and left the bar soon after Zeke, thinking that Old Steve was best left alone to ponder his life.

Shimshai trudged up the hill to home a puzzled man. He had known Old Steve and Mary all his life, he told his woman. All his bloody life, and thought he knew them as well as anybody on earth, only to learn now, at their age, that Mary had a son by a married man.

His woman turned from pouring milk into their nightcaps of cocoa. 'I can't believe it,' she said. 'What married man?'

'He didn't say.'

'Who didn't say?'

'Steve.'

'Steve told you? Himself?'

'Yes.'

Shimshai was evidently quite upset. Thinking, she assumed, of the years and devotion Steve had put into rearing another man's child. Even giving him his own name. It was unbelievable. After handing him his drink, his woman sat at Shimshai's feet. He hadn't changed, she was thinking. After all these years he was still the same. Still the same mischievous imp as he had been when they dropped the condom full of water on Quizzy Maggie's head. She began smiling, then quietly laughing. Perhaps meeting him would not be such a dreaded encounter after all. 'Tell me,' she giggled, 'just what he said. Exactly what he said.'

'I don't see what's so damn funny,' Shimshai said. 'Steve said that after their wedding Mary had a child by a married man.'

'Oh yes. So she did!' his woman cried, barely restraining her laughter. 'I remember now. I remember who the father was, too. His name was Steven Trevorrow.'

'Steve?'

'Of course. What married man would Mary have a child by, except her husband?'

When the penny dropped, Shimshai was angry. Really angry. He didn't see the funny side of it at all. It was a long time since he had lived in a community where you needed your wits about you for more than crossing the road. 'Why are they always taking the piss out of me,' he fumed. 'If they don't like me and resent me coming home, why don't they say so. Or shun me.'

She put her arms around his waist. 'They love you,' she said. 'Or they wouldn't do it. It's the way they are. You ought to know that. They never make fun of me like that.'

She was right. She knew us better than he did.

Old Steve was left in the bar alone. He wasn't the only one in there of course, there were quite a few of us and a few bleddy tourists propping up the bar. He wasn't on his own. Just alone. We didn't have to be clairvoyants or psychologists to work that out. We could tell he was getting maudlin, sitting there alone.

He left the bar just after his son and Katie had passed on their way back from the quay. He crossed the road and leaned over the railings. There used to be a low baulk of timber edging the wharf, he remembered, to stop the horse-drawn carts from being backed into the high tides. Come the war and they built a bleddy g'eat concrete wall to keep out enemy tanks. That had been scat down and replaced by railings when too many unwashed hippies sat upon it playing guitars. Totally unacceptable behaviour in any community. Such changes, Steve thought, so many lives we've lived. He heaved himself off the railings and made his way along the wharf. What am I thinking of, he thought. Down along the quay. Nobody there except bleddy tourists! All in bed or the pubs. He could never walk past the lighthouse without thinking of Sarah. And that got him thinking about Shimshai and his woman. How, he asked himself, could Shimshai do it? How could he come back here with his woman and tow all those memories behind him? How could he be so insensitive as to arouse all the old desires that Steve had suppressed for all these years. Every time he walked down here he got to thinking of what might have been. Having got his woman, that bleddy Shimshai should have taken her away and kept her away for the rest of their lives. Sometimes he thought how unsure he was of his own emotions, his own memories. Looking back, he thought, he should have realized that no woman could have loved him as she had done. And what man could love her as he had done? He wasn't happy and doubted that she was entirely happy, despite outward appearances. What had his actions denied them? Oh God! If Shimshai hadn't come back with his woman, their woman, none of these thoughts would have entered his head. He could have lived out his days in the manner to which he had become accustomed, he thought. But he didn't want that either.

Sometimes, when strolling down along the quay at night, pondering on the anomalies of life, he thought that sooner rather than later he would have to confront her and discover if she still loved him after all these years.

Sometimes, though, when strolling down the quay at night, he just thought of nothing, or what the hell was he going to have for supper.

TAPE SEVEN

...and one man among them was clothed with linen,
with a writer's inkhorn by his side...

Some of us are what you call figures of fun. To be honest, as people say when they're about to tell a whopper, most of us are figures of fun to some of us. The exceptions are usually those who try to be funny by telling jokes. We laughed at Shimshai's pretentiousness, Barny's intensity, Old Steve's cynicism, and our youngsters' mimicry of the so-called world of fashion. Zeke and Winnie were figures of fun for their eccentricity, though neither was daft. So were Collateral Fred and Theodora, he for his gullibility, she for her affectation of self-righteousness. We share all these traits in ourselves and need to be reminded of that at times. Some are not figures of fun, and these are the ones to be wary of. No names, no pack drill.

Henry Penny, nearly always referred to as Henny, except to his face, had a flat over his shop. From the sitting-room window he could just see over the roofs of nearby cottages to the horizon. Henny would stand there in the mornings where we could see him, in full view of the passers-by in the street below, wearing his luxurious Chinese silk dressing-gown, with his cup of coffee in his hand and cigarette smoke curling round his fingers. He saw himself as an example to the lesser men among us, a man who knew the value of fine living and good taste. In the evenings he stood there with his whisky and soda, surveying the view and passers-by in the streets below, congratulating himself on how well he'd done in life. Henny, like most of us, had a selective memory but his was selective to the point of denial. His long-distance memory was defective in that he forgot his upbringing, and his short-distance memory in that he forgot little details like the true value of items brought into his shop by people a lot worse off than himself. His silk dressing-gown was one such item, having been found in a load of junk removed from the glory-hole of old dead Cap'm Jack Thomas, who had been on the Far Eastern run for many years. If reminded of these lapses, he would say, 'It's business, old boy. Do you know the true value of a bottle of expensive and supposedly superior wine?' Well, no. Hardly any of us drunk the stuff.

After his breakfast he would descend the stairs to his shop. He called it his gallery of antiquities, for at times he acquired a bronze sculpture, a piece of silver or a painting which was above the value of the usual cracked china and worm-eaten commode. He made a study of the antique and art markets and followed the trends in anything collectable. The most interesting items that fell into his hands were never displayed on his shelves and walls but went straight to his connections at the London auctions. He knew his stuff, you have to give him that. He was expecting to do very well out of the bleddy tourists who would be coming for the eclipse. In anticipation of the thieving bastards crowding his shop and nicking his stock he had, at considerable expense, installed a new closed-circuit television system that covered every square metre (he was yards ahead of us in that respect) of the shop.

He was busy adjusting the prices of his stock to reflect inflation and the growing value of the market, just a penny or two here, a pound or two there, not enough to deter the indiscriminate when, through the window, he saw Ezekiel Endean trundling his handcart up the road and his heart dropped. There was a slight rain falling and the cart was groaning under the weight of items piled high and covered over with a piece of ancient tarpaulin. Zeke, who had never bothered about cars or learning to drive one, was pressing on up the slope totally ignoring both vehicles and pedestrians with heads held down under hoods or umbrellas. Henny had to keep on the right side of Zeke but, having him roll up and park that thing right outside the shop door, was an unbearable irritation liable to turn any prospective customer away on sight. He was suspicious at times that Zeke did it just to annoy him but, with Zeke's apparently guileless manner, he could never be sure. He watched as Zeke struggled to get his cart over the kerbstones and park it on the pavement, with the long handles close to the door and a piece of wood jammed under the wheels to prevent the whole thing running back down the street and ending up in the harbour. The bell on the door jangled as Zeke pushed his way inside. Henny had retained the old bell, despite the new surveillance system, as it gave the shop, he said, an air of genuine antiquity rare in these modern times.

'Loh,' Zeke said. 'Ow are 'ee?'

'I'm very well, thank you, and also very busy.'

'Gittin' ready for the 'clipse crowds? You should do all right out of that lot.'

'I doubt it,' Henny drawled, 'they'll probably be a tasteless shower of philistines.'

'Got some stuff for 'ee,' Zeke confided. 'Nice stuff.'

'I doubt that too,' Henny said. 'And you can't leave that cart parked right by my door. Take it round the back and I'll have a look.'

It was hard work trundling the cart further up the hill, round the corner and down the rough lane to Henny's back door. Zeke removed the wet tarpaulin and brought a couple of bundles into the shop, they in turn being wrapped in old rags.

'What rubbish have you brought this time?' Henny asked. There was not as much as it appeared while on the cart, just three rectangular parcels.

'These here paintin's,' Zeke said, as he unwrapped the parcels with great care to reveal a number of picture frames, some still holding filthy paintings. He leaned them in a stack against the wall at the back of the shop and stood back to allow Henny Penny to look at them one by one. Some were ornately framed, some bare canvas, and some on bits of old three-ply board.

'Not much demand for old paintings now,' Henny mused as he looked through them. 'Everybody wants modern stuff these days, abstracts. I can't stand them myself, but there we are, one has to make a living.'

Henny lifted another painting as Zeke was looking around at the stock on the shelves and in cabinets around the walls. There was a sudden stiffening of Henny's body and a narrowing of the eye, unseen by Zeke, Henny determined, with a quick glance in his supplier's direction. He looked back at the paintings and leaned them all against the wall as he regained his composure.

'Quite nice frames.' Henny observed. 'A bit old fashioned by today's taste. But quite nice.'

'I don't like most of them,' Zeke said. 'Too heavy.'

'Where did you say these came from?' Henny mused as he continued looking through them.

'In a attic down'long. Quizzy Maggie's that was.'

When Henny had seen them all he lifted them again, one at a time, looking more carefully. He let the paintings drop back against the wall as he thumbed through them. 'Very dirty,' he said. 'They'll take a bit of cleaning.'

'I cleaned some of them,' Zeke said, 'with turps.'

'Good God.' Henny muttered under his breath with his eyes rolling heavenwards. 'Turps!'

'Wudn proper turps,' Zeke said. 'Substitute stuff. It's all you can git these days.'

'Well,' Henny said, as he let the frames all drop back against the wall. 'There's nothing of great value here, as one would expect from an attic in Quizzy Maggie's house. But, if they were properly cleaned and the frames renovated, I dare say I could shift them eventually. Sometimes things come back into fashion. I'll be generous and offer you a hundred and fifty. For the frames, mainly. They are quite nice.'

Quite nice, Zeke noted with some satisfaction, was a phrase that Henny Penny would never use under normal circumstances.

'No,' he said. 'I'll take them up'long. You ceant fool me. They frames are antique. I know they're all the fashion. Gilt. Tha's what they are. Gilt.' He bent to wrap them up. 'I'm tempted to keep the paintin's for me'self, but I really don't like them, to tell 'ee the truth. I never was much for cows and windmills and they boats like a cheeld could do.'

'We...ll,' Henny drawled, 'as it happens, I have a London dealer coming to see me in a couple of days. In the hope that he'll be interested I'll give you... say... two hundred and fifty?'

'Three,' Zeke said. 'Three 'undred and fifty. There's twenty frames there, and tha's only seventeen fifty each for frames worth at least twenty pound. I can do sums you knaw. And they pictures might be worth a shillin' or two cleaned up. You ceant fool me,

Penny. I'm not that daft.'

'Well, very well,' Henny conceded. 'You're a hard bargainer, Zeke.'

'Cash?'

'As always.'

'Now!' Zeke said.

We were told that Henny sighed in resignation, but went to the safe upstairs and took out three hundred and fifty pounds worth of the oldest and dirtiest notes he could find. He hurried back down in case Zeke was checking the revised prices on his goods and hustled him from the shop, reiterating that he was very busy. He watched him load the tarpaulin and old rags in the rain, trundle back around the corner and go off down the hill until well out of sight. Henny then returned to the heap of junk pictures Zeke had just brought in and went through them very, very slowly, before covering them up and picking up the phone.

With longer summer days, Old Steve saw Shimshai's woman spending more time painting out of doors alone, for Shimshai was becoming ever more involved with his book in which he was recording the events leading up to the great day. The evening sunlight casts a certain glow over the old quay and the boats, especially when they're lying high and dry on the ebb. The warm sunshine also lingers on the old wooden baulks that have been sat upon by generations of locals and bleddy tourists alike before it disappears behind the roofs of the houses on the high ground to the west. These are the houses that both Sarah Stevens' father and Barny Baragwaneth's father had bought, as young men, at the most prosperous time of the fishing industry, when they needed to keep their eyes on their boats in the treacherous harbour. Houses with bay windows that take advantage of the view, where the families had lived a few doors apart and where Sarah still looked down into the harbour from her front-room window. She could see Shimshai's woman down there sitting under her wide-brimmed hat on a little collapsible stool before her easel. Blatant! Sarah thought. Coming back here utterly without shame or regret. Both she and that Shimshai, come to torment her in her old age. She who had never ill-wished a soul in her life was finding it very difficult not to curse the both of them with the vehemence of the Devil. What have I come to, she thought, to be so bitter at my time of life. And there was Katie, who knew nothing of past scandals, going out of her way to meet up with her. Going down over the quay steps with the *Morvoren* lying to her moorings and Boy Steve gone off somewhere just a few minutes ago and she with a bag of shopping slung over her shoulders and risking a fall on the seaweed just to meet up with that, that – she turned away from the window and those of us who saw her reckoned she nearly pulled the curtain off its rails in her anger – wuman!

That particular angle and intensity of evening light is short-lived. The shadows lengthen perceptibly across the sand and creep up the quay in an inexorable darkening of the tones of granite and timber and the artist must wait for another day to recapture the quality of the light and the lingering warmth on the stones. It never comes. No two days in the chronology of the world have ever been the same. A few minutes longer, shorter, darker, lighter, with the sun higher or lower, a cloud or a shower, perhaps a chill wind. There is no going back. The moment, like all moments, is fleeting, ephemeral, and the artist has only the pigment of the applied strokes and the promise of others with which to portray the unique moment in the harbour when Sarah's daughter, Katie, approaches Shimshai's woman across the wet sand.

'The light's gone,' the artist said, brushing a stray wisp of her greying hair from her brow. 'I was painting the light, rather than the scene.' She laughed at Katie, who stood, as she so often did by now, looking at the canvas glistening with wet paint. 'It's like trying to paint the twinkle without the stars.' She rubbed a brush into turps, and dried it on a rag. 'Impossible.'

'I envy you,' Katie said. 'Having the ability to express yourself.'

'Oh! If only,' she quipped as she stood up. 'I doubt if any of us can do that. Not entirely.' She took her eyes from her work and looked at Katie and her expression changed. 'Good Lord,' she said. 'You look exhausted. Are you all right. Have they been working you too hard in anticipation of all the expected hoo-ha. Come on. Let me buy you a drink.'

They went up the slip and into the pub. So early in the evening there were not many in. There was even space behind one of the benches for the canvas and paints and Katie's bag. Among those of us who were in were Ceecil and Boy Steve. The two were engrossed in deep conversation, with their heads close together, and it appeared, to the amazement of those who knew him, that Ceecil was doing the talking, emphasising a point here and there with an emphatic middle finger tapping the table. Boy Steve was so intently listening with his eyes on Ceecil's face that he didn't notice the entry of his girlfriend and Shimshai's woman. While the women were waiting at the bar for their drinks, Ceecil's narrative evidently came to an end and the two men leaned back against the wall, with Ceecil nodding affirmation of that which had transpired. Boy Steve suppressed a smile and looked around the bar, noticing Katie and her companion for the first time. He grinned and motioned them over.

Katie eased herself along the bench while Shimshai's woman looked at Boy Steve, thinking how incredibly like his father he looked, with the same dark hair and brows, the same build and, against her will, the old emotion flooded through her, the emotion that until now she believed she had overcome. The intense fire of love she had endured for the father was all rekindled by seeing the son so close, and she wondered if he knew anything of her involvement with Old Steve. She felt the hot blush of embarrassment flush her cheeks. None of them noticed. Both Boy Steve and Ceecil were gazing intently at Katie, who greeted them with a smile. 'I thought you might be aboard,' she said. 'I went down expecting to see you working on that hurdy-gurdy thing.'

It was another of those occasions, so common in this community, when nobody introduced anybody. All assumed that each was known to the others. And indeed these were all very well known to each other, even though Boy Steve had never spoken to Shimshai's woman or she to him or Ceecil. Ceecil was just Ceecil and hardly ever said a word to anybody, especially damn strangers and bleddy tourists, so didn't come into the equation of introductions. He greeted both Katie and the other woman with an equally brief nod.

'All done,' Steve said. 'It didn't take as long as I expected. Just needed freeing up.'

And Shimshai's woman smiled with relief. Upon hearing him speak, the similarity was gone. This voice was so different. That soft, deep, almost reticent, yet bemused tone, as if the whole universal situation was a subject of disbelief and amusement, was not here in this younger, confident, almost accentless voice. The confrontation with the old Steve still had to be faced. She could see why Katie had been so long the lover of this Steve. He had the handsome looks, the self-assurance that women loved, evidently intelligent but, ah but, there was no twinkle in the eye. No indication of mischief and folly. It seemed that he had outgrown his boyhood, something which his father, old as he was, would never do. She thought that Ceecil, on the other hand, might be a bit – now what are we allowed to say here? Dopey? Simple? Intellectually challenged? You decide, call it what you mind to – and, not for the first time, wished that she could have been part of a community where everybody regarded everybody as equals, rich and poor, bright and dim. They had differences, no doubt of that, yet the community was all inclusive. She wondered if it would be the same with the young ones here, if new generations would be willing to reveal as much of themselves as we did in order to be part of a whole. She thought not, for the world was changing and everyone would grow to be like her: a stranger everywhere.

You would have to know Ceecil for more than a few minutes to make judgements on his intellect. We can assure you of that.

'Have you decided,' Katie asked Steve 'whether to let the council use your boat when the Navy comes?'

'I s'pose I sh'll have to, as I'm still on the council. Nobody else will do it. They all expect to be making money taking trippers out. Same for the eclipse, if they're allowed to, that is. There's some talk about stopping all boats going out during the darkness. No point in fishing for a couple of days. They say the roads will be too jammed up to get the catch up to the markets.'

'The whole event is supposed to bring millions of pounds into the area,' Shimshai's woman said, 'but it seems that it might prevent all business for days. Shimshai has decided to go up to London for a week. Despite trying to record the events leading up to it, he says he just can't face all those millions of people. He wants us to let our house. Apparently we could get whatever sum we chose to ask. It's going to be horrendous, but I've never seen a full eclipse. I think I'll stay, just to see it.'

'Me too,' Ceecil said. 'I'm stayin' here.' A great decision for him, who had once gone to Plymouth.

'A lot of people are not letting anything just yet,' Katie said. 'Expecting the prices to rise nearer the day.'

More people were coming into the pub. They had to squeeze up along the benches. Ceecil downed the dregs of his half pint. 'I'm off,' he said.

'Me too,' Boy Steve said. 'Got work to do.' Katie looked at him with a query in her eyes. 'Paperwork,' he said. 'Everything comes down to paperwork these days.'

'How's your dad?' Katie said. 'I've not seen him for a while.'

'OK. I think. He doesn't say much.' He nodded to Shimshai's woman and left with Ceecil.

So the two women who had loved father and son were left alone. They decided to gather up their belongings and go too. 'I expect Shimshai has gone down for his evening walk,' his woman said. 'Then he might drop in at the plat for a while. Let's walk up to our place for a chat.'

Ceecil found a few of us at the railings looking at the flooding tide. Boy Steve joined us briefly on the way home. Then Shimshai turned up, and Old Steve, out for some company. Then, in town for a meeting with an old resident who had been persuaded to record his memories, none other but Barny the Bard Baragwaneth, in from the wilds.

'Lost your way, have 'ee?' somebody said. 'The bus stop is up there, look. Number seventeen just coming in.'

'My bus is number ten,' Barny said. 'I'm looking for Old Ben. Want 'n to record his memories.'

'Record his memories? Old Ben? Well, that weant take long. He abm ben nowhere nor done nawthen.'

'He's lived nearly ninety years. More than most. He must have seen things. Several wars. The coming of cars. Poverty. Hard times.'

'Hard times,' Ceecil said. 'We all seen they.'

Boy Steve then burst into laughter and turned to the railing for support. It was a long time since we'd seen him so helpless with laughter, instead of merely cynically smiling

'Nobody had so many hard times as you Ceecil,' Boy Steve eventually managed to say. He said no more on that occasion but, secrets being what they are, we all heard the yarn later.

Ceecil was a queer little fella. He was never very handsome and not much to look at, being squint-eyed and a bit short, in cash as well as stature. He was quite short in more ways than those, people said. Mind, some say that about Ezekiel Endean but they're on dangerous ground. The things people know about people are not always what they seem. In fact, how some people do know what they do know about people, we don't know.

'How they do knaw' Ceecil said, 'what they do knaw, I don't knaw.'

His name was Cecil, of course. The old people called him Ceecil, so the young ones do too. He would have been about fifty-eight or nine at the time of the 'clipse so a lot of us remembered him as a young man coming up. He was married and widowed. His misses was... well anybody who married Ceecil must have been, shall we say, a bit of a character. A bit of a *cok mabyar* she was, but, to give her credit, she didn't give a damn for anybody.

'She didn't give a damn for nobody,' Ceecil said, in reverent remembrance. In the pub he had been offering Boy Steve some advice on women. Seems he was one of the first to suspect that things were not all shipshape between him and Katie.

To see him now, listening intently to every conversation like a hungry owl listening for mice, you'd never believe how popular he was with women when he was younger, how he used to attract the girls. He was full of fun, mind, and girls seem to like that in a man. But then a lot of us were full of fun but we never had the conquests he had. He had them by the dozen. That's what it seemed like to us up on the plat, watching him walk by with one after another on his arm. He seemed never to have a problem getting girls. He had them queuing up.

'Had them queuing up,' Ceecil was telling Boy Steve in the pub that time and eventually confided in a few more of us when the plat was not so crowded.

We don't need to be told that, Ceecil. You must be hung like a bleddy donkey, we said.

'Ah,' Ceecil said, 'Not zackly!'

This may have been out of modesty but it was the first time we had heard him volunteer an original item of conversation for years, so all hands listened for more. You're never too old to learn.

He would not elaborate, not with so many of us lot all there listening. It was too personal he said. Private.

It was to Old Steve that he first told the whole yarn, beginning to end, in confidence. Steve was very good at getting people to talk about personal things. Better than Shimshai for his books or Barny for his tapes. It is a knack some people have, don't 'ee know. Ceecil told Old Steve therefore, in the knowledge that it would go no further, or was it the other way round, so that Ceecil could have a laugh at our expense, knowing that Steve couldn't resist but to quietly spread the word. You never knew with Ceecil.

His secret of success with the girls was very simple, really. 'They thought,' Ceecil said, leaning on his walking stick, 'that I had three.'

Old Steve looked at 'n like one touched. 'Three? What 'ee mean three? Three what?'

'Three,' Ceecil said, 'of what most men have two of.'

Old Steve said he kept a straight face at first, thinking that Ceecil had lost an oar or that his punt was capsizing a bit. Ceecil was giggling like a maid, Steve said.

'First of all,' Ceecil said, 'I only said it for a laugh, and I only said it once, jes once. It was to Joany Eva, the daft one. She wanted me to take her home after the dance. I didn' want to take she 'ome, for Christ's sake! She used to stink like a alley cat. So, to get out of it I said I wouldn' take her 'ome because I had a problem. I wudn normal. What 'ee mean, she said, not normal?'

Ceecil considered his words, Ceecil being a man of some eloquence, as you might say. 'On the spur of the moment, like they say, I told her I was embarrassed to take a maid home and get up to shenanagins because I had three. Thinking it would put her off. Not likely, you! I couldn't get rid of her. She chased me all over the auction, till I did take her home, past Mester sheds and, well... as I was saying. She must have up and told some of the other maids, no doubt saying she had first-hand knowledge, if you know what I mean. And word got around, Ceecil said. They all wanted to find out if it was true. All I had to do was to keep all hands to the mainmast, know what I mean? None of them were any the wiser and didn't like to say they never found out, I s'pose. Just hinted that they had.'

'And none of them ever told any of the boys?' Steve said.

'Well, I s'pose it was to save me any embarrassment. They didn' want to seem common. They were a nice bunch of maids, you know.'

'They were a damn sight nicer to you than to the rest of us,' Old Steve grumbled. You would think to hear Old Steve grumbling sometimes, that he never had none at all.

Ceecil reckoned he had said enough after that, and kept the remaining secrets of his life to himself, telling Barny to look elsewhere, there was not a chance of him recording his memories on they, what 'ee call it, tapes.

Sarah Sevens was about sixty-six at this time. If you saw them together from astern, wearing hats, you'd never tell her from her daughter. They had the same figure, and Katie had the lovely brown hair that Sarah had in her youth but now Sarah, while still very trim of figure, was getting grey. She had more grey than brown, yet it wasn't noticed, for her bright eyes held your attention to the exclusion of everything else. When she heard that Shimshai was coming home, home for good that is, she was angry with him. She hadn't ever spoken to him in her life, for he'd gone off to college and national service after the war and only came home for brief periods to see to his house or take short holidays in the spring. Few of us dared to cross Sarah, because she had the reputation of being forthright, for always speaking her mind, yet, to those who listened to what she actually said, instead of what she was reputed to have said, it was pretty obvious that this was a misconception. She was rarely heard to pass judgement on or condemn other people's behaviour. What she did have was such a frank look in her eye that there was never any misconception as to what she was thinking if she wished her thoughts to be known. If she had a mind to, she could wither the leaves on the trees with a glance. Despite this ability, Sarah was generally the most affable and easygoing of women, at ease in the company of men, like Katie, and tolerant of even the most erring of women, except one.

We could see her, when she was looking out of her window. As everybody knew, Sarah had only truly loved one man in her life, and he was not the father of her child. That child, Katie, now twenty-nine, was in the room, dropping off some shopping she'd carried up the hill, and Sarah was looking for the opportune moment to raise a difficult subject. She had brought Katie up to be as different from herself as possible, not wanting her to suffer because of the same disadvantages she had endured, but this had also caused difficulties and worries for Sarah. Now was no time, however, for beating around the bush.

'Shimshai's woman,' she said. 'You seem to be getting quite friendly with her.'

'Yes,' Katie agreed, 'she's very nice. She's like you in some ways.'

'Like me?' Sarah cried. Katie had never seen her mother react so violently to a casual remark. 'No fie! She edn like me. I certainly don't want to be like she.' She composed herself. 'I never thought to hear that,' she said. 'Like me! You don't know the half of it Katie.'

Her daughter said nothing. That there was more to come was evident. Sarah was trembling with emotion.

'I'll make some tay,' Sarah said.

Katie unpacked the shopping and put it away while Sarah went to make tea in the kitchen. It was a ruse to gain time, to prepare herself for some unpleasant discussion. Katie saw through this and allowed her mother all the time she needed. The tea was brought in on a tray and poured into cups with, Katie noticed with amusement, saucers. This was serious.

'You know,' Sarah said when the delay was becoming more strenuous than the statement, 'about me and Joe?'

'Yes.'

'And me and Steven Trevorrow?'

'Some of it.'

'Yes. Well, I'll tell 'ee all.'

Another long pause in which tea was sipped to moisten dry lips. 'I loved 'n. When we were young. And he knawed it. But he shunned me in our youth, even after I'd revealed my desire for 'n in our one and only passionate embrace. I kissed he, more than he kissed me. It was a mistake. I didn't know a thing about what I was doing. It frightened 'n off, I think, and he married another. Yes, he married Mary. And I'll say no bad thing about the dead. Mary was a good wumun. They jes wudn suited. I almost considered it an act of divine intervention when my daughter and Steve's son fell in love. No! Don't say nawthen. Le'me go on. I wasn't angry with or about Mary, although I could see from the start that they wudn't ideally suited and troubles would follow. However, they were as happy as many, and had a family and things seemed to be sailing along fairly smoothly when she come along.'

'Who?'

'Who? Why, she! Why, Shimsai's woman. The one you're getting so friendly with.'

Now, Katie thought, we're getting somewhere. 'Go on.'

'She come down here, with all her artist's immorality and seduced him in front of all of us. She was very beautiful, I ceant deny that, and she used her looks to make a damn fool of him and nearly break up the marriage. Blatant! That Shimshai's just as bad. Encouraging them, knowing nawthen would come of it and then stepping in and takin' her for hisself.'

This didn't sound likely behaviour of the Shimshai's woman that Katie knew. 'Are you sure that's the way it was?' she ventured.

'Sure I'm sure! And now Shimshai's brought her back and she'll be after Steve again. You mark my words.'

Katie marked her mother's words with care. After all she's taught me about not denying myself, being true to my passions and beliefs, here she is unable to accept her own. Good God, after all these years. She noticed the agitated way her mother poured more tea, spilling it into the saucers, and wondered if she herself could ever love with such fervour, over such a time, and with no intimacy. Certainly not with Boy Steve.

'I ceant forgive her,' Sarah said. 'But you must decide for yourself how you treat her. Just, be careful.'

'I will, Ma. Thanks for warning me.'

'I'm only thinking of your own good,' Sarah said.

Katie looked at her mother, who avoided her eyes. 'You have a good many years to live Ma. I think of your own good, too.'

Katie wondered why it was so incredibly easy to solve other people's problems when her own were so insurmountable. If she still loved him so much after all these years, and wanted to spend the rest of her days with him, why didn't her mother go and get Old Steve before he went after Shimshai's woman again. He was up for grabs. It was obvious.

TAPE EIGHT

...as the sea causeth his waves to come up... all hands shall be feeble,
and every spirit shall faint, and all the knees shall be weak as water...

According to Katie, what with all the last-minute panics over the impending invasion by hoards of trippers, many of whom were arriving already, the town clerk was buzzing around like a blue-arsed fly, wishing that Councillor Winifred Whistler had never heard of the Royal Navy.

The crush barriers were not up around the temporary stage, from where the event was to be broadcast to the whole world on the great day, there was some problem about keeping the roads clear for emergency vehicles, not enough signs had been erected to direct people to the camp-sites and the squire, by way of DDJ, was coming down on him like a ton of bricks.

Whereas anywhere else people would be fighting to be included in the ceremonies, here, for some perverse reason, he'd had difficulty in mustering even the small number required to be involved in the official reception, and was obliged to fall back on the councillors. It was his responsibility, he told the mayor and DDJ, to see that the town was well represented with presentable people, to create the right impression for both the naval officers and the general public all over the country, who would be watching the ceremonies with great interest. The television crews, who were here to record the events of the eclipse, would also be looking for items to fill the news bulletins all through the week. Our reputation as a tourist resort might well depend on it, he moaned in trepidation but, after much in-fighting, with people finding all sorts of reasons to be excluded, the final list came down to: his worship Mayor Timothy Penberthy; the town clerk; Councillor D.D. Johns; Councillor Reginald Hammond; Councillor Ms

Winifred Whistler (she of the red hat), with her escort, Mr Ezekial Endean; Councillor Theodora Yeoman (who had no escort, and who said she was far too modest to ask a man out) was persuaded that she might consider her fellow councillor, Mr 'Collateral' Fred, as escort, to which she reluctantly consented; the Brooks (as reserves).

The clerk had serious doubts about including Ezekiel, a man he didn't know, but was obliged to do so as Councillor Whistler had declared her wish that he should be her official escort. Surely, he thought to himself, among a whole town full of people there's somebody a bit more presentable than... that... that... than Ezekiel! There was also a problem with getting the dignitaries ashore after they visited the ship for, as Boy Steve had half-heartedly tried to warn them, the tide would be out at that time and there wouldn't be enough water at the quay steps to float the pinnace. They'd have to be brought ashore in a skiff. A skiff, for those of you who don't know, being a twelve-foot rowing boat with thwarts and a seat in the stern; freeboard, when carrying twelve passengers, about six inches. The mayor said he would sort it out and had a word with the harbour master, hoping to pass the buck, but the harbour master said none of the fishermen were willing to do it and the passenger boats were all going to be busy taking trippers around the ship.

'You can just imagine what a bleddy crant it's going to be with them all pissed up,' Boy Steve said.

'You'll have to do it,' Katie said.

'I'm not bleddy doing it. I'm standing by the lifeboat. They should've thought about it before. I did tell them.'

'What do they know about the significance of the time of high water? It certainly didn't occur to me. You should've explained. Besides, the lifeboat is only on standby and they can manage without you for once. As the councillor who seconded Winnie's motion, you'll have to do it.'

'I'll think about it.'

When the day of the official visit finally arrived, Her Majesty's Ship, *Median City*, steamed into view around the headland at the crack of dawn. She was a minesweeper, the best the Navy could do. We were lucky to get that, for Britannia doesn't quite rule the waves in the way she used to, but she could have put on a bit of harbour flash, with a wide sweep of the bay at full steam ahead, and given the early risers among us a sight worth seeing. In fact, she entered the bay at dead slow ahead. Despite the charts and echo sounders and other paraphernalia on the bridge, Captain Mathews took no risk, at this time of falling spring tides, of striking a sand bank or a submerged reef in this unfamiliar bay, to say nothing of the cost of fuel. So slow was she that she barely made headway against the tide, for the master was well aware of ships' officers meeting disaster in the waves of this bay before.

'She's brok' down,' Zeke said.

'I can remember the time,' Barny said, 'when they used to send a battleship here.'

'Battleship?' Old Steve said. 'How old are you for God's sake? I ceant remember no battleship.'

'Destroyer,' Zeke said. 'I c'n remember a destroyer.'

'That thing!' Steve said with a nod in the direction of the ship, 'is nawthen more'n a bleddy punt. That's all they think of us now.'

'We abm got no battleships now,' Zeke said. 'They're like we, obsolete.'

'You speak for yourself.'

Ceecil nodded a definite 'speak for yourself'. Ceecil was certainly not going to render himself obsolete before his time.

'I am speaking for myself,' Zeke insisted, 'and you too. We're all obsolete, all of us, young and old.'

Nobody was going to challenge Zeke on that one. There were more interesting topics to discuss, more interesting predictions to be made.

We all know that sometimes the sea can be flat calm in the morning on a rising tide. The flow comes up the coast, eddies around the coves and fills the bay with hardly a wave on the placid surface. The boats on their moorings in the harbour float off with scarce a ripple wetting the planks above the water-line. So it was it on the day of the official visit of the Royal Navy before the descent of the blackness upon us, when the sun was shining and there was not a cloud in the sky. What you might call a perfect day. Except that some of us remember it as being dull, overcast, with sharp showers and periods of drizzle. There are those among us who will deny that ship ever came here at all at that time and say we're getting events all mixed up. These we make allowances for; the young, who were too young to remember, and the old who have forgotten all about it. It happens all the time. Don't worry about it, we have the photographs. We all do know, however, that with a strong ebb flowing against a rising wind and a bit of a ground swell, conditions in the af'noon can be very different from they in the morning. That's why all hands turned out to watch the proceedings of the official delegation visiting from Her Majesty's Ship, *Median City.*

It was past high tide when the pinnace carrying Captain Mathews and his first officer, Mr Tomlinson, with the coxswain holding his boat-hook at eye-level, came alongside the quay steps, while the crew stayed aboard to prepare the welcome for the local dignitaries. The officers leaped nimbly ashore and skipped up the steps to meet the mayor. Both officers were a little disgruntled at this obligation, for they had joined the Navy to serve their country in battles with foreign powers, and to escape the boredom of civilian life. With no immediate armada to fight and the increasing obligation to attend official receptions, they had accomplished neither. They had learned, however, after many such occasions, how to relieve the boredom. The little wardroom was well prepared for the thirst that free booze can induce among civic dignitaries.

The rest of the council, together with respected elders of the community, met outside the town hall for the formal reception of the ship's officers. There was a small crowd of us onlookers standing in the road opposite the municipal building and we waited patiently for the sailors to arrive on foot. They had been escorted from the quay steps by his worship the mayor in his chain and robes, two mace-bearers in full regalia and the town's brass band. They were led by the town crier, wearing a full rig of ornate garments of indeterminate era topped by a tricorn hat, who stopped the procession every fifty yards to ring his hand bell, ding-ding ding-ding, and cry out to the four corners of the compass. 'Oh yes. Oh yes. Oh yes.' in a voice that carried all the way from the prom to the officials waiting at the town hall the steps.

'He's got that wrong, you know,' Winnie whispered to Zeke. 'It's supposed to be 'Oh yea.' Corrupted from the Spanish *oye*, the imperative of *oir*, to hear.'

Zeke turned to her in delight, his eyes wide in appreciation. Here, at last, was a woman as intelligent and knowledgeable as himself. 'Here, I tell 'ee, Winnie,' he said, 'We d' make a very good pair.'

'This to give notice!' the crier bellowed. 'His worship the mayor hereby...' The rest was lost in traffic noise from the crush of cars waiting to progress along the prom until, with three renewed breaths, the crier implored the Almighty, '...God... save... the Queen!'

Upon arrival at the steps, the sailors were officially welcomed by the dignitaries and, after being led through the oak doors, repaired to the mayoral chambers, where they were shown the town's history of association with the senior service, together with the historic regalia, and ancient documents, and were offered some saffron buns and a small glass of the best sherry the ways and means committee could afford. The duty of passing around this refreshment the bulky Reggie Hammond had graciously offered to perform as his contribution to the ceremonies of the day. With several of the recipients, however, Reggie, being of a sociable disposition, was obliged the join in the imbibing of a toast to himself. Cheers! Theodora, normally a strict teetotaller she reminded Reggie, had one generously poured glass to calm her nerves and then, in order not to appear unpatriotic, another to join in the toast to the Queen. The whole party eventually assembled once more on the steps where Captain Mathews presented the town with a shield bearing the ship's arms and the mayor presented the ship with a scroll of velum celebrating the visit.

The photographs taken on the town hall steps were later considered to be very good likenesses of one and all. There was the mayor in all his portly dignity, guarded by the two loyal macebearers accompanied by the town clerk in his dark suit, bow tie and bowler hat. Theodora, arrayed in a bright, flower-patterned dress and a broad white hat, stood between the two naval officers, smiling happily. Freddie was hatless, as a token to his indifference to the elements when roving the ocean waves, while Reggie Hammond, in his light tan overcoat was topped by a natty little trilby worn at a jaunty angle.

Winnie had bought a new outfit for the occasion. It was a blue and white short coat with a naval-style square collar over her shoulders and a short, white, pleated skirt. Her hat was a small affair modelled on the hat of a sailor, red as always we noticed, but with patriotic trimmings of white and blue as was fitting for the occasion. Ezekiel Endean, in order not to let her down, had scoured every charity shop in the town and eventually procured a pair of dark green corduroy trousers and a tweed jacket of the Norfolk type, with four large pockets and a cloth belt. The pockets, he explained to Winnie, would be ideal for carrying his digital camera, wallet, purse, mobile phone and a copy of *Jane's Fighting Ships*.

It was unfortunate that during the posing for one picture, Councillor Mrs Theodora Yeoman's high heels, to which she had never become accustomed and only wore to compensate for her diminutive stature among so many tall men, caused her to turn her ankle and stumble. The photograph of her nose buried among the brass buttons on a manly chest, with her hat awry and arms grasping Mr Tomlinson firmly about the waist, while never published in the press, became the second most sought after by the citizens of the town for their private collections of local memorabilia.

When Theodora had been disentangled from Mr Tomlinson's brass buttons and medals and dignity had been restored, they lined up behind the town crier and macebearers preparatory to returning to the ship in a further procession through the streets and along the prom. They could have hired taxis or given the sailors a lift in their own cars, but the town clerk advised that public profile on the part of the council was as important as that of the Royal Navy in the proceedings, especially as there were already so many extra people crowding the harbour in anticipation of the impending great event of the eclipse.

Boy Steve had given in to Katie and was standing by in his skiff off the steps, in case the tide left them high and dry and he would be obliged to give them a shove-aboard as well as a shove-ashore. He sat on the thwart with his arms on the crossed oars and waited, in anticipation of disaster.

Under the watchful eyes of the likes of Old Steve, Shimshai, Sarah Stevens, Ceecil, and a crowd of bleddy tourists, one of whom was a blonde party in a short skirt who looked at Boy Steve in open admiration, the delegation descended the quay steps that were wet behind the falling tide. With Zeke sneaking the odd photo when he had the opportunity, the official party boarded the little pinnace at the quay steps with the men showing off their sea legs by disdaining assistance from the sailors, and the women accepting all the help they could from such handsome matelots, especially Theodora Yeoman who was passed from hand to hand as she smiled absently under the influence of her two whole glasses of sherry. Reggie Hammond, whose duties with the sherry, together with a couple of scotches he'd had prior to the gathering, were having an effect, was a little more circumspect in boarding than most, looking forward as he was to the reception on board. A slight lurch as his bulk rocked the launch brought a 'Whoops! My soul!' from Councillor Winifred Whistler as she grabbed her red hat to prevent it falling overboard. She was in very high spirits to think that all this came about as a result of her own far-sightedness. There was a last-minute hitch when the clerk was summoned by an urgent hand-delivered message and he had to disembark and return to the municipal hall. He watched with some misgivings as the pinnace embarked from the quay steps with the coxswain again doing his stuff with a boat-hook held horizontally at eye-level and standing four square against the slight ground swell. The clerk was thankful that his ruse had worked and he wouldn't have to go out there, hoping that the threat of the sack would force his minion messenger to keep his mouth shut about the non-existent content of the said urgent message.

Boy Steve shipped the oars, with a glance up at the watchers on the quay. That blonde party in the short skirt put one foot on the lower bar of the railings. He wondered if that was an unconscious movement or deliberately done for his benefit. There was no one else who could see up her legs.

Upon arriving at the ship, the party climbed up the ship's gangway, with the bosun blowing the hornpipe, and was welcomed aboard by Captain Mathews, who assured the mayor that he had ancient connections with the town, as his great-grandfather was from here and had run away to sea at sixteen and eventually settled in Rochester. There followed some discussion as to which family of

Mathews now living here the seaman was related. If they had but known, arrangements could have been made to reunite the distant cousins while they were ashore.

In the little wardroom there was a plentiful supply of delicacies to assuage their appetite, for the ship's cook had been busy preparing various patties, sherry trifle, rum truffles, brandy snaps and an even more plentiful supply of alcoholic drinks to assuage their thirst. The ship's silver, such as it was, was on display and included some cups won by the crew at naval regattas throughout the world, and a finely worked silver cigarette case that the steward kept replenished. Mr Tomlinson ensured that glasses were never empty as they were led around while Captain Mathews informed them of the features of his ship. She was not a minesweeper, he said, but a mine counter measure vessel, or MCMV. He told them of her displacement, length, beam draught and top speed, as they perambulated around the decks and through bulkheads. She was, he informed them as they inspected the crew's quarters, fitted with two Rusten-Paxman deltic 9–58k, developing 19000 horsepower. Plus one Deltic 9-59 diesel for pg and ad. She had two shafts plus bow thrusters, upon which intelligence Theodora burped alarmingly. Her armaments, the captain continued, were one DS 30b 30 millimetre and 2 BMARC 20 millimetre. To all of which the delegation listened intently while Mr Tomlinson and a couple of ratings refilled glass after glass. There was also, Captain Mathews confirmed to his attentive audience after questions from Zeke, which funny little man, he observed, was the only one who seemed to have a bloody clue what he was being told, two Pap one-o-four Mk5 RCSs, RMCDS, Mk1 Tag, Mk 8 Oropesa sweeps, SCARAB RCFM towing devices. The compliment was 45.

'And compliments to you, Captain,' said Theodora, raising her glass, evidently forgetting that she was a lifelong abstainer. To which they all responded, 'To the captain.'

Back in the wardroom, Reggie thanked the captain and proposed 'Compliments to the ship and all who sail in her,' and downed another scotch.

Councillor Freddie expressed his appreciation that such a ship was used in the protection of our vulnerable fishing industry. To which Mr Tomlinson proposed a toast to the fishermen of England, which was accepted with good grace by Zeke, who would normally object to being called English.

Mr Mayor assured Mr Tomlinson, between mouthfuls of pastries, that our little port had every facility should the admiralty ever wish to base any of Her Majesty's ships here. Mr Tomlinson promised to remember that. 'A toast to the ladies,' he said.

'And the gentlemen,' Winnie giggled when her glass was empty.

Reggie Hammond suddenly became aware of the motion of the ship from a rising swell, and held on to the wardroom table to steady himself, taking yet another cigarette from the case when he felt more stable.

DDJ, whose eyes had become somewhat glazed under their drooping lids, was reassured to learn that taxpayers' money was being so well spent and expressed the council's gratitude to those responsible for such efficiency, but remembered he had not proposed a toast. Unwilling to be outshone in protocol by the likes of Reggie Hammond he whispered to the mayor, 'We must'n fergit the officers,' with somewhat less that his usual pomposity. He gathered his wits and hung on to the wardroom table with his left hand and raised his glass in his right, swaying slightly to the motion of the ship. Between hiccups he proposed, 'To th'hociffers of Her Majesty'sh shipsh.'

The Brooks, who were already feeling decidedly unwell, were trying to think of an appropriate toast but after conferring between themselves could only come up with 'And here's to the next time!' but everybody responded wholeheartedly and downed another.

The steward brought round more trays of patties and Zeke, after yet another flash photo, and being a man of the people, thought it about time somebody remembered the crew, so that was another glass all round, by which time everybody was agreeing what a thoroughly good day it had been and, before they went ashore, Captain Mathews proposed a toast to Councillor Winifred Whistler for her foresight and imagination in making such a brilliant day possible. Winnie responded with a dismissive wave that continued in an arc to grab the bulkhead as the ship rolled in response to the rising swell.

A couple of ratings guided the party to the gangway, where Boy Steve was waiting in his skiff to take them ashore. The ship was rolling a bit, with the bottom steps of the gangway awash and Boy Steve was holding on to keep the skiff steady as the party came down the steps and scrambled aboard. First was DDJ who sat quietly in the stern, followed by Theodora, then Freddie, who sat close to her. He was followed by the Brooks, holding on to each other in terror, with Zeke and Winnie finally sitting opposite each other in the bow. Tim shook hands with the captain and after putting his mayoral chain in his coat pocket, scrambled aboard and managed to fall on top of Freddie, who was hanging on to the gunnels for dear life.

Boy Steve was anxious to shove off, for the rise and fall of the swell, while nothing normally to worry about, was increasing all the time and liable to jam the skiff's gunnels under the gangway steps and ship a few gallons of water aboard. He shipped the oars in the rowlocks and was about to shove off, when they realised that Reggie was missing and looked up to see couple of sailors propping him up at the top of the steps.

'A life on the ocean wave,' Reggie was singing, 'dee dada dedaah de da.'

'Oh, shite!' Steve said.

The fresh ocean breeze had hit Reggie like a bag of spuds. He could barely stand on his feet, but was blissfully happy and unaware that he might go hurtling down the gangway and into the drink, or into the skiff and capsize them all, at any moment. The two strong sailors hung on to his arms and kept him upright, but there was not enough width on the gangway for them both to guide him down and he was too big and heavy for one man to cope with.

Steve told us later that the crew were, to his way of thinking, just a bit too ready for this contingency and one had already prepared a rope with a skilfully tied man-sized double bowline on the end. There was, Steve noticed, a pulley block and swivel bound on to the davit over the gangway and the far end of the rope was passed though it to where a further half dozen ratings were standing by in preparation for immediate action. Captain Mathews and Mr Tomlinson were standing po-faced at the rail watching the proceedings with not a word or a glance between them.

'Now just sit still,' Steve said. 'Don't none of 'ee move 'less I tell 'ee to.' He brought his oars aboard and prepared to receive and stow cargo in the form of Reggie, who was being fitted into the double bowline with one loop under his armpits and the other tight under his knees. Following a nod from Captain Mathews one rating kicked Reggie's legs from under him and he fell into the cradle and those on the end of the rope all heaved together and Reggie was airborne. They swung him out on the davit and began lowering him slowly down into the skiff as he changed his tune from 'Life on the ocean wave' to 'The daring young man on the flying trapeze, he flies through the air with the greatest of ease.'

Theodora looked up and, seeing Reggie hanging over her head and about to come crashing down on top of her, moved closer to Freddie, who put his arm protectively around her. She looked up into his half-closed eyes and belched alarmingly in surprise and began a series of hiccups that would last until they were all safely shore.

Reggie was lowered down to the bottom boards and sat there with his hat down over his eyes and fell into a peaceful sleep.

Steve shipped the oars in the rowlocks and began rowing slowly to the harbour. After every ten strokes or so the boat was rocked by the broadside swell and a drop of water splashed aboard, wetting the seats. Ezekiel, sitting up in the bow opposite Winnie, produced his camera from one of his voluminous pockets and took a last photo of the ship and the officers at the rails, and then one of Steve's back and the passengers clustered around Reggie's inert form in the stern.

Now, a skiff like Steve's is built to carry weight in shallow water, built with very little draught. Do 'ee follow our meanin'? Another thing you have to understand is that when there's a little ground-swell running, like there was on that day, they little waves d' build up as they roll into shallow water. That which is, say, no more than nine inches out in the bay can be twice that by the time it breaks on the sand. Ask any surfer. And you remember that a skiff like Steve's has a freeboard of say six inches when loaded. Waves three times as high? OK? Well, as Boy Steve rowed slowly in towards the quay steps, they little waves, so small that he would never have noticed them had he been aboard on his own or with a crew of fishermen, began slapping against the starboard side and splashing the passengers a bit. You also understand that they little waves building up can smack against the side of a skiff and send her rocking from side to side. First they lift the weather side and, as that settles, the other side comes up with a heave-ho here and drops back to even keel before the next little wave comes rolling in. It happens all the time when the boatmen are ferrying passengers back and forth from the launches. Absolutely nothing to worry about.

As they approached the quay head, Winnie's new pleated skirt was getting a bit wet from the splashes on the seats, as was the backside of Zeke's new pants, so Zeke suggested that they both sit up on the gunnels. OK, she said, and sat up on the starboard gunnel of the bow while Zeke eased himself up on the port. They were just about to come alongside, now, with we crowd all up there watching, when Zeke decides to take Winnie's photo, just as one of they little waves skat her broadside, and as the camera clicked Winnie fell backwards with her legs in the air and her skirt up around her waist and tipped overboard into the sea. Zeke was so astonished at what he had seen in the viewfinder as the camera clicked that, as a cry arose from the onlookers, he threw both hands in the air crying 'YES!' But, as the wave passed under the skiff and sent her rocking the other way, he too lost his foothold, dropped the camera in the skiff and fell back overboard on the other side, with his legs still hooked over the gunnel.

There they were, with one overboard on each side. The water was, as we said, only about a foot deep, so Zeke untangled himself with a bit of help from Steve, who turned on his thwart and flipped Zeke's legs overboard to stop him drowning upside down. Zeke then rescued Winnie and her red hat, retrieved his camera and they waded ashore, hand in hand, to the shouts and cheers of all hands on the quays. Steve brought the skiff alongside the steps and helped all the others ashore. They managed to hang on to the handrail, carefully ascend the steps without further mishap, and make their way home. All except Reggie, who was still asleep on the bottom boards, so Boy Steve, having no rope for a double bowline, pulley block or gangs of matelots to man the rope's end, beached the skiff, anchored her from the bow and left his oblivious passenger there to sober up and wade, swim or row ashore when he was able.

The show was all over when Katie left the gallery and strolled along the front for some exercise en route to Shimshai's house.

TAPE NINE

The morning is come unto thee... All the bright lights of heaven will I make dark over thee, and set darkness over thy land...

Katie saw Boy Steve next morning, evidently just ashore after mooring his skiff, with salt water still wet on his jeans.

'How did Reggie get home?' she asked.

'I've no idea! I got a kid minding a punt to bring him ashore. I'm not his nursemaid. What a bleddy crant the whole thing was.'

'So, was Zeke right, or not?' Katie laughed

'What 'ee mean?' Boy Steve said. 'Right about what? What're you talking about?'

It seems that Steve, with his back to the main event of the day, was the only one present not to witness and join in the controversy over Ezekiel Endean's long-held conviction regarding the wearing of red hats. Both Zeke and Winnie, being unwillingly baptised by the elements at the time, were also unaware that the controversy about what had been revealed was universal. Suffice it to say that after a day or two, what with the passing of the phenomenon preoccupying everyone's mind, the incident, together with any reference to red hats, while not exactly forgotten, was rarely mentioned in polite society.

Boy Steve uttered a cynical laugh. 'The whole business was nothing but a farce,' he said. 'Nawthen but a bleddy crant! Are you on the way to the town hall?'

'No,' Katie said. 'Why?'

'Tim has called an emergency meeting. Phoning people to get there as soon as poss.'

'Oh! Don't know what it's all about, do you?'

'No. But I don't know why the Navy's still here, either. They were supposed to sail an hour ago.'

The mayor and town clerk were waiting in the former dignitary's parlour, and, as the councillors filed in, they were astonished to see that Captain Mathews was also standing in the room with his hat under his arm. All summoned had been aboard the ship on the previous day except for Katie who had assumed, wrongly, that the meeting was open to all the council. All summoned were not present, however. Reggie was not too well, Ms Whistler had a chill, D.D. Johns was at a meeting with the squire. Zeke, while being a member of the party, was an invited guest and not entitled to attend closed council meetings.

No one attempted to eject Katie and no one was invited to take a seat and it was the clerk who addressed the gathering. His normally taut features were yet more taut and drawn as he spoke. Ever the avoider of responsibility, he passed the buck to the captain. 'Mister Mathews,' he said, and Steve raised his eyebrows at Katie, implying 'Mister for God's sake'. 'Mister Mathews wishes to address the members on a matter of some gravity.'

'Good morning,' Captain Mathews said, omitting the formalities of 'Mr Mayor', etc. 'I trust you enjoyed a successful visit to my ship.'

There were murmurs of assurance.

'Yes. Well. I am not a man to avoid the unpleasant when it must be faced, and I am obliged to face it, together with yourselves, at this moment.'

Tim hung his head to avoid confronting anyone, while the clerk, with twisted lip, found some absorbing pattern among the thin cracks of the ceiling that would have to be seen to when the place was redecorated.

'Upon your disembarking from my ship,' the captain said, 'it was reported to me that a valuable item was missing from the wardroom. I am sorry to say that the implications are obvious.'

There were gasps of protest, especially from Theodora. 'What are you saying, Captain? I mean suggesting. I mean implying. That something was stolen?'

The captain was in no mood for euphemisms but with ladies present he restrained his nautical language. 'I said 'missing'.'

'Perhaps, 'Theodora said, 'you mean lost. I mean mislaid.' The clerk looked at her with a narrowed eye. There was, he thought, always more to these people than he gave them credit for. This woman, in her inarticulate way, was giving the sailor opportunity to retract accusations and could be a formidable opponent under certain self-righteous circumstances.

'Everything seemed bolted down,' Freddie said. 'Wasn't much that could be stolen.'

'The cigarette case,' Captain Mathews informed them, 'that was on the wardroom table, is a very valuable item of ship's silver that we would not like to lose.'

'Is that what's gone adrift?' Boy Steve asked.

'Yes.'

Steve too was not one for avoiding the unpleasant when it had to be faced. 'You've checked the ship?'

'Of course.'

Katie scowled at Steve. She was sure that Captain Mathews, she said, would not have made enquiries ashore without first being sure of his crew. She remembered those who went, and considered how the theft could have taken place. The women could have hidden it in handbags. No. Impossible that Winnie or Theodora could have done it. Freddie wouldn't have the guts. DDJ? No. Not your petty thief. What about Ezekiel? God, those voluminous pockets in his Norfolk jacket. No, surely not. Zeke was no thief. Or Reggie Hammond with his overcoat? Oh shit, she thought. Reggie! The bloody idiot.

The mayor assured Captain Mathews that if any member of the visiting party was guilty of theft the culprit would be apprehended with alacrity and all possible measures would be taken to ensure that the property of Her Majesty's Royal Navy would be returned to the ship. The officer left the meeting to board ship after promising to delay legal proceedings for twenty-four hours, when the ship would be obliged to leave the town under a cloud of animosity.

'What a mess,' Mayor Tim said. 'What a scandal. The whole town will be aware of this. We're all under suspicion. We must find the culprit and return the damned cigarette case as soon as possible.'

'Such a small item will not be easy to find,' the clerk reminded them, with barely constrained glee at the thought of one of these country bumpkins spending a few weeks in the nick. 'I intend to notify the police forthwith.' He noted the alarm on their faces with well-concealed delight. 'For the sake of the council's good name,' he added, to assure them that there was nothing personal in his intention to involve the law.

Tim suspected the town clerk was really enjoying their predicament and expecting to take charge, as he alone among them had not been among the official party, and was therefore beyond suspicion. There was no way Tim would let the smug bastard take over. 'Hang on!' Tim said. 'We don't want any of this getting out until we've dealt with it. Somebody has got the bloody thing. Leave it to me. I'll summon everybody into my presence and grill them all. What a bloody mess.'

'I suppose,' Katie said, 'that if the thing was returned, that would be an end to it.'

'Well, yes.' Tim said. 'That's what he said. If it was returned in twenty-four hours.'

'Then, don't worry,' she said. 'Well get it back to the ship by tonight.'

'Tonight?' Theodora said 'How?' She was appalled at the scandal that might besmirch all their good names.

'I think we'll hear no more about it,' Katie said. 'Come on, Steve. Let's get it over with.'

Boy Steve was taken aback. He had been looking forward to the scandal sweeping the town like a tidal wave. It would keep the pub and plat in mirth for weeks.

'Come on,' Katie insisted, 'let's go and get the damn thing,' and left the room with Steve following behind.

'What do you mean?' he said. 'Go and get it? Where are we going?'

'To see Reggie Hammond,' she said.

'Reggie?' Boy Steve shook his head and laughed. 'I expect Reggie is very poorly.'

Reggie was very poorly. With the tide rising, we had seen him sleeping like a log in Boy Steve's gently rocking skiff for hours. He slept until he had a shove-ashore by a boy minding Silent John's skiff. Not being a particularly agile man Reggie managed to get two wet sockers from the surging swell and squelched his way home to collapse, fully clothed, in his chair in front of the telly. His hat fell low over his brow and he observed with incredulity the salt water from his wet trouser legs and socks oozing through the lace-holes of his brown brogues.

He hadn't moved, and was still contemplating the accumulating pool of water on his carpet, when the two entered his cottage without so much as a knock. Reggie roused himself with an effort. 'I say,' he said, 'what's…?'

'Stand up, Reggie,' Katie ordered him, and Steve helped the dozy Reggie to his feet.

'Pockets!' Katie said. 'Empty them!'

The overcoat pocket holding the cigarette case was, as the result of Reggie's prevarication, the last one he reached into. After the penultimate grope, he brought out an empty hand with a co-operative smile and shrug. 'What am I supposed to be looking for?'

'Oh Reggie!' Katie remonstrated and reached into the final pocket of his overcoat where she found the missing item.

They pumped him full of coffee, changed his socks and shoes and, well after dark, marched him down to the quay where he was put aboard the *Morvoren*, unseen by all but a few, and taken out alongside the *Median City*. The gangway was lowered and Steve guided Reggie aboard.

'I don't know why I did,' Reggie shamefacedly told Captain Mathews. 'I only wanted the fags. As if I can't afford a few fags. I really don't why I did it, old chap. Not like me. I'm terribly sorry.'

Captain Mathews could see that he was telling the truth and was feeling just a little apprehensive about the consequences if he were found guilty of plying his guests with overdone hospitality. 'I think we might put it down to high spirits,' he said magnanimously and ambiguously, 'and forget the incident.'

When the deputation had gone ashore Captain Mathews poured his first officer another black coffee. 'Phew!' he gasped as they heard the rattle of the anchor being weighed. 'That was lucky escape, Number One. It would have raised one hell of a stink for us if he'd fallen overboard drunk and taken the bloody box with him to the bottom of the bay.'

Zeke decided that his many-pocketed jacket had been a very judicious purchase, what he called an A1 garment and, after drying it before the fire, resolved to wear it on days when his voluminous overcoat was too warm. Life had never held such promise, he vowed. There was nothing like a blossoming love affair and a few good deals in the offing to make a man feel self-assured. We saw him passing Henny Penny's shop with a confident stride. To his amazement, the new-found confidence was evidently apparent to all, for Henny actually opened the door to greet him.

'Good morning, Ezekiel,' Henny said, with a new degree of respect apparent in his voice.

'Hulloh,' Zeke said. He was a busy man, and was not intending to waste time talking to the likes of Henny Penny today. He had an assignment.

'Those frames,' Henny said.

Zeke stopped in his tracks. 'Yeah? What about them? Wha's wrong with them?' he demanded.

'Well,' Henny said. 'It seems I was mistaken and you were right. My London dealer took them all.'

'What I tell 'ee? I knawed they was valuable.'

'Yes. Well it seems he wants more. Not the pictures. They were worthless. There's no more rubbish from Maggie's attic is there?'

'No, nawthen,' Zeke made to shove off. 'Oh, hang on,' he suddenly remembered, 'There is a frame, with a old picture in 'n. Old boats all skew-whiff and the houses all capsizin'. Is on a bit of wormy plywood. I ben using 'en to block the draught down the chimbly. You wouldn' want that.'

'Well, no. Obviously not. Ha ha.' Henny cleared his throat. 'Boats did you say?'

'Es. They old sailing boats. Schooners, what they d' call.'

'Ah well. You might bring it along some time if you want it off your hands. Seems some old frames are worth fifty pounds in London if they're of, of, you know, a certain period.'

'If they're worth fifty quid up London,' Zeke said, 'they're worth fifty quid here. Maybe a bit more.'

'Well. Maybe. Anyway, I'll have a look at it for you. Bring it in. When you're passing. No hurry.'

'All right,' Zeke said. 'When I'm passing. If I remember.'

Sarah was highly amused to hear Katie's account of Reggie's mis-demeanour. Although she could never condone the excessive consumption of alcohol, she sipped the occasional glass of wine when dining with Katie, and had taken advantage of the abundant sloes growing in the countryside round about. Katie's statement that Sarah 'had a good many years to live' had meant more to her than her daughter realised, and had induced thoughts about her future. She had neither ache nor pain, she mused. Could walk up and down that hill without getting out of breath. She had neither varicose veins nor ingrowing toenails. Her hair was getting grey, true, and she had a few lines, but she had all her own teeth and, to her surprise, although this was something she kept to herself, occasionally felt randy.

'I have a good mind,' she said to herself, 'to go for 'n! Everybody else do, so why shouldn't I?' What a crant, she thought, if me and Steve and Katie and Boy Steve was to get married. Oh, dear, dear. What a crant.

'What are you laughing at?' Katie asked her.

'Oh, just a thought.' But then, she also knew that if Steve was interested in anybody it would be Shimshai's woman, the fool.

'A thought? OK...' Some of the thoughts that went through her mother's mind were best left unexpressed Katie knew, without hav-ing any idea what those thoughts might be. Her mother was as close with some particulars as she was open with others. Some thoughts were best left to herself. 'What shall we do for the eclipse?' Katie ventured. 'Have 'ee thought about it?'

'No. Not really. There's going to be complete chaos, from what they're saying.'

Sarah had thought nothing about the eclipse. She was thinking more of her daughter's long-term future. Katie never seemed to con-sider the prospect of loneliness, presumably because she had never experienced it, yet there was a certain sadness in her that Sarah had never fathomed out. It was as if there was a dark secret somewhere, and Sarah knew only too well what a burden that could be.

'I've been thinking about you,' Sarah ventured. 'About you and Boy Steve. He's a very nice man. You shouldn't be having him on. Having him on with doubts, I mean. You know what I mean.'

Here we go again, Katie thought. Her mother had far too much concern about her, and never thought about herself. What can she see that causes her so much distress? Was it Katie's own father and his tragic death that made Sarah overly concerned about the future? Who could tell? Here was further indication that Sarah, while always advocating openness and honesty, was herself very reluctant to disclose certain aspects of her own life. Especially what went on in that intelligent mind of hers.

'Don't worry about Steve,' Katie said. 'It's pretty well over between us. We haven't fallen out. We just know that we're unsuited.'

'Unsuited?' Sarah said. 'Unsuited. And you've ben together all these years. Tha's fine and queer, if you ask me.'

'It's not a question of asking,' Katie said. 'More of telling. Well, not telling.'

'Not telling what?'

It's gone on too long, Katie decided. There and then, on the spur of the moment she decided that, despite promises made to Barny and Boy Steve, her mother should be told. There would be as much pain in the telling as in the hearing. Where should she begin?

'My father,' she said.

'Joe. Yes? What about him?'

'Did you love him?'

'Yes.'

'Yes? How can you say yes?' Katie said with irritation. 'You only knew him for one night.'

'That was enough. I've told you before. I loved him. Loved him a damn sight more than many wives d' love their husbands. I can tell 'ee that.'

Katie could not dispute that.

'I knew him all my life. He was a good man. I've told you all about him. You can ask anybody in the town about him. He was a good man. He died trying to save another, as you know full well.'

'I wish I'd known him before then.'

'You did know him. He was always very good to 'ee.'

'I didn't know he was my father. I had no proper relationship with him.'

Perhaps, Sarah wondered, that there lay the problem. Perhaps Katie had difficulties with relationships with men. If so she had never shown it. 'He was a good man,' Sarah insisted. 'He was always very close to 'ee.'

'He was. I regarded him as a friend.'

'Well, that's more than some can say about their parents. Just remember the friendship as more than that. He loved 'ee till he died.'

'I know,' Katie cried, 'I know.' Sarah was utterly disconcerted to see Katie break down in tears. 'I know he loved me.' Katie moaned. 'Oh God. How I know.'

'Oh, my dear cheeld,' Sarah said, suddenly as disconcerted as her maid. 'Why whatever's the matter with 'ee?' She rose and put her arms around her daughter. 'We don't belong to see 'ee like this. What's upsettin' 'ee so. For pity's sake, stop crying. You're breaking my heart.'

Katie dried her eyes on a proffered hanky and composed herself after a few trembling sobs. 'You know,' she said, 'that time in the mine. That time when that man was found dead in Wheal Dowr shaft.'

'Of course I remember. After you were found by the adit, unconscious. Some thought that Boy Steve had something to do with it.'

'Some thought that Boy Steve had killed him, mother. Let's not avoid the truth.'

'Nobody believed that. Not for a minute.'

'The police did. And a few others.'

'Well, you never did,' Sarah asserted.

'I had my doubts. I can't deny it. Steve was very hot-headed at the time, remember.'

That was true enough and Sarah had to agree. We all knew Boy Steve had hated the man who had made lewd remarks at Katie. Threatened to kill him if he didn't lay off her, as most of us had chosen to forget.

'It was because of all that. Because of all that, that Boy Steve and I are still together after so many years. That's why I'm so close to Barny Baragwaneth.'

'I'm sorry,' Sarah said. 'I don't understand what you're trying to tell me.'

'When Joe died, drowned, while trying to save one who he thought was Boy Steve after the lifeboat capsized, he left a tape for Barny. You know he was dyslexic, couldn't read or write.'

'Yes.'

'He recorded a message for Barny, who was to pass it on to Boy Steve and me if circumstances demanded it. It was recorded in case Joe died and Boy Steve was still suspect or convicted. The verdict on he in the shaft, after weeks of suspicion, was eventually of accidental death, so when we'd listened to the tape we destroyed it.'

Sarah went to the window. There was slight drizzle beginning. She looked across the bay and saw nothing of the eastern shore or of the surf or the boats fishing off the head. She saw only kindly old Joe, Uncle Joe, who had been her only lover. One of the roughest, toughest, most uncouth, roguish, kindest, gentlest men she had ever known. Had it not been for that other love, she would have married Joe. If he would have had her, he would have been the perfect father for Katie. But over the years her love of Steve would have been an unacceptable cruelty to Joe, who had never a shred of malice in his whole being. He was best left a bachelor to watch his daughter grow up from a distance.

'What did he have to say?' Sarah asked in a voice so soft as to be barely audible across the quiet room. 'On the tape?'

'He said,' Katie paused but was now committed to tell. 'He said that he knew I was interested in going down the mine to look for bats. He was worried in case I had some accident down there alone and decided to follow me. To keep an eye on me. That man, the surveyor, was already down there. I think Joe knew. I didn't know. When he saw me down there alone he attacked me. Tried to... to rape me. I know I knocked my head and fell down and he came on top of me. The next thing I remember is being outside the adit. Found by Ezekiel, as you know.'

'I didn't know Joe was down there.'

'Neither did anyone else. He came into the adit and saw what was happening. He dragged the guy off, you know I can't bear to utter his name, and he killed him. He was out of his mind with rage and killed him. He hit him with his fists and then an iron bar and threw him down the shaft. It was Joe,' Katie said. 'Joe, my father, who killed him. For me!'

'Oh my poor cheeld,' Sarah said. ' How could you have borne it over the years?'

'Barny played the tape to Steve and me, so that I would not suspect Boy Steve for the rest of my life, and to keep us together. Only we three knew the truth about what happened down in that shaft. Only us. I think that when Joe saw that man in the water and he thought it was Boy Steve, he gave his life willingly trying to rescue him, as recompense for his crime.'

Sarah came from the window and sat in her chair while Katie bit her knuckles in an effort to control her emotions. A long silence prevailed with neither knowing what to say.

'I don't see,' Sarah eventually sighed, 'that Joe committed any crime. Why, even a dove will fight to protect its young.'

'This is between us, Ma,' Katie said. 'I only told you so that you could see the difficulties in my relationship with Boy Steve. It must go no further. For Joe's sake. And for Barny and Boy Steve's sake. You must promise me that.'

Don't worry, my cheeld. I'll put 'n in with all the other secrets I've kept over the years.'

It was raining quite steadily when Katie went down the hill and along to Shimshai's house. He was away. His woman let Katie in with a welcoming smile. Gave her a towel to wipe the rain from her face and eyes. She made coffee in silence and looked at Katie as she passed over a mug, waiting to be informed of the reason for this visit.

'These men of ours,' Katie said after a while. 'Father and son. How can they be so different? What did Old Steve have that made you fall so madly in love with him when you were young?'

'I wasn't that young. And Steve was in his forties.' She angled her head with a slight shake, as if not accepting the thoughts that came into her head. 'He was very handsome.'

'So is his son 'ansome,' Katie said, 'but when you've been with someone for a while, their looks become irrelevant, you don't notice what they look like. It takes more than that to rouse the intense passion you seem to have shared.'

'Yes.'

Katie almost hoped the woman would say no more. She was evidently aware that Katie was disturbed. There was a very charged atmosphere building in the room. Katie really had no right to ask for such personal revelations. It was her own motives that were actually under discussion.

'It was the sun,' Shimshai's woman said quietly as she looked at the view between the raindrops slithering down the window pane. 'The summer sun and the sea. The sensuous sun and the emotional sea. We would lie – he would never tell you this – naked in the sun and watch the powerful, restrained, surge of waves with their murmurs rising and falling with the swell.'

Katie refrained from commenting on the sensuality of sunshine, while Shimshai's woman seemed to have been transported back in time, like one recalling dreams. 'Steve,' she mused, 'once said *Yma levow yn mordros*. There are voices in the sound of the sea.'

'*Mordros*?' Katie queried. 'He actually said *Yma levow yn mordros*?'

'Yes. He couldn't speak the language, but sometimes he would look things up, or ask someone. That was the only phrase I learned. It seemed to epitomise our relationship. There are voices in the sound of the sea. Have you heard them? Yes, of course you have. They sometimes whisper, he said, telling intimate secrets. At times they shout warnings or cries of exultation. He made me aware of them, and to see that most people are deaf and blind to all about them. He showed me dolphins, seaweeds, birds, colours in mosses, things I'd never noticed, and I the artist. He wasn't talkative. Far from it, he was very reticent about revealing himself, but by just a look, or a wistful smile or a glance at some trifling phenomenon he made me aware of everything about us in a way I'd never experienced before. We could lie together for ages, side by side in the sun, not speaking, and listen to the voices in the music of the summer swells. It was almost as if we communicated our love through those voices in the sea. I had never experienced anything like it.'

'I find it hard to believe we're talking about the same man,' Katie said. 'There's evidently a side to him I've never seen. And he's very different to his son, I'm afraid.'

'Perhaps.'

'Perhaps Boy Steve is more like his mother, who was very conventional and conservative. But my mother said that Shimshai wrote it all down. In his books. Didn't you mind?'

'No. It's what we do. We artists. We prey on each other. The point is that we know it's impossible to expose anyone, or anything, entirely. There's always an element undiscovered, undisclosed, that hides the ultimate reality of things. People are led to believe that art is the revelation of truth. It's very difficult to accept that art is all lies and illusion. A mere exploration.'

'Sometimes I think that all life is but lies and illusion.'

Shimshai's woman laughed. And here was something else that Katie envied in her. That infectious laugh, so open and, like everything else about this woman, so uninhibited.

'I can understand why my mother was so crazy about the old bugger now,' Katie mused. 'She saw more in him than she's ever let on.'

'I didn't know about Sarah then. It would have been even more difficult for me if I had.'

'She hates you.'

Shimshai's woman looked astonished. 'I expected a lot of people would hate me when we came back and the tongues began wagging. But I did your mother no harm. I didn't know her, don't remember her at all. Why does she hate me now?

'She sincerely believes that you will entice Steve Trevorrow again.'

'Ah! Well, in that, she's very much mistaken. He avoids me. And, to be honest, I avoid him. I think we're afraid of each other. That the whole fire might be rekindled.' That laugh again.

Katie thought the denial might have been too quick. 'What does Shimshai make of all this?'

'Shimshai would never have brought me back here if there was the slightest risk of losing me to Steve for the second time. Remember, it was Shimshai who brought me here in the first place. I loved him a bit before, and I love him very much now. Nothing will part us.'

Katie thought about that. Of those who couldn't be prised apart with a crowbar now gone their separate ways. 'I'm sure,' she said, 'that Old Steve would never attempt deliberately to steal you away, but sometimes our emotions run out of control.'

'Yes,' Shimshai's woman whispered with a sigh. 'How well I know that.'

'Did you know Joe?'

'Uncle Joe? Yes, of course. Everybody knew Joe. He was lovely. I was very upset when Shimshai told me he'd drowned. Rough as rats, as they say here. But a truly lovely man.'

'My father,' Katie said.

For the first time Katie saw her new friend suddenly disconcerted. 'Oh, I didn't know that. He was rough... but... I didn't mean to offend. He truly was a lovely man.'

'I know. Don't worry. My mother says the same. But Shimshai never told you?'

'No. Never.'

'He must think it's still a secret. And it is, but everybody knows.'

They sat for a long time in silence.

'I think I'm slowly getting myself sorted out,' Katie said.

TAPE TEN

For the day is near, even the day of the lord is near, a cloudy day, it shall be the time of the heathen...

And now, we come to the crunch. Shimshai went away, leaving his woman all alone here for the first time since he brought her back. 'Shimshai's going away,' somebody said, so all hands turned their eyes to Old Steve Trevorrow who could now have unhindered access to the woman Shimshai had contrived to steal from him all they years ago.

Her daily schedule, like that of so many who lead a casual existence, had become predictable. She was not an early bird, at least not outside her home. She would do a bit of shopping at mid-morning, go back, drink coffee, think, look at her work, add some refinements, and then, after lunch, depending on her mood, either paint outside or go for a walk.

Old Steve, on the other hand, having settled into a regular routine in his solitude, was utterly unpredictable. He came down to the plat every day after reading the newspaper and getting into a tizzy over the state of the world and the way things were deteriorating. You could rely on him being there, regular as clockwork, unless you wanted to see him, when he wouldn't appear for days. He was still a solitary walker, as he had always been, and some days he'd pack up a few bits of crouse and take off for the day, as he did in his youth, some of us remembered. Some of us thought he might like a bit of company on his walks, but no, he liked the solitude, where, presumably, his thoughts were still the thoughts of his youth, unfettered by the conversation of others. Not even with Barny Baragwaneth would he go for a walk out along the cliffs they both knew so well, so here were a few hours of a life in our community of which we knew, and know, nothing. Old Steve was so reticent about where he went, what he did, what he thought about on these solitary excursions that about them we could say we know absolutely nothing, which would be true, but, on reflection, we can't really see much difference between absolutely nothing and just... nothing. Can you?

The last lone walk of Old Steve, the last time he went off along the cliffs by himself, was one that we might have dissuaded him from had we known the consequences. It was a sunny day. (Don't start that again! It was a sunny day, and that's that! If it were raining, he'd never have gone.) Some say that he knew before starting off that she had also gone out there along the cliffs, and that he followed her. That he had a determined expression on his face, there is no denying, but we shall never know if he set off that day in deliberate pursuit of Shimshai's woman.

The coastline meanders west with the cliffs, protruding in a series of headlands of elvan and granite, descending steeply to the boulders and islets washed continually by surging waves. It is a beautiful scene whatever the weather, there's no denying that, but if a man, or a woman, was to fall into that sea on a ground swell their body would be torn to shreds in hours. From prominent points on each headland it's possible to see the path, and who is on it, ahead to the west and behind to the east. The way is tortuous and winds through both bog and boulder, with steep descents and climbs that deter many a would-be venturer after but a mile in their open-toed sandals or high-heeled shoes. It is not a path for a casual stroll. Most people seen after the first headland along the path are long-distance walkers, heads down and striding out to traverse their allotted mileage before the sun sets and they are benighted on this isolated track.

He saw her in the distance. She was walking slowly on the narrow path between bracken and gorse, pausing frequently to appreciate the view or some item at her feet, so he stopped to let her stay well ahead, only resuming his walk when she was out of sight. She never looked back. Neither of them, he became aware, was as fit and agile as in the days when they came this way together, eager for the solitude in the sun by the edge of that seething, sensuous ocean. How their one short summer of those distant days had changed them. His life's emotion, under the shield of cynicism that we all saw, had been one of melancholy, and Old Steve decided he'd enough of it. He and she were as wild animals trapped and caged together in the passions of the past, and the time had come to release each other and open the gates to freedom. She stopped on the path after passing the last cove, where grey seals were sleeping in the sea with their noses pointing skywards. She looked about, saw no one, and made her way through the gorse to the headland. She had not forgotten, Steve thought, she still remembered the way down to that pool of clear still water where their naked bodies had roused each other to such unbridled passion. It was a dangerous descent, even for those in their prime, but it would have to be there. He hitched up his pack and set off after her. This was, Steve mused, a journey on foot along a familiar track, one he had traversed so many times in his mind since those sunny days so long ago. By forging ahead he was about to retrace the steps they had taken together towards passion and remorse. To go back was the only way forward.

The features along the way, those they had passed or paused beside, were still there to remind him of those short journeys which had led them so far into the unknown country of ardour. There was the grey stone, encrusted with yellow lichen, protruding over the track. There was the bog they had waded through looking for sundews between the fronds of royal fern. There, gushing from the spring where they had drunk the cool water, was the stream, glistening over pebbles and gravel. Ahead, at the bottom of the cliff where he would face her at last, was the rock beside the tidal pool where she had painted his portrait. Still there, there for ever in the cool blue elvan rocks, was the ledge where he lay as she painted his portrait, nude and aroused as she laughed aloud with her blue eyes twinkling and her flaxen hair caressing her breasts. And there, always in his inner vision, was her reflection as she gazed into the depths, her naked body, tanned thighs, flaxen hair and blue eyes forever tormenting him from the dark depths of the pool, clear and limpid with its encrustations of coral and sinuous weeds. That one so sophisticated could be so primeval, so shameless and licentious, aroused every emotion his mind and body had ever dreamed of.

And here was his anger. That those moments so natural and uninhibited then should have plagued him for the rest of his days as being the decisive emotional experience of his life, never to be repeated or equalled. She had robbed him of, no, he had given her, the ultimate passion, lust and love, to be unattainable with any other.

The way down to the pool was impassable. The path, always obscure, was completely overgrown, which served to remind Steve how long it had been since his last visit here. He found her sitting among the boulders out on the headland where thick tangles of blackthorn scrub had encroached the cliff. The sun was warm. Heather was in flower. The swell around the rocks below sent subdued murmurs up from the foam. There were bees, busy in the purple bells. Her face was lightly lined, her hair becoming grey, her eyes still that intense blue that had haunted him for so long. She was as beautiful as ever, but she was not his. She was Shimshai's woman. He would have to say her name.

'Hullo, Cleo.'

She didn't reply, not with her voice, but that smile was an invocation of all those distant days. The mischievous narrowing of the sky blue eyes, the white teeth between open lips. It encompassed all the memories that they shared together.

He also smiled and shook his head in disbelief that this could be so easy, there was no hint that she suspected his fury. His smile became an open laugh. 'I followed 'ee,' he said, 'all the way from town.'

'Yes. I know.'

On the eve

Freddie said, 'Henny's shop is deserted. He's gone off. There's a notice on the door.'

Henry Penny had indeed gone off. A few days previously, he just happened to be passing Zeke's door and thought he might as well have a look at that old frame with the picture on a bit of wormy plywood. Zeke agreed to sell it, but it had not been a happy negotiation. Zeke was like every other greedy dealer in the world, Henny mused. Glad to be rid of his junk at any price, but obstinate as hell when it came to parting with something in which Henny had inadvertently shown an interest.

'You don't belong to come down here, 'Zeke accused him. 'You habben ben down'long for years. Wus so wonderful about it now? Ha! You're after that there frame,' he cried.

'Well,' Henny agreed. 'I thought I could look at it, as I was down here anyway.' He had heard of Zeke's romance with Winnie the Pew, and thought he might be in need of some extra cash. 'I thought fifty quid might be useful to you in your present circumstances.'

'Leave my circumstances out of it,' Zeke said. 'And anyway, the price has gone up.'

'What?'

'All they people coming down here will be looking for old things like picture frames and fishing gear and stuff to put in their lounges and new conservatories. And you abm even seen 'n yet. I'm not daft Penny. I know they'll be in demand. Seventy-five quid or nawthen.'

'Let's have a look at it.'

Zeke would not let him in but, through the cottage door into a room that he had never seen before, Henny could see that the picture and frame were in Zeke's grate, as he had said, blocking the draught from the chimney. He could also see a roomful of items that Zeke had accumulated out of interest and curiosity over the years, items that would fetch a small fortune in a London auction. The dopey idiot, Henny thought, why doesn't he let me help him out with a little purchase of something of interest now and then. He decided that it might pay him to pander to Zeke's eccentricities for their mutual benefit. 'OK,' he said. Seventy-five. I'll take a risk, as it's you.'

Zeke went in and brought the frame to the door. 'Shall I scat the ol' picture out?' he asked, raising his boot.

'No!' Henny cried. 'I mean, it might damage the frame. Leave it to me.'

'OK,' Zeke said and the money and frame changed hands.

We saw Henny Penny walking past the plat with the frame under his arm and an irrepressible smile on his chacks that would frighten the devil. Next thing we knew about Henny was he'd gone up London and would be away for the 'clipse, saying that the shower coming down for it were unlikely to appreciate what he had to offer them.

While Henny was away, we saw Zeke load up his cart with bits of old cardboard, plywood and ancient tins of hardening paint he had retrieved from Maggie's attic and glory-hole, together with a catalogue of Alfie's exhibition with descriptions of his style and materials. He trundled off to the council rubbish skip wondering why, if Henny was so clever, he could fall for one of the oldest confidence tricks in the world.

He felt a bit guilty as he pushed his cart through oncoming traffic up the one-way Fore Street in the wrong direction, but mused that if Henny was a 'onest man, if he was a 'onest man like Ezekiel, and the London dealer was a bleddy shyster, if he let the London dealer make an offer for they frames and pictures, not telling Henny what he thought they was, and if Henny kept his mouth shut and said nothing about Alfie or anybody else, Henny would do very well out of the transaction as a innocent man knowing nothing about fakes or copies, like Zeke himself, who sold him only a few old frames. And good luck to 'n. Whichever way it went, he would think twice about what he offered Zeke for a sweet pea vase in future. Their business dealings could flourish on a more respectful relationship to their mutual benefit. As to what happened to the London dealer when they pictures were examined by a expert, well, who could tell. Who were we to evaluate works of art? Down here, a expert was somebody from up there.

On the eve

Squire Chygwyn was not a very happy man. Just a few days to go, he fumed at DDJ, and he had not a single booking for the whole event. What, he wanted to know, had happened to all the people he had spent a small fortune and weeks of work preparing for?

Neither DDJ nor Denzil could explain it. There had been so much publicity about the event, they told him, that some in the tourist department were complaining that there was no money left for anything else. There was a whole year to think about, they were moaning now, not just one day, apparently forgetting who had been urging that this golden opportunity should be exploited for all it was worth. The squire phoned around and discovered that there were others in the same boat. Nobody was booking anything. It seemed that the alarms about blocked roads, masses of disruption to all public services had put people off and they seemed to be staying away. His associates on other camp-sites were cancelling portable loos, mobile offices, water bowsers, discos, marquees and shop-bought home-made pasties by the dozen. What with the dismal weather forecast, the whole thing looked like being a damp squib all round. We heard that they demand-ed an explanation from the town clerk, threatening him with the sack for incompetence. That worthy, whose job it was to be cognisant with the laws that applied to himself and his circumstances, directed their attention to the minutes of the council meetings, where, he assured them, there was no record of his ever mentioning the matters in ques-tion so no blame for any misconceptions or misinformation about the phenomenon could be laid on him. Off the record, he hinted, the forth-coming turn of the millennium could well be an opportunity to utilise the preparations for a celebration of some kind, such as a massive fancy-dress music festival. This intelligence was passed on to the squire, who saw it as insider information and set in motion immediate plans to exploit the new situation for the benefit of all. Then, acting on further insider intelligence from his contacts in official positions, he heard that even Robin Rainey's ten thousand capacity camp-sites, such as his own, were closing down through lack of bookings all over the area. All the facilities had been taken away or the bookings, for mobile toilets, shops, and stalls cancelled. He was a very worried man but, at the last minute, he phoned around and discovered that all these facili-ties that had been brought in were lying idle. He booked a few on the cheap and opened up his site with capacity for five hundred in the hope that, by getting his own employees to man it he would at least get some of his money back. Arthur Pender would grumble at that, but that was unfortunate. If he didn't like it, he knew what he could do. There were plenty of unemployed gardeners out there.

On the eve

Freddie, as the councillor elected by the tourist industry and the one most susceptible to pressure from vested interests, was also in trouble, he moaned to us on the plat, being besieged by letting agencies demanding recompense for the results of misleading information the council had given to the media. The hype, they said, had the opposite of the desired effect. The initial high prices for accommodation had led potential visitors to delay booking and the dire warnings about traffic chaos had persuaded people to keep away. There were empty properties, now, right now, at the height of the season, which was unprecedented. People should have been given incentives to come here not disincentives to keep them away. After all, the thing could be seen a hundred miles nearer home for most of them anyway. Freddie, while wondering if he'd been pushed on by Tim Penberthy's enthusiasm, wished he'd kept his mouth shut through all the council deliberations, at least when the press were in the gallery. People had invested so much collateral with no hope of profitable return, and he was being blamed. The day was going to be a disaster.

On the eve

Boy Steve felt a weight off his shoulders now that he and Katie had finally admitted that there was no future for them together. It was a queer world, he thought as he sat there in the stern waiting for the tide, while Shimshai's woman painted the scene from further up the foreshore. I'm a painting, he thought, I'm *Waiting For The Tide*, nothing more than a seascape in oils by Shimshai's woman. Who the hell was she? There was something going on between her and the old man; that was obvious, if only from the way he avoided her, in public at least. God, he was a secretive old bugger.

Boy Steve had been away at the time and it seemed that none of us had ever told him what went on between them. How could we? We would have to say 'Your old man had it off with Shimshai's woman' or something equally forthright, there would be no point in telling half a yarn. Even Katie, who had just recently been told the tale by Sarah, couldn't face telling him about his father's infidelity.

From the plat we could see him there, musing to himself, like you do when there's nothing to do but wait for the tide, or a bus, or a kettle to boil. Perhaps some of these here hartisses ought to paint that for a change... *Waiting For The Kettle To Boil* by a young master. If it was daft enough somebody would be sure to acclaim it as a work of genius.

Who would know, Boy Steve thought, about his father's relationship with that woman over there painting him? Sarah? No hope of getting anything out of her. Katie? What did she know that he didn't? It was certainly a queer world. Here I am with one of the most attractive women in town and I'm glad to be rid of her. She's glad to be rid of me, no doubt about that, but I don't mind. At least I'm free, but for what?

Why, damn it! he thought, here I am talking to myself about things I should have talked about with Katie. Why couldn't we be honest with each other instead of living these past years under stress? Who knows?

That young party came across the foreshore (the times we've seen this happen) and went right up to him just as the first of the flood reached his moorings. Brazen!

'Young women today,' Collateral Fred said as he looked down into the harbour with incredulous eyes, 'don't give it a thought.'

'Don't give it a thought,' Ceecil said.

She leaned over the gunnel, elbows akimbo, fair-haired, straw hat, tanned arms, short dress rucked up to show her calves and shapely knees. (You, *one*, d' notice these things.)

'Wudn like that with we,' Freddie mused with a degree of remorse in his voice. 'We never had sex like they do today.'

We looked at him with some pity.

'I've heard them say,' Freddie informed us as he wrenched his eyes away from the girl talking so blatantly to Boy Steve, 'that in America, ol' man, young people today... young people today,' carefully choosing his words, 'don't give it a thought.'

'Not a thought,' Ceecil agreed.

'I've heard them say,' Freddie said, in an incredulous voice, 'that in America today, ol' man, in America today, young people today d' have,' (in a whisper), '*intercourse* on average of,' (incredulously), 'two times a week!'

'Tha's twice,' Ceecil said. He's pretty good at mathematics.

The rest of us nodded but made no comment, reckoning that, even though he had lived a life of abstinence, with a wife like his he had no idea what a blessing-in-disguise that was. During Freddie's marriage he would have been lucky to have had it twice a year and even those of us who'd had it as often as young people in America today, wished we'd had a bit more of it. That's old age.

'Waiting for the tide?' she asked.

'Yeah!' Boy Steve agreed. 'That's what we do.'

She laughed as the second surge came around her shoes.

'We wait for the tide to come in and sometimes,' Boy Steve said, 'we even wait for the tide to go out.'

'That sounds like a waste of time. There must be better things to do.'

'You're right! I was just thinking what a queer old world it is.'

The *Morvoren* was moored on a bit of a sand-bank that had come in on the last ground swell. It's a darned nuisance. You get your moorings all set out to take advantage of the first of the flood and the sandbank d' shift right under 'ee. Happens all the time. It can't be predicted. That maid would have to get her shoes and socks off to get to the quay or the foreshore.

'She'll be cut off, dreckly,' Zeke said.

Old Steve saw history repeating itself and said nothing as Shimshai's woman packed up her artist's things and retreated before the tide.

The maid from up-country climbed aboard the *Morvoren*. Boy Steve cast off. She'll be put ashore at the quay steps, some thought, but no, not they, off they go out into the bay and she with nothing on more'n a thin frock.

'She'll be cowld out theer,' Ceecil said, making one of his very few original observations.

'Not if the boy has any bleddy sense,' Old Steve said, with ill-concealed exasperation, as we watched the boat leave harbour and head across the bay.

There was an awkward silence on the plat as people remembered things best forgot. We watched Ezekiel Endean go by arm in arm with Winnie the Pew and sighed at the terrible things love could do to a man.

'Shimshai's coming home,' Barny said, eventually, and wondered why Old Steve burst out laughing, shoved himself off the railings, and blatantly made his way down to talk to Shimshai's woman on the foreshore without a word to none of us.

'Any of us,' Ceecil said.

'What?'

'Any of us. Not a word to *any* of us.'

On the eve

As a precaution, for the weather forecast was doubtful, it was decided that Kate's gallery would close for the day. Just the suggestion that people might fall through the huge windows while watching the eclipse was enough to put the fear of the gods of litigation into the managing committee. Some said they up London really hardly knew the eclipse was coming and they were all too busy thinking of ways to appropriate a bit more of the town land to expand the gallery. Well, to expand the tasteful gift shop and cafe with a view over the coast, where a dish of tay would be dear as saffron, but nobody who had a vested interest in the proposals believed a word of that.

'That's not so.'

'Yes it was.'

'No it wudn! They have the town's interest at heart and Katie had the day off! The 'clipse came on a Wednesday, and that was her day off.'

'You're getting old and totalish. Your memory's gone adrift, we tell 'ee.'

Katie mentioned it to Boy Steve, what a worry it all was, the possibility of rain driving hundreds of people crowding in to watch the eclipse from the gallery, and he said, 'Buy them a compass.'

'A compass?'

'Es. A cheap wan'll do. Or get them to look out the winda.'

'Look out of the window?'

'Es. They'll be lookin' pretty well nor-nor-west by west. I b'lieve the 'clipse 'll be somewhere about sou-sou-east by east.'

'Oh. Yes, of course!'

Well, whatever! Her mother wanted to know what she was going to do. Where she was going to witness the phenomenon. 'I'm staying here,' Sarah said, hoping that Katie would do the same. 'Our view will be as good as anywhere.'

'I'm not sure yet. I'll see what Boy Steve is doing.'

'I thought that was over.'

'It is. But we're still friends. We haven't been more than that for ages, Ma. Nothing has changed except our acceptance of the situation.'

Sarah sometimes found it difficult to adapt to the way things were. In her youth, when people, couples, broke up it was usually with acrimony and bitterness that lasted through their and all their families' lives. Now it didn't seem to matter. Sarah wondered if it was a good or bad thing to be so easy to part. She wondered what would have happened if Old Steve and Mary had realised where they were going all those years ago and called it a day. What if they had parted amicably instead of fighting like cat and dog for most of their lives? She could see the sadness in his eyes, the growing cynicism, regrets. And now he was about to settle the unfinished business with Shimshai's woman. She could feel it coming.

'Steve doesn't seem keen to be with me when he comes ashore,' Katie added.

'I heard he was seen with some party from up-country,' Sarah said. 'A stranger.'

'First I've heard of it,' Katie said. 'But in that case, I might get away from it all and go down to see Barny Baragwaneth for a bit of peace and quiet.'

'You must do what you think right,' Sarah sighed, as Katie left to go to her own rooms, implying that she understood more than she was saying about her daughter's relationships. And thinking that it wouldn't be much fun left on her own.

She made herself a pot of tea, covered it with a tea cosy, put it on a tray, together with a jug of milk and her single cup and saucer. If she was obliged to do things fitty for other people when they called then it was worth doing things fitty for herself, she maintained. There was a small table and a chair in the bay window, from which she could look across the bay and down into the harbour where the rising tide was gently flowing into the rills and ripples left in the sand by the ebb. It was a scene she had witnessed countless times, sitting here alone. And what of Katie? After so much time with Steve's son, during which Sarah continually hoped for but never mentioned the prospect of their marriage, was she also to be relegated to a life of loneliness? Sarah's body rose and collapsed as she exhaled a great sigh of resignation as she remembered her own hours of solitude. 'Ah, my dear cheeld,' she said. 'I only want for 'ee to be happy.'

The harbour now was busier with bleddy tourists than with the industry of the sea. On the ebb boats come in to catch the tide and unload their catch with cranes and ropes, while lorries loaded with ice and fish make their way up and down the narrow quay and the bleddy tourists impede their passing with their loitering. On the morning flood, the boats belong to go out straight from their moorings and the tourists have the quays to themselves.

As Sarah watched, the *Morvoren* floated off, went alongside the quay. Boy Steve made fast. The exhaust from the engine was spitting drips of moisture into the sea, so, with his engine running, he wasn't expecting to be there long. A few idle bystanders leaned over the railings to watch the picturesque fisherman stow his gear ready to face the mighty ocean. One of the idle bystanders was Old Steve, the boy's father. Just leaning over, arms and elbows on the rail, with no hint that they were even acquainted, let alone so closely related, although each was well aware of the other and knew exactly what was in his mind.

The old devil, the young man in the boat was thinking, hasn't been down to the end of the quay for months. Why today, of all days?

The silly fool, the old man leaning over the railings was thinking, why doesn't he put to sea? He's about to make a damn fool of himself.

The girl in the straw hat skipped down the steps and stepped aboard, as sure-footed as a cat, and the painter was let go. Boy Steve went astern with not a look ashore or up to the top of the steps where his old man shook his head in resignation. It had been only a matter of time, he thought. The *Morvoren* came about and put to sea.

Sarah, up in her window sipping her tea, saw Old Steve go to the end of the quay and watch the *Morvoren* go out around the headland. She saw Shimshai's woman come on to the quay and walk down towards him. She lowered her cup carefully back to its saucer and placed then on the table. Brazen! The woman was brazen. Steve turned, and there she was, right behind him. She gave him a kiss on the cheek. They walked up the quay together.

Ceant he see? Sarah was saying to herself. Ceant he see what he's doing? Don't he realise what he's doing to himself, to his son, to Katie, even to that brazen woman, betraying her husband the minute his back was turned? The silly old fool had learned nothing. A whole life gone and he had learned nothing; neither from his own nor other people's follies. She had been lucky, she realised with relief. His refusal of her had been a lucky escape and his affair with that woman a disgusting scandal known to all the town. And now he was about to disgrace himself before another generation. Oh, she thought. The man was mad, irresponsible and insensitive. Why hadn't she seen it before? My Lor,' she said, 'I must've been blind!'

TAPE ELEVEN

Behold the day, behold it is come: …I will cover the sun with a cloud, and the moon shall not give her light.

After being away for just a few days, Shimshai came home. It seemed to some of us that that's all he ever did. The times we've heard it… Shimshai's coming home… Shimshai's going away… Shimshai's home… Good God! Who cares whether he's going or coming or just breathing heavy. We knew very well he'd come home for the 'clipse, there's no way he would miss it. As if he, of all people, could go away and not witness such an extraordinary event. He's still too bleddy aloof to admit he was as thrilled by it as anyone else and pretended to be an indifferent observer recording the matter for posterity. Ha! Who does he think he fooled when he wrote:

Meanwhile, all along the shoreline, and on the tops of the surrounding hills, the crowds were gathered in their thousands to witness the ultimate obliteration of light from the world. There was a certain trepidation that comes with facing an inexorable but unforeseeable experience. As the umbra followed the path of totality strange rites were being performed in hidden glades and on remote crags, the like of which had not been since the demise of the great god 'Ilumquh from the pantheon of deities.

That's the way Shimshai began describing it before it even happened, but then, he would, wouldn't he?

Writers! What did he know? Did he know, for instance, that his woman met Old Steve out the cliffs that day while he was away up-country? Does he know what transpired between them, out there alone on the cliffs where they had spent so many passionate hours together? We don't think so.

One thing is certain (we think), that wherever you were on that auspicious day, there was a sense of impending awe and a strange silence descended like an invisible acoustic blanket that muted all hilarity and celebration. There was indeed, as Shimshai said, a certain trepidation that comes with facing an inexorable but unforeseeable experience. It seemed that there were those who, unable to face such natural phenomenon with equanimity, were equipped for making as much damned noise as possible, with the intent, it seemed, of sending shockwaves into outer space that would shift the heavenly bodies from their preordained orbits for ever. They had bands, groups, gigs, massive loudspeakers and any other contrivance for making as much noise as possible to hide their anxiety, but even these were muted as the time of the awesome event approached.

At least the weather was kind. With blue skies and wispy clouds, it was a glorious day.

'No it wudn!'

'Yes it was. We ought to know, we were there.'

'It was, why, dammee rainin'. How're you so?'

'It was scorchin' hot. We were there too, don't fergit.'

It was dull and overcast, with just the occasional break in the clouds. Anybody would think we were blinded by looking at the sun, the way some go on. It didn't happen on one square yard, you know, it happened all over. Some did have sunshine, so they said. Or was that for the eclipse of the moon?

Never mind. The point is that nobody saw it all. The most amazing thing was that the crowds of people appeared as if by magic out of thin air. It seemed that the whole region suddenly became chock full of people from far and wide intent on sharing the experience of a lifetime. Long before the darkness descended, the harbour and headlands were crowded to capacity as was any spot with a reasonable view of the bay and the town and the sky. It was the same all along the predicted line of progression, hoards of people out to witness the celestial event of a lifetime.

We can report that, despite it being as dark as a dog's guts, a good time was had by all. Some went to the cliff, and nobody fell over. Some went out in boats and nobody drowned. Some drank but few, if any, were drunk and disorderly as far as we could see except for one noticeable exception who has never lived it down. On the hills surrounding the town gathered the unorthodox and alternative, preparing for outlandish rites performed by priests and acolytes of obscure sects. There was the smell of bonfires and burning aromatic herbs in the air and some made innocent oblations of garlands of flowers, but nobody was offered to a pagan god, not in public anyway, despite a few willing virgins of both sexes being eager to make the ultimate sacrifice.

We crowd decided the best place to witness the event was from the same best place to observe everything else, up on the plat by the lodge by the railings above the harbour sand, aware that this is still one of the most advantageous locations for observing all the phenomena of the universe. From here we could see all. Most of us had the same idea. In fact nearly all hands went up there and most got there early, for the bleddy tourists would also see the plat as a good viewpoint open to all and nothing more, having no knowledge of tribal rites and sacred territories and no compunction about invading them if they did. First to arrive was Old Steve. His boy was to be on lifeboat standby, off the harbour mouth, so both had risen early. I s'pose, he thought, Shimshai and Cleo will be here dreckly. Sarah Stevens will be here too, to scowl at me if I have a yarn with them. He watched the approach of Mr Ezekiel Endean of the voluminous coats and Ms Winifred Whistler of the red hats, who were the next to arrive, having also decided the only place from which to view the phenomenon was along with the rest of us on the home ground of the plat, where Zeke spent most of his free time anyway. He guided Winnie carefully through the crowds where her red hat stood out like a beacon in a dark sea of motion. The alleged correlation with respect to certain items of headgear and certain items of underwear was a subject discreetly avoided since both had gone overboard from Boy Steve's skiff. The fact that a red hat was still the most prominent item of Winnie's outfits, whatever the occasion, did however lead to a great deal of unspoken speculation, although, truth be told, we don't give a toss what people wear, or don't wear, on their heads or anywhere else.

Wudn long before Freddie, Collateral Fred, turned up. Then, lo and behold, who should appear but DDJ and the town clerk, with

Robin Rainey in attendance. Then Shimshai and his woman, came down'long, together mind you, arm in arm, an unusual occurrence sure 'nuff. They went straight to Old Steve, who was leaning over the railings and was tapped on the shoulder by Shimshai and kissed on the cheek by his woman. 'Mornin' Shimshai,' Steve said, 'Mornin' Cleo.'

'Wus goin' on here?' we could but ask.

They were followed by the Brooks. The Brooks were undecided how they could witness and celebrate the eclipse. Mister wanted to drive out away from the crowds and climb Carn Cawrvargh where they could take a picnic with a bottle of wine and the view would be uninterrupted for scores of miles. Misses said she had never heard anything so absurd. Did he realise how high the carn was, how much gorse they would have to struggle through, that all the godless pagans from miles around would be up there performing obscene rituals? And as for the view, was he not aware that a twenty-mile vista was irrelevant while the bloody sun and moon were directly overhead? They compromised and headed for the headland north of the harbour, stopping briefly at the plat to exchange a few pleasantries with the locals on the way.

Reggie Hammond, who, after and despite his misdemeanour afloat, had at last fulfilled one of his ambitions and become a bit of a 'local character', arrived and was greeted by surreptitious winks and nods of conspiracy, as happened whenever he appeared in public. He was greeted warmly as almost one of us, vulnerable and liable to transgress.

We weren't sure when Ceecil arrived, as always he seemed to have materialized out of thin air. He could come and go like a will-o'-the-wisp, appearing at your elbow before you knew he was there and be as quickly gone, for his departures were as unobserved and surreptitious as his arrivals. He would interject one of his repetitions of your own last spoken words and melt away in the crowd unseen. But then, as somebody said, 'Tha's Ceecil for 'ee. Goes without saying.'

Theodora Yeoman arrived towing behind her a rickety shopping trolley with a buckled wheel. This damage had occurred when she had inadvertently backed the trolley into the path of a speeding skateboarder roaring down the harbour slipway and sent the poor kid flying headlong into an enormous sandcastle complete with crenellated turrets and heraldic banners. The trolley was now full of emergency food supplies and first-aid kits, into which was jammed a folded umbrella protruding at a dangerous angle. Finding most of us engaged in serious uninterruptible discussion, Theodora latched on to Ceecil.

'Hullo,' she said, 'isn't it wonderful, I mean exciting, awesome.'

'Awsome,' Ceecil said, thinking that there was no way he intended be lumbered with she beside 'n all through the 'clipse and looked about for somebody to have a proper yarn with.

Then, can 'ee believe it, none other than Henny Penny came sauntering along the prom with a haughty look in his eye and swinging his cane, much as to say, I deign to favour you with my presence. We thought he really would be up London doing deals, but he was home and actually came up on the plat, and we thought, look out here, there'll be ructions about they pictures when he sees Zeke over there with Winnie the Pew. Funny thing, though, they just looked at each other, Henny as haughty as ever and Zeke with that innocent look of enquiry with which he looked at most of the world, each giving nothing away.

'Inscrotable!' Ceecil said, and, considering his reputation, we wondered if his diction was really that bad.

Of the people we are concerned with here, the last arrival on the plat was Sarah Stevens. Early in the morning, Katie set off to see Barny Baragwaneth, who had decided to stay at home for the occasion. There would probably be no buses running, and he didn't fancy walking back from town in the rain. Sarah, being left to drink yet another solitary dish of tay, decided that enough was enough. Solitude was one thing, something she was well used to, but the prospect of being alone during a communal occasion when all others were joining in a grand party was loneliness, altogether a different matter. She donned a lightweight coat, no hat. If it rained, it rained. He would be there, she thought, but so what? She couldn't live out her whole existence in evading him. He was never worth it. Shimshai would be there with his woman. Two people she'd never spoken to, yet felt as if she knew as well as anyone she'd met in all her life, and was prepared to confront as the circumstance required.

She went down the hill. The hill that kept her fit when walking up it, the hill that separated her from the community down'long, which, since Quizzy Maggie died, had been reduced to just Ezekiel Endean, a few retired incomers and a continually changing population of what used to be called visitors and are now bleddy tourists, although they never toured anywhere except along the roads from attraction to attraction, as if they were but particles of iron filings drawn unwittingly to magnets. Poor souls, Sarah thought. What a life they must lead, saving and scrimping for a whole year just to get away from it for a fortnight down here going from heritage to zoo to various tourist attractions of vicarious experience. Not for her. She had never travelled anywhere. Had no desire to. Have I missed anything, she asked herself. Am I completely out of empathy with the rest of the world who seem to enjoy these things? All her acquaintances seemed to have travelled. It was something innate in the people here, a wanderlust that took them to the four corners of the earth before returning, having found nowhere better. Barny the Bard had worked abroad. Steve, like all his contemporaries, was an ex serviceman from the days of conscription and had seen service in the far east. Periods in all their lives that were never mentioned, as if they were the lives of others. Our young people are scattered all over the world. And there's that Shimshai, who's been everywhere, and his woman from God knows where, also come back. They go, they return, while I stay here, set in my ways and getting old. I am like the town, the community, constant and reliable, welcoming the prodigal sons. Together, the town and I weather the subtle currents and storms of change that batter the harbour walls, the gentle but insidious, persistent, cold easterly winds of progress that wrinkle our skins, erode the ancient granite of our houses and chapels and bring water to our eyes. Now, as we enter a period of shadow, I am Sarah Stevens, spinster of this parish, showing with it the signs of age and degeneration, nostalgic for the beauty of our youth. I am the spirit of the cobbled streets. It is for me they return, for I am the constant, the anchor that holds them fast in the currents of progression. I stay, while they go and return to me, unaware of my influence. Their times away are lives unknown to me. How remote we can be from those so close. I haven't even asked Steven Trevorrow about his experiences abroad, so far away under the searing sun of the distant east.

She had got down the hill as far as the end of the railings that edge the steps, as the sky began to darken. She stopped, holding on to the last cast-iron post. However, she laughed at a private joke, I am like Thoreau, and have travelled extensively in Concorde, though I've never been in an aeroplane in my life.

Then, as she paused there, a chill of apprehension shuddered down her spine at the sudden realization that, from fear of revealing her feelings, she had never asked Steve Trevorrow about anything. In all these years of loving, lusting, after him she had not spoken to him, more'n to say hullo, how do, and how are 'ee, as they passed in the street. That couldn't be so! Was it so? She hung on to the railing, breathing deeply, and a passer-by might have come to her aid as one suffering from some seizure or a spasm of cramp. The realization that she and Old Steve Trevorrow had never spoken about anything of any significance reinforced itself, as a the symptom of a dreadful profligate error that had wasted her life. Why, what a fool I've been, she thought, I mean nothing to him! Why should I? That woman is the only one who has enraptured him. And why should he mean anything to me? she demanded of herself. I've been daft! She composed herself and took the last steps down to level ground.

So all were there in good time, yet some didn't stay long. The Brooks were the first to leave after being accosted by Councillor Theodora Yeoman, pulling her trolley away from the uncommunicative Ceecil.

'Hello,' Theodora said. 'You're the first people I've found, I mean met that I recognise, know, that is, to talk to. These crowds are a brea thing,' she said, 'I'm glad I fell in with 'ee, I mean met 'ee, eh, you, I mean.'

The Brooks were not glad of the encounter. They had no intention of being lumbered with Theodora Yeoman and having to decipher her dialect and diction on an occasion like this.

'Hullo,' they said. 'Isn't it terrible. We can't stand any more of it. We're just going home.'

To their relief, they saw Collateral Fred approaching and, to his suspicion, greeted him enthusiastically before making off towards the headland. Theodora, was thankful that the red-hot flush that coloured her cheeks was not seen by any of the three as they looked at each other and she looked at Freddie. Since that day on the ship she had somewhat changed her opinion of Freddie. He had been the only one, she observed, who had retained any degree of decorum on that dreadful day, although she would never dream of saying such to a man's face. She remembered his strong, well, quite strong for a man of his age that is, arms protectively around her in the skiff. By his brave action he had thereby made something of an adventure out of what otherwise would have been an utterly disastrous and shameful occasion.

She was quite happy for the Brooks to go off and leave her with Freddie. She said goodbye and coyly, as coyly as she could manage, informed Freddie that she was still a bit concerned about the dangers of staggering around in the dark amongst an inebriated hoard of unpredictable heathens, hinting that she would appreciate the company of manly protection for the duration of the penumbra.

Freddie, painfully aware that his marriage had been somewhat dominated by a hard-minded and hard-bodied partner now deceased, remembering the vibrant proximity of Theodora's ample curves pulsating to the rhythm of her hiccups when that idiot Reggie Hammond had hung over them and terrified her into his arms, decided he could do worse than spend a few minutes in the dark with one so buxom. It was, he said, going to be increasingly crowded here on the plat, or anywhere else near the harbour. 'Praps,' he suggested, 'it would be wiser, safer, more convenient, I mean we'd have a better view of things, wudn' us, from my attic winder.' He might even persuade her, he was thinking, when Theodora agreed to his proposal, to partake of a very small celebratory drink... or two, if she so desired, to which end, on the way home, he called into Landers that was, and invested some of his collateral in a selection of miniature liqueurs. He and Theodora were seen weaving their way through the crowds hand in hand, as he towed her behind him like a punt in a storm while she, with her shopping trolley bouncing behind, indifferent to, or in ignorance of, the damage done to shins and ankles in her wake, eagerly followed her pilot and protector to the security of his top-floor flat, from whence, he reiterated, they could watch the event in peace and seclusion away from the aforementioned mad heathens in the streets.

Long after the event, Freddie was later heard to declare, during a discussion of matters fiscal among the chaps on the plat, who are all experts in financial transactions, that an outlay of collateral on a small collection of miniature liqueurs was one of the most profitable short-term investments he'd ever made.

Despite all the preparations and early arrivals, some didn't see any of it. Reggie Hammond, for instance, developed a burning thirst a short while before the light began to dim and decided to get in the mood of things by going into the pub for a quick one. The pub was packed with people doing the same but one of the barmaids went outside for a quick look and never came back, so Reggie, while accepting drinks from friends, took a long time to get served, by which time it was all over

The three dignitaries in the forms of DDJ, Robin Rainey and the town clerk had decided to forgo personal celebration of the eclipse as a matter of civic duty. Together, they decided to perambulate around the streets, beaches and harbour to ensure that everything was proceeding in accordance with the health and safety rules drawn up by the council's solicitors. Neither had close friends or relatives so the sacrifice was not that great. They were each, however, as we were well aware, really seeking an excuse for bringing themselves together so to avoid facing the thing alone. They had tried to persuade Mayor Tim Penberthy that he should accompany them, when they could be seen by the millions as a joint token of welcome and hospitality. Tim had other intentions, with two lady-friends from up-country coming to stay, and remembered the town clerk's desertion in the face of the enemy on the occasion of the visit of the Royal Navy. As the dimity drew nigh we saw the trio approaching through the crowds. They normally hated each other's guts but, on such a communal occasion, were desirous of any human company with whom to join the celebrations.

Robin Rainey, proud of his efforts in making this stupendous occasion such a resounding success and not wishing his efforts to go unnoticed, was saying to the clerk, in the hope that DDJ would also

be impressed, 'The effort expended into developing an entrepreneur-
ial culture among the locals has begun to reap rewards in terms of
product and process innovation which will underpin our platform
for further growth in targeted consumers...' And, when DDJ looked
at him in utter incomprehension added, 'At this moment in time, we
can be proud to be part of a dynamic team leading the community
forward into the twenty-first century from a position of strength.'

'What the hell are you talking about,' DDJ demanded, and Robin
Rainey, for once, felt bold enough to further his vision.

'I am saying,' Rainey said, 'that, if we wish to establish ourselves
as a top destination and growth town, providing good, well-paid
jobs, then we need to build from a strong foundation and climb stage
by stage; setting a course of direction and developing steadily;
enhancing and improving our facilities and establishing markets
within our capabilities to encourage investment that shows a return.'

DDJ scowled and decided that, after all, the best place to be at this
time of lunacy was with someone who spoke his own language. He
nodded 'Good-day' to his companions and hastened to the car park,
from whence he drove his Rolls Royce at unaccustomed velocity to
the camp-site of his friend and mentor, Squire Chygwyn.

The squire, having discovered a couple of days before the event
that most of his rivals had closed down their empty camp-sites in
despair, hastily rebooked a beer tent and disco and put it out on the
Internet, radio and press that his site was open and ready, and found
himself liable to be full up following last minute enquiries. He
placed his own estate workers at strategic points along the approach
roads and they directed traffic to his camp-site, allocating tent sites
and selling ice-cream and pasties and beer, lots of beer. Arthur, as
being the most reliable and honest man in his employment, the
squire realised with some reluctant respect, was allocated to be in
charge of the beer tent, which Arthur was quite happy to do. There
had been only a few early arrivals but on the day of the eclipse
the squire himself was on duty at the gate from dawn, taking the
entrance money. People had been travelling all night and arrived in
hordes. They came in cars, caravans, buses, by bicycle and on foot,
willingly paying what they regarded as a moderate charge after
hearing so much about the likelihood of being ripped off at every

opportunity. They handed over their money and were directed to sites over the field, filing the whole farm with laughing picnicking people with every regional accent the country had ever heard.

Squire Chygwin had never seen so much money, real money, paper tenners and fivers and the new, round, tin pound notes, in his life. His money was usually just figures on a balance sheet, left to others to manage. As the morning progressed he realised he would not make a loss, might even make a small profit, and was a happy man. When he thought more arrivals were unlikely he stuffed the money into the pockets of his threadbare old jacket, and baggy pants, delegated a stable boy to stay there on duty, and made his way to the beer tent to ascertain that there was no fiddling going on. Even Arthur might to succumb to temptation under the influence of alcohol.

He intended to buy a little beer for his employees as a token of thanks. The money would go back into his pocket eventually, but he found himself accosted by punters who were already somewhat merry, had no idea who he was, and, seeing his threadbare clothes, took pity on him as a poor old peasant thirsty for a pint. 'Come on, ol' mate, have a drink. Join in the celebration,' the men said, sympathetically but firmly, while the women fed him pasties and cakes, leading him about with arms over his shoulders and pouring beer into him between kissing him on the cheeks, not accepting refusal in the assumption that, like many simple country people, he was too proud to accept charity.

'Thank you,' he kept saying, 'Thank you . Thank you. Very kind, I'm sure.' As he eventually became pissed as a newt, staggering about the site with a glass in his hand drinking the health of Arthur and his astonished workers when he met them in the fields.

As it was getting dark, DDJ's Rolls Royce came to a halt beside the beer tent and its disgruntled driver alighted onto the grass, where he was astonished to find the squire outside with two cockney ladies hanging onto his arms.

'I'm under the affluence of incohol,' the squire cried to DDJ, 'whee hee!' as he threw his hat into the air and the two fell upon each other, laughing more than they had done for years.

For most of us the rain kept off. The weather was like it belongs to be when there's something special on. It was dull, with a light sou'westerly that shifted the thin clouds over the face of the sun in waves of dark and light. There was a rising hope that the sky might clear for the moment of climax. Just before a quarter to ten o'clock the sun's outline was clearly visible like a dim headlight in fog on the road to Penewlek. All eyes were skywards. Some had dark glasses, some had special ones with special dark lenses bought special for the job, but they didn't work. You couldn't see nawthen through them. Some had cardboard squares with pin holes through that were supposed to project an image on white paper. They didn' work either, the sun wudn bright enough. Some, well, one fella, came up on the plat with a telescope on a tripod that did project a faint image onto a dark card until it got scat over by somebody wearing a welder's mask, trying to shove his way to the front with outstretched arms like one playing blind man's buff. Daft, when it was all about to happen right overhead and he would have been better off lying prostrate on the sandbank.

'Supine,' Zeke said, 'better off lying supine on the sandbank.'

'Supine,' Ceecil confirmed, with a succession of affirmative nods, like one of they dummy dogs you used to see in cars' back winders.

Then, through the clouds, the north-eastern corner of the sun was seen to be indented by a faint crescent of shade. A dark shadow began to gather to the west, where the hills became black silhouettes against an ominous, threatening sky.

All fell quiet. The thousands of people seemed in awe of what was happening. The celestial bodies, the sun and moon, that control our very being, were about to demonstrate their inexorable complexities. As the thin crescent gradually enlarged and encroached across the dimly apparent sun, the world darkened as if at dusk. Over the sea, the swell became obscure, and pale, ghostly gulls gathered in a silent flock over the darkening harbour mouth, wailing in perplexity at this sudden approach of night. They flew off in the direction of their roost across the bay, over the navigation lights of the lifeboat, standing green and red and white. Around the town, sparrows gathered together and flew to holes in walls and under eaves, twittering an evening chorus as cats and dogs set off for home. Rooks hung over the trees around the manor-house, cawing in subdued confusion like black demons awaiting their fate from the gods.

The darkening increased, gradually, stealthily, until it became so dim that security lights began to operate, illuminating doorways and porches until people turned them off, not wanting the natural phenomenon to be interrupted by artificial daylight. For an hour the world became darker, and darker, and the thin crescent of shadow over the sun increased to a complete disc of the earth's black shadow. The thin clouds added to the impression of impending doom at the approach of the apocalypse, with no sunshine to promise the return of light to the earth ever again.

At the precise moment of the commencement of the totality, Zeke took out his watch. 'Right on,' he told Winnie. 'The eleventh hour, eleven minutes and forty-five seconds zackly.'

We weren't sure whether he was checking the accuracy of his watch or the reliability of the sun and moon in this uncertain day and age.

For just two minutes the sun was completely obliterated by her lesser sister and we were cut off from the source of light and life. The gloom and eerie silence persisted and the darkness was pierced only by thousands of brilliant sparks of light as flash cameras were set off all around the bay. We could see the momentary specks of light from over on the eastern shore, where hundreds of others had gathered to witness the phenomenon in the open air. All this, after all these months, years of anticipation, finally here, experienced and gone, already a memory as the first glimmer of light appeared from whence the darkness began and the sun was once more beginning to glow through the obscuring clouds.

The racket that then began was an explosion of emotion, the thrill of having just witnessed such an event, relief that the light had returned, a celebration of the wonders of our universe, and the beginning of a good old shindig by all hands from far and wide.

People left the plat. Collateral Fred and Theodora Yeoman, as we have intimated before, were already otherwise engaged. Kate was gone off to see Barny the Bard, of whom more dreckly. Ezekiel Endean led Winnie the Pew away to who knows what. Henny Penny sauntered, he never just walked other like mortal souls, back to his shop and opened up the door. Boy Steve came ashore from the lifeboat standing by and was met on the quay by that blond party who had been seen with him on a number of occasions lately. Ceecil disappeared into the crowds, bent on some personal quest. Shimshai, and Cleo after she had pecked Old Steve on the cheek, went up the hill to home so that he might set it all down while fresh in his author's mind.

Of those relevant to our yarn, only Old Steve and Sarah were left up there, finding themselves close together, leaning over the railing on the plat.

Now, what they two had to say to each other, we can't say. Not that we're sworn to secrecy on the matter, or that we wish to keep anything to ourselves as being too personal to relate. No, we can't say what they had to say because we don't know zackly what they had to say, any more than we know what Shimshai's woman and Old Steve had to say, or what they did, when he followed her out there along the cliffs and they met again after all they years. We can only relate that which has been related, or as they say up there, leaked, to us. If only two of us are engaged in conversation or other forms of intimacy, and those two choose silence, there is nothing the rest of us can do about it. Not even one as skilled in the subtleties of interrogation as Quizzy Maggie could draw intimacies from Old Steve, Shimshai's woman or, most definite of all, Sarah Stevens, if they wished to keep them confidential. That must be obvious if you have followed the narrative of our apocalypse thus far.

There is nothing to prevent conjecture, though. We mean to say, both Sarah and Steve are well enough known to us. As are her daughter and her old friend, Barny. We know their history. We know how their minds work. We know how they relate to each other and to others. We also know the outcome of that conversation on the day the sun was obscured. If, therefore, we use our imagination, which some say we've been doing all along, implying that this account is nothing more than a pack of lies, *an scavel an gow*, then we can follow them and speculate.

TAPE TWELVE

Son of man, Behold, I take away from thee the desire of thine eyes
with a stroke; yet neither shalt thou mourn nor weep.

We heard that Katie arrived at Barny's cottage two hours after setting off. She went along the road, taking a couple of short-cuts through the field paths where the road makes those long sweeping curves around the tops of the valleys. In the fields, from farm to farm, she met no one apart from the campers in a site near to town. Both road and footpath were deserted under the leaden sky, for any walkers out to see the scenery would have taken the path along the cliff and car drivers were already in position to see the eclipse from the few unblocked lay-bys. Remember that anywhere where there was enough space for a car to park off the tarmac, and at the entrance to fields and lanes, where the uncontrollable rabble had been predicted to invade, the access was blocked by massive boulders. (Some of them are still there).

Katie was a troubled woman and she walked quickly, head down, deep in thought. In a way, she was wishing the gallery had stayed open and she'd been obliged to go to work, her day's actions predetermined. It was her free will that was the reason for her troubles. In deciding to walk out and visit Barny the Bard instead of joining in the general celebrations in town she had also decided to resolve her future, a momentous achievement to undertake consciously. We originally said to consciously undertake but have been assured by Shimshai, the pedantic old tuss, that to deliberately split infinitives is to definitely reveal ourselves as illiterate, so we decided to immediately revise our manuscript. 'You've still got it wrong,' Old Steve said, 'You can't say that.'

'Now wha's wrong?' we said.

'Manuscript,' he said, 'it's not PC,' he said. 'You have to say personscript.'

Oh, for God's sake! we told him. Let's get on with the bleddy yarn before everybody dies off.

Steve might laugh, but it wasn't funny for Katie, about to challenge Barny. When she arrived at his cottage he was working. He was not out digging the garden, clipping his escallonia or shovelling barrow-loads of cow shit from the neighbouring farm, actions which he saw as pleasure. He was sitting at his old, chaotically laden desk, transcribing a tape of reminiscences. The job was to play a section of tape, then write out this dialogue in full on his word processor, trying to remember each sentence, verbatim, so that there was also a written record of the recordings. 'Come in!' he yelled when she'd already taken off her muddy walking boots and was closing the door behind her.

'I don't know why I agreed to do this,' he grumbled. 'It's a hell of a lot of work.'

She flopped into his threadbare armchair. 'Yes!' she said, 'thank you very much. I would love a cup of tay after walking all this way to see 'ee.'

He grasped his electronic mouse and pressed its backside a few times until the bright screen faded into darkness. 'Sorry. *Drok yu genef. Da tha welles. Tay yu!*'

She sat in the chair in silence while he fiddled in the kitchen and eventually came back with an enormous steaming pot, milk and two mugs on an old wooden tray. She said nothing, following him with her eyes until he sat opposite her on his rickety sofa. As always when sitting here, she considered the incongruous room, the so-called state-of-the-art electronics, in his hi-fi and computer, surrounded by all the old stuff that he could well afford to replace but never noticed. One could sit in an old chair as comfortably as one could sit in a new chair. The old tea tray carried pots and cups as efficiently as any new one might. The chaos on his desk was no enigma to him. He knew where things were. Everything necessary was filed in his equally chaotic brain or over there in the filing cabinet, if one could find it under the heaps of books. All so different from her own tidy rooms at home with a place for everything and everything in its place. Only, she mused, because her own mind was so chaotic that without consciously ordering things her life would be impossible, a total mess.

Barny watched her when her eyes fell upon the tray and down to her mug, with the tea swirling like a miniature maelstrom from her over-vigorous stirring. Not like Katie, he thought, to be disconcerted and silent while sitting here. Her short skirt revealed her tanned legs, muscular calves, shins in her thick, crumpled socks. She must be nearly thirty, he thought, but you would never think so. There's something in the genes of the women in that family that keeps them young forever. She could sit there, in the same old sofa that the other had sat in, and erase all those regretful memories that had plagued him for so long. Katie's presence always eliminated all the remorse and despair of those days which had almost been his last. She, more than any other, made him appreciate the gift of life. Was she not aware, as she lay back against the sofa's arm, that her short skirt was rucked up so high over her legs as she lounged there opposite him, tempting him, arousing him. If only she knew how he lusted after her she would never sit in such a flagrant pose, with one knee raised and her legs apart, apparently indifferent to his feeble attempt to avert his gaze. If I do, he thought, if I do, if I even give her a hint of how I feel, I might scare her off, lose her precious friendship forever. No! How I hate getting old.

'Aren't you going to watch the eclipse?' Katie said. 'It's nearly time.'

Her voice brought his mind back from thoughts of carnal pleasures. He came right back to his usual defensive self. 'I've seen it get dark before,' he said.

'Not in the middle of the day, for heaven's sake!'

He laughed, having also roused her out of her own deep thoughts. 'I was intending to go down to the cliff,' he said. 'Shall we?'

Outside it was already getting dim as they set off for the cliff, which is just a ten-minute walk from Barny's place, down the lane that is a stream of mud in winter and a dusty track in summer. In August its hedges (stone walls) are aglow with mists of flowers above the rutted track. On that day there would have been pink campion, stonecrop on the top, and sparkling yellow heads of a few late dandelions.

'Do you know all these flowers,' she said.

'Not very well,' he mused. 'They keep themselves to themselves. It's like that, living out in the countryside.'

'Their names!'

'Oh! Well, let's see.' He looked along the hedge, pointing out the various blooms. 'That's hawk's beard, cat's ears, birdsfoot, sheep's bits, birdseye, cranesbill, and there's coltsfoot, cocksfoot, oxtongues, goat's beard, horsetails, marestails, kidney vetch, liverfoot...'

'Enough!' Katie cried. 'You make the lane sound like a bloody knacker's yard.'

They laughed together and she took his hand as they continued on to the cliff. All the colours of the landscape were muted under the dreary sky, the sun a faint disc of light that faded and intensified, continually breaking its promise to shine as the thin clouds passed it by. Sitting on a lichened rock, they waited for the shadow to pass, waited for the moment that had induced years of anticipation and dread. There was a thin sliver of light illuminating distant waves out near the northern horizon but inland the clouds thickened across the face of the sun, its disc eventually lost in grey obscurity. The world was dark to the western horizon and, as for us in town, all fell silent as the gloom approached. Far below them a few confused kittiwakes circled low over the water. A flock of jackdaws gathered on a crag, uncharacteristically quiet. It was an eerie shadow that enveloped them, silencing speech and even thought as the black gloom intensified. Out there, on the isolated cliff almost under the centre line of the path of totality, there were no flashbulbs, no car headlights, no artificial light or man-made sound. A total darkness descended and they watched in silence, some primitive fear gripping them, the same irrational fear that had terrified both ignorant and learned for millennia. It was the fear that light had left the earth, and might never return. The sea became black; even the swell, far below, seemed suppressed and muted under the pressure of diurnal darkness. They each put an arm around the other.

They saw no Baily's beads, those weird lights like strings of pearls that border the moving moon, neither the crescents of the chromosphere, which were to have been the climax of the experience. Through those gloomy clouds there was no light whatsoever for the two whole minutes that they sat there together under the passing umbra.

As imperceptibly as the gloom approached, so did it pass. There seemed no moment when the light returned, no precise moment of jubilation. Eventually, their primitive doubts and fears were assuaged, as a thin, watery sun gradually reappeared, enough to brighten the world with promise.

'Wow!' Katie said.

Barny made a short expelling of breath, lost for words. 'Phew!' Both were overwhelmed by the experience.

They went back to his cottage in silence, still overawed by the eclipse, until, near the top of the lane he stooped and picked a flower from the base of the hedge. He gave it to her and she held it in her hand.

'A wild pansy,' he said, and watched her eyes. 'Heartsease.'

Her eyes narrowed as she turned to him, each searching for something more than the spoken word. Barny was the first to avert his eyes, disturbed, it seemed, by some recollection of a previous intimacy in this blossom-spangled lane. He led the way back to his cottage, too deep in thought for conversation.

The old armchair and sofa were awaiting them, and Barny once more organised drinks, this time the only resemblance to tea being in its colour. 'With soda?' he asked.

'No. No thanks.'

She was curled up on the sofa, he sat beside her. 'Cheers,' he said. *'Kernow Bysvyken.'*

'Kernow Bysvyken!'

They sipped the liquid, letting the amber fluid warm their innards. Katie rolled her lips around the taste. Another sip. They sat in silence, each deep in thoughts that they wished to but could not reveal to the other. It was Katie who broke it.

'Tell me,' she said at last.

'What? Tell you what?'

'You know. All that! All that stuff you keep on suppressing.'

It would require more than that to induce Barny to go back to those memories that plagued him daily. He had become increasingly adept at avoiding mentioning them to anybody. It was all too personal and painful. He just shook his head and smiled. Then came a direct, unavoidable question.

'What was she like?' Katie demanded.

He capitulated, having anticipated and, if he were honest with himself, even hoped for this question from Katie for years. Its abruptness disconcerted him, however. 'You mean, you never met her?'

'No. She was never here when Boy Steve and I came to see you around the time Joe died. I only know that she made you very happy for a while, and after she went, you became even more of a recluse than before. I could see you were in pain. Even more than I was.'

'Yes. We don't have to go into detail.' Barny exhaled a deep sigh. 'She was very beautiful to look at. Delicate. Vulnerable. I fell in love with her. And I saved her life. Not something I do every day.'

'You loved her, then?'

His response to that was merely a slight nod, as if the reminiscence was too painful to articulate. His body slumped into the cushions, limp with emotion. 'I'd rather not talk about it.'

'I want you to talk about it. It's very important to me.'

'Is it?'

'Yes.' He rose up and looked through the window across the dark moor to the distant carn, composing himself. 'The fact is,' Barny confessed, 'that I made a damned fool of myself. She was far too young. There was never, realistically, any hope that she would stay with me as I got older.' He sat beside her again, with a wistful smile. 'I've always fancied the young ones.'

'You don't seem to do much about it.'

'No, and I don't intend to. I couldn't go through all that again.'

'I don't see why not. You still have a lot going for 'ee.'

'Katie,' he said. 'I am still randy, full of lust, longing for love and sex, but, oh no, never again.' He paused for breath and composure, wondering if he could ever impart to her the pain he had endured through loving. 'All right,' he said at last. 'I'll tell 'ee. You and no other. She came to me as a wreck, after several attempts at suicide. I cured her, gave her strength, my strength, and she recovered.' He paused at the memory, smiling a rueful smile of remorse. 'It was almost a biblical cure. She took up her bed and walked. She walked right out of my life as soon as she was strong enough to go. Went.

No goodbye. No nothing. And that nearly killed me. I mean I really nearly killed me. I was within minutes of doing it.' He twisted his lips in a wistful grimace. 'I still have the rope.'

She let the revelation sink in, aware that she'd suspected something like this had occurred. 'And nobody knew? You've kept all this to yourself? For what? Ten years?'

'Is that all?' Barny couldn't believe it was only that. It seemed ages since he'd recorded it all in that cathartic typescript shoved away in the filing cabinet together with the floppy disc that contained all his inmost secrets. 'I wrote it all down,' he said. 'Everything. It took months, over two years of purging. That's why I seemed to become more withdrawn, I suppose. I wrote it all down. Her story and mine. Yours. The shipwreck. Joe's death. Everything. It's all there.' He laughed a rueful laugh. 'If it weren't so personal, so painful for all of us, it might make a good novel. No one would believe a word of it.'*

Katie was not deceived by his cynicism. 'It's a wonder you're still sane.'

'I'm not!' he cried, 'I'm not. I'm just as crazy as ever. Can't you see? I'd be ready to go through the whole awful bloody business again if I didn't keep control of myself.'

'I think,' Katie said, with a meaningful look in her eyes, 'that we've both been keeping too much control of ourselves.'

Now, more than that about what occurred then between they two we can't tell 'ee, and what they said to each other was mostly in the old language anyway. If you've read through these reminiscences expecting to have your prurient curiosity satisfied and lusts aroused by a lurid description of what happened next, as they revelled in all the erotic and sensuous indulgences that you imagine doing and having done to 'ee in your wildest fantasies, then too bad, as there are some things that even we party will not reveal to a microphone. Use your imagination!

Behold, everyone that useth proverbs shall use this proverb against thee, saying, As is the mother, so is her daughter.

See postscript on p.202.

And the other way round too, it seems to we. When all hands had left the plat, leaving he and she there together, almost a purpose lie, if you know what we mean, neither of them knew what to say. They'd known each other since childhood, mind you, and didn't know what to say.

What they were thinking... what they were both thinking... was about that time, so long ago, when they'd exchanged a kiss in the moonshadow of the old lighthouse, after going to the Saturday night dance, when the Blue Rhythmics had played the last waltz so low and slow that they could have stayed in each other's arms forever. A mere moment in their lives that neither had ever been able to forget. They were remembering the touch of the other's lips, the proximity of their bodies, the restrained passion, the lust they had felt for each other and never gratified or even mentioned again during the past forty-odd years. It had been so intensely sexual that each one believed that some metaphorical line of decency had been irrevocably crossed and were ashamed, though ever wishing, to repeat it.

'Well,' Sarah said when the crowds had departed. 'That was some sight.'

'A brea thing, sure'nuff.'

'All over. After so much fuss,' she said.

Old Steve Trevorrow, after all the years of avoidance, finally turned to look Sarah Stevens in the eye (we saw that) and she looked in his. She was a very attractive woman, he thought. Still a very attractive woman, at what, sixty? She was grey, but who wasn't? Her figure would shame many a youngster these days when so many were over-weight from eating too much clidgey nicey. Her eyes, that had condemned him in silence so many times, now held his in a look of candour, revealing little of what was in her mind. He raised his eye-brow, in that quizzical way that had been so characteristic of his youth, expecting that now, in confrontation at last, she would belabour him with reprimands for a life of indiscretion. If only, he thought. If only she hadn't been so bleddy *pure*. So unapproachable.

'Es,' he said, 'all over at last.' There was a look in her eyes that he couldn't fathom. It had been there all along if only he'd had the courage to look at them, all those years, but he was seeing it for the first time. It was a reassuring look, a frank look of amusement at his disconcertion. 'Nothing now until the millennium,' he said.

'Isn't there?'

Steve thought he'd said the wrong thing in his apprehension of her response, but as she turned away from his eye to look at the ripples on the rising tide he wanted her to stay with him, to clear up all that stuff that had been bothering them for such a long time. He might even sum up the courage to tell her how he felt about her. How, over the years, she had come to occupy more and more of his thoughts. 'I was thinking of taking a turn down the quay,' he said, 'Do 'ee fancy a bit of a walk?'

'I'm not going down there,' she said.

I've done it again, he thought. Said the wrong thing. Of course she wouldn't go down the quay with me. Down where it all began when we kissed each other there by the lighthouse when we were young. She would be reminded and ashamed.

'The quay is stemming,' she said. 'Look at them. I don't want to be in that crush. You ceant move down there.'

True. The quay, all the harbour, was packed with people, as were the pubs and cafés all over town. It was the crowds that she wished to avoid, and there was only one place where they could do that, with Boy Steve liable to go home at any minute.

'We can go up my house,' she said.

'Up your house?'

'Why 'es. Wus the matter? Idna grand enough for 'ee?'

Steve laughed at this old challenge, and heaved himself off the railings. 'Come on en,' he said. 'Up your house.'

So long, he thought as they came into her sitting-room overlooking the harbour, so long since I've been in this room. So long since her parents died, leaving her to cope alone. It was almost the same as it was then. The same old fireplace with lotus tiles and oak mantle, the same ornamental ceiling that had been there since it was built, now all back in fashion and looking as good as new.

'You used to have me up doing work for 'ee,' he said. 'Years ago.'

'I still would, if anything wanted doing.'

'Would 'ee? Perhaps she was not holding him in total contempt. 'You only have to ask.'

'You don't wear things out very much when you live on your

own,' she said. She remembered the old pretexts she had used, just to see him, to have him in her house for a few hours before he was married. And afterwards too, for as long as she dared. Jobs she could well have done herself. 'Sit down,' she said, and went over to her sideboard. 'What'll 'ee have? Sherry or sloe gin? It was a good year for sloes last year. I abm got no beer nor fancy cocktails.'

'Well,' he said, taken aback. 'Well, a drop of sloe gin, eh? We can drink to the 'clipse.'

'Bit late for that.'

Her tots were a bit above the standard amount in any pub, he noticed, but decided he might need it. She seemed in a very determined mood. He wondered what was to come. She held her glass up, but he could think of nothing to drink to and took a sip after a mere raising of his own glass's height. 'This'll set a few tongues waggin,' he said.

'That'll be nawthen new!'

He registered that they'd both reverted to the broad accent and dialect of their past, as locals did when among their own. Evidently at home with it when there were no outsiders to accommodate, just the two of them, just two of the remaining generation who had witnessed the dilution of their community and all the old ways go. Through the window he could see the crowds milling about around the harbour, a few boats going out, Boy Steve and his new girlfriend, reminding him of times past.

'No,' he said. 'I s'pose we both set them waggin at one time or another.'

The sloe gin seemed but a sip, so dry was his mouth. He could see the sky lightening over the eastern shore. 'A drop of good stuff that is,' he said. Sarah refilled his glass, topped up her own in silence.

Now, at last, determined to guide the conversation to where she wanted it, she looked directly at him and said, 'What do you think of me, Steve?'

'What? What do I think of 'ee? Well. I don't knaw. What should I think of 'ee?'

'You mean,' she challenged, 'that you never think of me?'

'Tha's not what I said. I think of 'ee a lot. I just don't knaw what I think of 'ee. It's hard to say.'

'Well lemme remind 'ee,' she said, 'what they all d' think of me.' She took a deep breath before continuing. 'Sarah Stevens, the self-righteous town prude. Bleddy dried up old spinster who only had one man, for one time, in her life, a man she used, just used as a convenient sperm donor and would have no more to do with 'n, though he thot the world of her! Is that what you think, too?'

He was noticeably shocked by this. For one thing, no one had ever heard Sarah Stevens utter a profanity in her life, and for another he was appalled that she regarded herself as a pariah in the community. 'For Christ's sake, Sarah!' he cried, 'What are you saying? Nobody ever thot that about 'ee. We all know 'ee and we all knew Joe. It's be'n long forgot. Joe was my best pal, remember. I knew him well enough to know that he must've been well aware what you wanted, and agreed to it.'

He thought about what had been said. 'And you couldn't have chosen a better father for Katie. Pity she didn' knaw before he died.'

'Yes,' she said, regaining her composure. 'I think that's my one regret.'

They sipped their home-made sloe gin, and Steve was secretly amused to see her lips pucker at the unaccustomed burning in her throat. 'You don't look like a bleddy old dried up spinster,' he said, risking a compliment.

'I don't feel like one either!' She fiddled with her glass. 'People think, I used to think, that we lost all our desires when we got older.'

'So did I,' he replied with caution in his voice. Thinking, now what, exactly, is she telling me? 'I tho't that too,' he said. 'I can remember looking forward to it as the end of all my problems. Ha! Some hopes.'

She asked him, though she must have known to the day, 'How long have you ben on your own?'

'Over five years. I'm quite happy to be on my own most of the time. Me and Mary never got on all that well in latter years.'

'I'll hear no bad thing about Mary,' Sarah said. 'She was a good wife and mother.'

Steve didn't answer. What the hell do you know about being a good wife and mother, he thought, but immediately remembered Katie, a lovely daughter for anybody to have reared. It was shame that it was all off between her and the boy. 'I do miss Mary,' Steve said. 'Sometimes.'

Sarah expelled a long sigh, followed by a thoughtful silence before she said, 'I think about Joe, sometimes, wondering if we could have made a go of it. Can you imagine what it's like to be on your own for a lifetime? To have no one to confide in. No one to share intimate moments of happiness and sorrow. Never to be able to cry except into your pillow in the dark lonely nights.'

This was a Sarah Stevens Steve hadn't met before. Revealing her vulnerable side. 'No,' Steve said, his voice softening with sympathy. 'No. I ceant imagine that.'

'Well I can!' Sarah suddenly exclaimed. 'And I've had enough of it.' She took a determined swig at her glass. 'I can,' she repeated, 'and I'm sick and fed up with sitting here night after night with my hand down my drawers. I still have a few good fuckin' years ahead of me and I intend to get a man and make the most of them.'

Steve coughed up a half tot of gin and looked at his glass. Hell's bells, he thought, that's strong stuff, but surely I'm not drunk already. Did she say what I thought she said? Was that Sarah Stevens speaking, or am I hallucinating? My wishful thinking, maybe. 'Pardon?' he said, 'what did you say?'

'You heard!'

She could hardly believe she'd said that herself. But it's true, she mused, that's just the way I feel, so he might as well know it. He can take it or leave it. Pretending indifference to her own incredulous self.

Now, Old Steve was not so insensitive that he was unaware that he had been propositioned. He was also aware that this woman, who he had set up, stereotyped for over forty years, had been a stranger to him. Also, and this made him think very carefully where this conversation might lead, that in revealing herself she had assumed his trust and confidence. He sat in silence for a long time, remembering the past, hearing her breathing heavily in anticipation of his response. This time, he must get it right, however much she might be disappointed. Not say the wrong thing, for once. What, he found himself thinking against his will, had it been like for her with Joe on that one occasion? Steve's own response to her desires could be a disappointment for her and a humiliation for him. With Joe? he thought. Never mind about Joe! Think about we. She was talking about the rest of our lives. He also could not face another disastrous relationship.

'You want', he said quietly, 'to be fucked.'

'Yes,' she said in a voice barely audible.

'By me? For years and years. The rest of your life?'

'Yes.'

'Well, I'm sorry,' he said. 'but I don't want to do it. I don't want to fuck 'ee. We're too old.'

He watched her inscrutable face as she shrugged off her fate. She'd always been so clever at hiding her emotions when she felt like it, he thought, but now, despite showing no emotion, she had revealed all, committed herself without the prudence of first ascertaining his likely response.

'You abm,' he reminded her gently, 'asked what I d' want.'

'No,' she said, desperately trying to hide the humiliation of his refusal, 'I didn'.'

'Well, if you must know,' he said as he approached her chair and took her hand as if to soften the blow of rejection. 'I'll tell 'ee what I want.'

'What I d' want,' he repeated as he dropped to his knees beside her, 'is to hold 'ee in my arms and kiss 'ee the way we kissed in the doorway of the lighthouse that time. The way I've been wanting to kiss 'ee again for years. And I d' want to make the most tender love imaginable…' Her arms came around him and she began to giggle with relief and joy as Steve continued, with the old, mischievous gleam returning to his eye, '…until we're beside ourselves with passion, lustin' for ever more intense sexual gratification before collapsin' in ecstasy and anticipatin' the next time.' He paused for breath as Sarah looked at him with the sparkle returning to her eyes and a spreading smile on her lips. 'Do 'ee think you can cope with that, my flower.'

She blinked away a little tear of glee. 'I can gibm a try,' she said.

Their mouths met in the soft, sensual kiss that each had spent years longing for, with their bodies trembling with rejuvenated passion, and it wudn long before they tumbled to the carpet laughing loud 'nuff to frighten all the gulls off all the roofs of down'long.

APOCALYPSE DRECKLY

Thus; Ezekiel is unto you a sign..

Next day, with the sun shining brightly (note use of adverb), most of the hoards of people had dispersed back up'long where they came from. Only the usual number of regular bleddy tourists were here to keep us in the manner to which, thanks to them, we hope to become accustomed by their spending money on rubbish and junk called souvenirs.

As Ezekiel, the other Ezekiel, the prophet one, who those of us who know the bible have been quoting all along at the beginning of the tapes, put it:

And they shall come thither, and they shall take away the detestable things thereof and all the abominations thereof from thence.

Hee Hee! No, we're jokin'. We don't mean it. We're bleddy tourists too when we go up London and buy postcards and plastic models of Tower Bridge.

As we said, next day, the sun was shining fit enough to crack the hedges. The harbour was full of light and colour, the way it belongs to be in summer, tide out and sea sparkling. Semi-naked bodies were cooling off in the shallow water of the harbour mouth and lying scattered along the foreshore sand, laid out like ling. That familiar aroma of summer, that delicious perfume that permeates the air in the heat of day like the scent of tropical blooms was arousing our olfactory senses like a powerful aphrodisiac. From factor four, right up to fifty, the sun-tan creams and oils were being lavished on naked skin below the plat, sending the responding pheromones into the air like a cloud of spanish flies.

'Giver her the lotion, boy,' said Ceecil, the man of many parts, 'Give her the lotion.'

'That wudn Ceecil!'

'Wudn Ceecil said that!'

'And it wudn the day after the 'clipse.'

Well, next day, next week, what we're telling of happened a while back now, so what does it matter? The next day, the next week, it's all part of the same happy memory of a story where everything turned out all right in the end. Whenever it was, it so happened that by coincidence all hands turned out one day and contemplated the eclipse from the viewpoint of retrospection, when it was decided to make these tapes for posterity. Ceecil was up there early. So was Henny Penny, taking a quick saunter before opening his junk shop. Tim and DDJ happened to be passing on their way to the town hall. Along came the one that Mary had by a married man after she and Ste' were wed, Boy Steve, and his new girlfriend. (What was she called again?) Then came a flowing over-coat accompanied by a red hat as Zeke and Winnie broke with tradition and nailed up on the lodge wall a notice of their impend-ing wedding (instead of the many years of funerals) to which all were invited. Collateral Fred and Theodora Yeoman had formed a business partnership that required long periods up in his attic dis-cussing matters of mutual interest and they came by, bleary-eyed, after a long night of intense negotiation, they said. Barny was in town to pick up Katie, who was, to everyone's surprise, moving from her mother's house to live out there in the back of beyond with a man old enough to be her uncle. That left Old Steve able to move in with Sarah, and Boy Steve free to have whoever he had a mind to living with him in their family home. The town clerk and Robin Rainey were passing and saw an opportunity to receive the well-deserved public approbation for all their hard work.

'I think we can say,' Robin Rainey informed us, as the town clerk, the mayor and DDJ listened in the background, 'that the whole occasion was managed by the council and officials with impeccable precision. We can now look forward to the advent of the millennium with equal confidence in our corporate identity and ongoing endeavours to maximise the opportunities for the community at large.'

The Brooks couldn't understand why nobody but they two clapped. Not another bleddy crant, the rest of us were thinking, with threats of millennium bugs causing mayhem with computers, disas-ter all round and everybody going mad over nawthen till the end of the year.

'But,' Ezekiel Endean emphatically insisted to the officials for the umpteenth time as he repeatedly banged his fist down on the railing, 'the... new... minellium... does not... begin... until... the end... of the old bugger... and the bleddytwothousandthyear! How ceant you see that?'

An deweth a'n dalleth.

POSTSCRIPT

Events in the community, first revealed in Shimshai's notorious novel *The Saffron Eaters* were further exposed when Barny Baragwaneth eventually published his own cathartic experiences under the title *Horn of Strangers*.